Mystery Bre
Brett, Simon.
Blotto, Twinks and the
Maharajah's jewel

Blotto, Twinks and
the Maharajah's Jewel

Also by Simon Brett

Blotto, Twinks and the Ex-King's Daughter
Blotto, Twinks and the Dead Dowager Duchess
Blotto, Twinks and the Rodents of the Riviera
Blotto, Twinks and the Bootlegger's Moll
Blotto, Twinks and the Riddle of the Sphinx
Blotto, Twinks and the Heir to the Tsar
Blotto, Twinks and the Stars of the Silver Screen
Blotto, Twinks and the Intimate Revue
Blotto, Twinks and the Great Road Race

Blotto, Twinks and the Maharajah's Jewel

Simon Brett

CONSTABLE

First published in Great Britain in 2021 by Constable

Copyright © Simon Brett, 2021

1 3 5 7 9 10 8 6 4 2

A CIP catalogue record for this book is available
from the British Library.

ISBN: 978-1-47213-390-8

Typeset in Palatino by Photoprint, Torquay

Printed and bound in Great Britain by Clays Ltd, Elcograf S.p.A.

Papers used by Constable are from well-managed forests and
other responsible sources.

Constable
An imprint of
Little, Brown Book Group
Carmelite House
50 Victoria Embankment
London EC4Y 0DZ

An Hachette UK Company
www.hachette.co.uk

www.littlebrown.co.uk

Lynne Truss,
with admiration

1

Abroad Thoughts from Home

'Do you know the Nawab of Patatah?' asked Ponky, whose surname, though spelt 'L-a-r-r-e-i-g-h-f-f-r-i-e-b-o-l-l-a-u-x', was pronounced, as anyone in his Old Etonian social circle (in other words, anyone who mattered) knew, 'Larue'.

'No, sorry,' said Blotto. He was always ready to admit ignorance, which meant that, given the sieve-like quality of his brain, his life contained a great many such admissions. 'I can never remember songs. And I'm a real empty revolver when it comes to tunes. Ears made of the finest Cornish tin, I'm afraid.'

'We're not on the same page,' said Ponky. 'The Nawab of Patatah was actually one of our fellow muffin-toasters at Eton.'

'Oh, we're talking about a boddo, not a song, are we?'

'Yes. Surely you remember him? His school trunk was encrusted in diamonds.'

'Not tinkling any tinkerbells, I'm afraid,' said Blotto.

'He was rich beyond the dreams of avarice.'

Blotto shook his head. 'Don't know her either.'

'Who?'

'This Avarice droplet who does the dreaming.'

'Also, he had dark skin,' said Ponky. Such details might

have been noticed in the predominantly white Anglo-Saxon environment of Eton before the Great War.

But Blotto again shook his fine head of blond hair. 'Nothing rattling in the old memory box, I'm afraid.'

'He did play cricket,' Ponky offered.

Enlightenment spread immediately across Blotto's patrician features. 'Oh, that Nawab of Patatah!' he cried. 'Once carried his bat with an unbeaten hundred and two in the Eton and Harrow match.'

'That's the Johnnie!' Ponky confirmed. 'Tiddle my pom!' He lay back, lanky, goggle-eyed and chinless, a representative product of the British public school system. Ponky Larreighffriebollaux permanently wore the expression of someone who had just been informed that his great-grandfather was a tadpole.

'Ah, yes,' Blotto continued. 'I've popped the partridge in the right pigeonhole now. Mind you, I never called him the Nitwit of Pyjamas or whatever it was you said.'

'No?'

'No. I always called him "Foursie".'

'"Foursie"? Why?'

'Because he kept hitting fours.'

'Ah.'

'If he'd kept hitting sixes,' Blotto elaborated, 'I would have called him "Sixie".'

Ponky Larreighffriebollaux nodded at the unarguable logic of this. He thought he could contribute something to the discussion. 'And if he'd kept hitting tens, you'd have called him "Tensie".'

'Good ticket,' Blotto agreed readily. Then he was struck by something which a person more versed in the works of Shakespeare would have recognised as 'a pale cast of thought'. 'Except you can't hit a ten in cricket.'

'No,' Ponky conceded. 'You've pinged the partridge there, Blotters.'

Blotto, more formally known as Devereux Lyminster,

younger son of the late Duke of Tawcester and younger brother of the current one, lay contentedly back on the greensward at the edge of the Tawcester Towers cricket pitch. It had been a good day, the annual match between the home team and Ponky's occasional line-up called the Peripherals. Most of Ponky's boddoes were old muffin-toasters from Eton, whose every googly and cover drive Blotto had studied since he first donned long white trousers. Though his own team was made up mostly of Tawcester Towers domestic staff, with the chauffeur Corky Froggett as wicketkeeper, Blotto, as ever, had led them to victory. His own contribution of an unbeaten total of two hundred and thirteen runs, together with bowling figures of eight for forty-three, had obviously helped, but Blotto wasn't the kind to see sport in terms of personal achieve-ment. It was the team effort that meant everything to him.

He looked through half-closed eyes, lids reddened by sunlight, at the scene before him and reflected how fortun-ate he was to live in the most beautiful countryside in the world. (There was a great deal of the world that he hadn't actually seen, but Blotto felt supremely confident that no other vista could hold a candle to the splendours of the Tawcester Towers estate. It was one of many things that he felt supremely confident about. Such an outlook was just one of the advantages of being born into the British aristocracy.)

It was an evening in late summer. The heat of the day still hung on the breeze that gently rustled the leaves of ancestral oaks. Swallows climbed and swooped in the sky, feeling there was no point in flying South while the weather in England remained so clement. (Indeed, if they'd had any sense, they never would have flown South at all. Abroad was never as nice as home.) Blotto, while not recognising the reference, would have agreed wholeheart-edly with Robert Browning's observation that 'God's in His heaven – All's right with the world!'

'Anyway ...' said Ponky diffidently, 'I asked if you knew the Nawab of Patatah ...'

'Yes,' Blotto agreed. 'And we established that I did.'

'But, actually, Blotto, me old Victoria Sponge, I wasn't just asking if you knew him ...'

'No?'

'No. I was asking if you knew him with a view to my saying something about him ...'

'Oh,' said Blotto, utterly bewildered.

'Sort of initiating a conversation about him ...'

This only confused Blotto further. All the word 'initiating' brought to his mind was unsavoury recollections from early days at Eton of heads being pushed down into toilet bowls while the chain was pulled.

'Well,' Ponky went on, 'the fact is, the Nawab of Patatah was recently in this country, pongling round various cricket pitches and playing the odd game ...'

'Toad-in-the-hole!' said Blotto. 'Was he?'

'Yes. He's on his way back home now. Sailed from Southampton last week. But I met him at a match we played against the Oxford Occasionals and we got talking. And – tiddle my pom! – he's only invited me to take a Peripherals Eleven to play a series of return matches out there.'

'"Out there"?'

'In India, Blotto, me old tub of tooth powder.'

'"In India"? But surely, Ponky, the Indians don't play cricket in the winter, do they? They must get as cold as bare feet on an iceberg.'

'No, they do play and they don't get cold. You see, Blotters, the Indians have different seasons from us.'

'Do they? Well, I'm totally crab-whacked. That really is a bit of a rum baba. What's wrong with the old spring-summer-autumn-winter routine? It's worked all right for us for a good few millennia.'

'No, you're still shinnying up the wrong drainpipe.'

4

Ponky tried to explain. 'In India, they do have the same seasons as us, but just have them different times of the year.'

'Why, in the name of snitchrags, would anyone do that?'

'It's because of the climate. In the winter it's warm in India. And they couldn't have their cricket season at the same time as us, because of the monsoon.'

Blotto's furrowed patrician brow now showed such befuddlement that Ponky decided to cut to the chase. 'Blotters, you just take my word for it – out there, cricket will be played right through the winter. And all I'm asking is: would you be up for beating the blithers out of a few balls in India?'

'Would I, by Denzil? Nothing would tickle the old trouser-press better!'

'So, you're up for it? You'll sign on the dotted?'

The answer was so obvious that Blotto just asked, 'Is the King German?'

But then a cloudlet of doubt shadowed that same patrician brow. The doubt was prompted by a recollection of the Tawcester Towers plumbing. While an untutored observer might wonder about the relationship between cricket and plumbing, anyone inside Blotto's family circle would instantly recognise the problem.

Tawcester Towers, in common with many English stately homes, prided itself on tradition. The fact that little had changed on the estate since one of William the Conqueror's co-conquerors had witnessed the laying of the building's foundation stone, was regarded very much as a plus rather than a minus. What had been good enough in the eleventh century should be more than adequate for the twentieth. In Blotto's circle, there was still a definite twinge of regret about the ending of the feudal system.

Change came slowly to places like Tawcester Towers. The convenience of electricity had been grudgingly allowed on to the premises, but the expense of updating

5

the ancient pile's ancestral plumbing was a constant source of anxiety. Ripping out the whole system and replacing it with 1920s state-of-the-art piping and radiators was beyond the dreams of that ancient Greek king whom Blotto always referred to as Creosote.

As a result, a series of botched repairs and short-term fixes ensured that the plumbing was a constant drain on the Tawcester Towers resources. And a recent flood on the premises, which had put the kitchen out of commission for a month, meant that Blotto was in no position to contemplate expensive foreign travel for no more lucrative purpose than the playing of cricket.

But quite how he should spell out this problem to Ponky Larreighffriebollaux presented another difficulty. Nothing was worse form for people of their class, particularly people who had been fellow muffin-toasters at Eton, than talking about money. And the situation was even worse in the case of Ponky who, although he never talked about it, was well known to have the old jingle-jangle pouring out of his ears and every other available orifice. To mention to him that things were a little tight in the trousering department would be way beyond the barbed wire.

Blotto tried to think what excuse he could come up with to get him out of the current gluepot. He wasn't good at trying to think. He wasn't good at thinking either, come to that. He wished his infinitely brainy sister Twinks was on the scene to help him out. She was a whale on having spoffing good ideas of how to get a boddo out of a hole.

But she wasn't there. She'd watched some of the cricket and then pongled off into the house. Probably now in her boudoir, employed at one of her leisure activities . . . like translating Dante's *Divine Comedy* into Urdu. Blotto would have to sort this thing out on his own.

He racked his brains. It didn't take long. There never had been much there to rack. He focused his mind (such as it

6

was) back on their days at Eton. What had been the only excuse then for a boddo not to do something?

Injury! Yes, that was it – injury.

'Sorry to put lumps in your custard, Ponky me old sausage skin, but I'm afraid I can't take the Indian commission.'

'Why ever not?'

'Crocked my kneecap.'

'When was this? It didn't seem to affect you out on the pitch. You were playing like a Grade A foundation stone.'

'Yes, well . . . It hasn't happened yet.'

'What do you mean?' asked a bewildered Ponky.

'Crocking the old kneecap. The moment of crockdom hasn't yet arrived.'

'So, when is it going to arrive?'

'Between now and . . . erm, when you're due to export the Peripherals to India.'

'Ah.' This explanation did not seem to lessen Ponky's bewilderment. 'How do you know?'

Blotto hadn't prepared properly for these supplementary questions. 'Erm . . .' he said. 'Because it's happened before.'

'Oh?'

'Yes, I get a fumacious twinge in my knee about . . . er, two months before it's going to crock itself.'

'And you're feeling that twinge now?'

'Yes. Just a little flicker of a twinge.'

'Well, that's a tick in the tickety-boo box,' said Ponky.

Blotto's fine brow furrowed. 'Sorry, not on the same page, me old butter knife . . . ?'

'The Peripherals take ship in a fortnight. Journey to Bombay round three weeks. Out there making with the willow on leather for a month, then back to Blighty. Your kneecap won't crock till we're on the return voyage.'

Rodents, said Blotto to himself, unable to share his old muffin-toaster's enthusiasm.

'Oh, do say you'll join the cavalcade, Blotters,' Ponky

pleaded. 'The Nawab of Patatah will be so disappointed not to get our best bellbuzzer of a batsman . . .'

'Sorry, me old collar stud. I'd be worrying all the time about the kneecap crocking.'

'. . . particularly since he's offered to pay all the expenses of the trip.'

'"All the expenses of the trip"?' Blotto echoed, cautious about trusting his ears.

'Yes, the whole shooting-match is going to be the Nawab of Patatah's treat.' Ponky looked with concern at his companion. 'What's that strange expression on your old tooth-trap, Blotters?'

'It's just my twinge untwingeing.'

'What, you mean you will join the Peripherals' tour to India?'

Blotto could have asked again whether the King was German. He didn't. He just said, 'Toad-in-the-hole!'

And, goodness, he meant it.

2

A Peripheral Problem

Ponky Larreighffriebollaux was very pleased that Blotto had consented to join his Peripherals tour. Disproportionately pleased. 'Tiddle my pom!' he kept saying. 'This really is the panda's panties! With you on the strength, Blotters, we'll be rolling on camomile lawns! Assuming, that is, that they have camomile lawns in India.'

He kept saying things like this so often that even someone as slow of perception as Blotto started to suspect an overreaction. 'I'm as tickled as a ticklish trout that you're such a happy hedgehog, Ponky. But you don't have to spill over the froth. This is only me agreeing to go on a cricket tour, not the second coming of the Memsahib.'

'I think you possibly mean "Messiah", Blotters.'

'Ah yes, perhaps I do.'

'"Memsahib" means something else. You'll see a lot of them in India, though.'

'Messiahs?'

'No. Memsahibs.'

'Ah. I'll look forward to meeting them.'

'Wouldn't be so sure about that, Blotters.'

'But, come on, Ponky, uncage the ferrets. Why are you so fizzulated that I'm on the tick-in?'

'Erm . . .' His old muffin-toaster looked slightly shame-faced. 'Fact is, Blotters me old shoelace-threader, I was finding getting an eleven together a bit of a tough rusk to chew.'

'Well, I'll be jugged like a hare! Surely not? An all-expenses-paid cricket tour to India is the real meat and two veg with lashings of mustard. Any of our old muffin-toasters from Eton would give their left ventricle for a chance like that!'

Ponky Larreighffriebollaux shook his head sadly. 'I'd have thought the same, Blotters, but you wouldn't believe the fumacious gluepots that some of our best and bravest have got themselves into.'

'Toad-in-the-hole! What, you mean trouble with the Boys in Blue?'

'No. Well, a few have pongled off down that road, obviously. Whiffy O'Nostril is in Dartmoor at His Majesty's pleasure for passing off leadpenny fivers at Ascot, and Bubby ffrench-Leeve is doing a stretch in Parkhurst for impersonating a policewoman, but that's not what's really thinned the ranks.'

'Then, for the love of strawberries, me old wingnut, tell me what has put lumps in your custard?'

'Two terrible things, Blotters. The first is . . .' Ponky Larreighffriebollaux shuddered '. . . marriage.'

An instinctive, parallel shudder ran through Blotto's finely tuned body. 'Marriage?' he echoed fearfully. Then, appalled, 'Not you?'

'No, no. My wrists are still free of the handcuffs, but as for the rest . . .' Ponky shook his head grimly. 'I'm afraid the scourge of matrimony has cut a swathe through the brightest and best of our generation. A lot of the old thimbles with whom we used to share our youthful dreams and muffins have succumbed to . . .' another shudder '. . . wives.'

Blotto matched his old chum shudder for shudder.

'Some,' Ponky went on, 'have even got children.'

'Surely,' Blotto protested, 'boddoes of our breeding don't need to let details like that get in the way of their enjoyment? Throughout my childhood, my aged Ps showed no signs of being aware of my existence.'

'That's all changing,' said Ponky dolefully. 'A lot of our contemporaries feel that having wives and children are an impediment to going to play cricket in India for three months.'

'The stenchers . . .' Blotto breathed, in a state of shock.

'But that's not the worst thing . . .' Ponky continued.

Blotto, whose imagination could not come up with the notion of a worse thing, steeled himself for the next revelation.

'A distressing number of the boddoes I asked,' said Ponky, 'said they were unable to join the Peripherals in India . . . for reasons of work.'

'Work?' Blotto felt his very saliva sullied by the unfamiliar word.

'Yes, me old windscreen wiper. I'm afraid a lot of our old muffin-toasters seem to have taken the commercial shilling.'

'But why?' asked a bewildered Blotto.

'Because a lot of them are short of the old jingle-jangle.'

'People of our breeding have always been short of the old jingle-jangle,' Blotto asserted, 'but that has never before driven us to *work*.' He encrusted the word with disdain. 'People like us live on inherited wealth.'

'And when our inherited wealth runs out . . . ?'

'Then we borrow more and build up more credit with tradespeople.'

'But what happens when those tradespeople demand payment?'

'We tell them to remember their place! That's how things have always worked for the aristocracy, from the feudal system onwards.'

11

'Hm,' said Ponky with gloomy thoughtfulness. 'I've a feeling things may be changing, Blotters.'

'Don't talk such utter globbins! You know what you sound like, Ponky me old horseshoe nail?'

'No?'

'A Socialist.'

Both men were silenced by the pronouncement of that terrible word. Blotto was profuse with his apologies. 'Sorry, don't know what came over me. Didn't mean to say it out loud. Just shock at your talking about some of our muffin-toasters actually . . .' He had a couple of runs at the word before he managed to articulate it '. . . *working.*'

'I feel bad for mentioning it, Blotters me old Victoria Sponge.'

'Don't don your worry-boots. No icing off my birthday cake, Ponky.'

'No, but . . .'

Blotto now felt more in control of himself. 'When you talk about some of our muffin-toasters actually *working*, you mean managing their estates, don't you, not actually *going out to work*?'

Ponky Larreighffriebollaux was unable to provide the reassurance his friend required. 'No, I'm afraid some of them do go out to work.'

'What, like common people . . . oikish sponge-worms like doctors and stockbrokers and solicitors?'

Ponky nodded ruefully.

'Well, I'll be kippered like a herring!'

'Tiddle my pom!' Ponky agreed. 'It's absolutely the flea's armpit. A lot of the boddoes from the old school whom I've asked to join the jollities say their bosses won't let them have the time off.'

Blotto's noble brow furrowed. '"Bosses"?' he echoed the unfamiliar word. 'And what's a "boss" when he's got his spats on?'

'A "boss" is someone for whom another person works, someone they have to obey.'

'But surely that doesn't apply to people of our breeding, does it, Ponky me old wireless valve?'

'Increasingly it does, I'm afraid. The days of the private income are numbered.'

'Broken biscuits,' Blotto murmured in shock. 'It's that murdy Socialism again, isn't it? Next thing they'll be banning fox-hunting.'

Both of them had a good laugh at the incongruity of the idea. Then Blotto returned to less frivolous matters. 'So how many boddoes have you got for your Peripherals line-up?'

'You bring the tick-up to eleven, Blotters.'

An indrawn breath. 'No twelfth man?'

'No twelfth man,' Ponky confirmed lugubriously.

'And you've popped the quezzie to everyone?'

'Every last muffin-toaster. The bottom of the Old Etonian barrel has been scraped dry.'

'Hm. Bit of a risk taking no twelfth man cover . . .'

'Don't I just know it, Blotters.'

'Particularly going to India,' Blotto added darkly. He'd never tasted Indian food, but it had a reputation. 'Only takes one iffy curry . . .'

Ponky finished the sentence for him. '. . . and the Peripherals would be making the wrong kind of runs.'

'You've popped the partridge there.'

'As you can imagine, Blotters, I've been wringing out the braincloth, trying to come up with a name for a suitable twelfth man.'

'Good ticket,' Blotto agreed. Then that rare phenomenon, an idea, irradiated the echoing spaces of his cranium. 'Of course, as you saw in today's match, my chauffeur, Corky Froggett, is no dolly with the wicketkeeper's gloves on. And something of a boundary-basher at the crease.'

13

Ponky Larreighffriebollaux didn't say anything, but a look at the pain etched in his old chum's face told Blotto how far he'd overstepped the mark.

'Sorry, brainbox not in gear. Of course, wasn't thinking. Didn't mean to play the dunce's part. Momentary mind malfunction. Corky's a Player, not a Gentleman.'

'You're bong on the nose there.' Ponky couldn't keep a note of reproof out of his voice. As he knew well – and Blotto would also have known well if he'd been concentrating – in the world of cricket there was a very rigid distinction between the two categories. Gentlemen were gifted amateurs with private incomes who played for the sheer pleasure of the sport. Whereas Players were professionals who stooped to the ignominy of being paid for their services (and, to make things worse, sometimes actually *practised*). To put it simply, Gentlemen were Blotto and Ponky's 'type of people', while Players were oikish pond-life from the lower reaches of the British social system. (But, to demonstrate the selfless magnanimity of the upper classes, the Gentlemen behaved towards the Players almost as if they were normal people.)

'So Corky's way beyond the barbed wire,' Blotto confirmed gloomily. 'Are you sure you've tried all our old muffin-toasters? Including the ones we didn't like?'

'I even got as low down the barrel as "Snotrags" Prideaux.'

'"Snotrags" Prideaux?' Blotto echoed in disgusted amazement. 'The stencher whose father, at the beginning of every term at Eton, used to deliver him in a baker's van?'

'The very same.'

'The "Snotrags" Prideaux, whose grandfather sold jellied eels in the Balls Pond Road?'

'None other.'

'The "Snotrags" Prideaux, whose school fees were paid for by the estate of a thimble-rigging bookmaker in

Shoreditch who'd been sharing the same umbrella as the boy's mother?'

'That's the Johnnie.'

'The "Snotrags" Prideaux who was never invited to anything because he was, by five circuits of the Grand National course, "not our sort of boddo"?'

'You do know who I'm talking about, then?'

'Do I, by Denzil! You asked him to join the Peripherals?'

'Yes.'

'That's not scraping the bottom of the barrel. That's halfway through to Australia underneath the barrel!'

'I know.' Ponky Larreighffriebollaux hung his head in shame.

'Anyway, what did the bucket of bilge-water say?'

'Said he couldn't do it.'

'"Couldn't do it"? He'd never had an offer like that in all his bornies. Why, at Eton "Snotrags" Prideaux was not even asked to act as a human toasting fork at the Bullies' Bonfire. What limp-rag excuse did he offer for turning down the Peripherals?'

'He's touring the world in his luxury yacht.'

'Toad-in-the-hole! Did he buy that with more jingle-jangle from the squiffball bookie in Shoreditch?'

'No, he made it in the City. Flaunted his Old Etonian credentials to get a berth in a stockbroker's, bought the right shares at cat's meat prices and, when the whole rombooley went belly-up, licked off the cream. Made millions.'

Blotto allowed himself a patrician shudder. 'How vulgar,' he said. At least the money the Lyminster family didn't have was inherited.

It was silently, but mutually, agreed that there would be no more mention in their conversation of 'Snotrags' Prideaux.

'So,' Ponky recapped ruefully, 'I'm still missing a twelfth man.'

A beam spread over Blotto's face, heralding the arrival of that rare visitor, an idea.

'Rein in the roans there, Ponky,' he said. 'I think I know where we might find something to fit that particular pigeonhole.'

3

Twinks Is Out of Sorts

Twinks's boudoir was as elegant and fashionable and feminine as its owner. The décor of the rest of Tawcester Towers favoured the traditional. Indeed, very little had changed there in the previous century. The Lyminsters were, generally speaking, not the kind of people who noticed their surroundings. They only noticed if something was different. And anything different was, by definition, unwelcome. If dark wood panelling broken up by dusty family portraits and rusty suits of armour had been good enough for the last three generations, then surely it was good enough for the current one? And if the panelling was here and there stained and distressed by the passage of the years and by flooding from the Tawcester Towers plumbing . . . well, only nitpickers with too much time on their hands would notice details like that, wouldn't they? Dust, as all the Lyminsters knew, was the patina of good furniture, and every part of Tawcester Towers was generously spread with it.

The boudoir, however, could not have been more different from the rest of the house. It was the private domain wherein Twinks communed with herself. (She did in fact spend a surprising amount of time communing with herself – she so rarely encountered anyone else of comparable intellect.) Though not a slave to fashion, in the boudoir she had matched the best efforts of London's top interior designers with distinctive touches of her own. The result was a welcoming nest of pale silks, laces and brocades which breathed aristocratic femininity.

(A question that had frequently occurred to Twinks was whether her mother, the Dowager Duchess of Tawcaster, had introduced comparable evidence of a woman's influence into her own bedroom and boudoir. Her instinct was for an answer in the negative. But it was a response she would never be able to prove. In common with most young people of her breeding, Twinks had never been inside her mother's bedroom or boudoir. The Dowager Duchess was a great believer in the old adage, 'Children should be seen and not heard.' But, during Blotto and Twinks's childhood, she had ensured that they weren't seen much, either.)

Many young women of Twinks's age would have made their boudoir a base for the military planning that went into the secret and mysterious processes of beautification. Their dressing tables would be sentried by bottles and pots and powders and potions, which would be used with punctilious and time-consuming skill to produce the perfect image for a Hunt Ball. But Twinks had been endowed with such perfect natural beauty that the only enhancements it ever required were a thin lick of lipstick and the occasional dab of rouge.

So, her boudoir was dedicated to more cerebral pursuits. It was there that she applied her colossal brainpower to problems of translation. Instead of make-up, the surfaces were piled high with dictionaries in languages ranging from Serbo-Croat to Shoshoni. Her eager intellect experimented with languages in the same way other girls might with hairstyles.

And it was also in the boudoir that Twinks did the basic

thinking involved in her other great passion, the business of detection.

On the day that Ponky Larreighffriebollaux suggested the Indian cricket tour to Blotto, his sister was out of sorts. She had just thwarted yet another of her mother's matrimonial plans for her and, as with anything involving the Dowager Duchess, the process had been a sticky one.

Though her upbringing had taught her that the discussion of money was vulgar, the old battleaxe was not unaware of its importance. Amongst her class, of course, the only respectable way of getting money was by inheritance, and if you hadn't personally inherited enough of the old jingle-jangle, the solution was to marry someone who had. This was why the Dowager Duchess devoted so much energy and scheming to the business of finding a suitable husband for her only daughter. It was not only the family honour that was at stake, but also the Tawcester Towers plumbing.

As a result, over the years, a wide array of amorous swains had been lined up as potential husbands for Twinks, and she had had to use all of her considerable ingenuity to frustrate the plans to entrap her.

One problem afflicting many aristocrats in her position mercifully passed the Dowager Duchess by. Paddling exclusively in the same gene pool for many centuries did not necessarily engender beauty in young women of their class. Prominent teeth, flat chests, emaciated gangling and its reverse, a very English kind of curtailed dumpiness, bedevilled the matrimonial ambitions of many mothers. But the perfection of her daughter's beauty removed all such anxieties from the Dowager Duchess of Tawcester. The infant Twinks had charmed everyone she met and, as she grew into womanhood, men fell for her with the frequency of guardsmen during a heatwave. A single look at

19

her reduced ducal heirs to ever deeper levels of patrician inarticulacy and persuaded confirmed bachelor earls of the benefits of matrimony. Twinks, in spite of her brilliant head for figures, had long ago lost count of the number of proposals she had turned down.

Though of impeccable breeding, none of the candidates, of course, could hold a candle to Twinks intellectually, and in many cases she only had to wait until the poor greengage in question did something stupid enough to rule himself out. It wasn't too tricky. Like the girls who were her contemporaries, most of the men she was dealing with came from depleted stock, weakened by generations of effort trying to cultivate chins.

But Twinks could never quite relax. The Dowager Duchess's determination was only matched by her daughter's and, as the years passed, the struggle between the two superpowered women grew in intensity.

Her mother's latest offensive had been the most difficult yet for Twinks. Because somehow the Dowager Duchess's trawling through the depths of Debrett's had contrived to ensnare someone with that most unlikely of aristocratic qualities – intelligence.

His name was Barrington Flexby-Cruise, and he was the second son of the Earl of Worthing. Now normally second sons were bad news. They didn't inherit the title and, their noses permanently out of joint, had a propensity for getting into scrapes and dubious company. One had only to look at the British Royal Family to find plentiful examples. Except for shining paragons of chivalry like Blotto, second sons were not the kind of people a boddo would want to go into the jungle with. Jealousy of their older siblings warped their minds. The law of primogeniture was not conducive to familial harmony.

But Barrington Flexby-Cruise was an unusual second son. His late father had solved the perennial aristocratic problem of too little jingle-jangle by the extreme measure of marrying an American. His bride had arrived in Britain from Texas with, not only inexhaustible oil wealth, but also some very startling American ideas. Among these was a resistance to the principle of primogeniture. Yes, she was happy for the title to pass to her elder son, but on her husband's death, she insisted that the money should be distributed equally between all of their children, even – and this caused much harrumphing in stately homes – the daughters.

So, untrammelled by any title beyond 'Honourable', Barrington Flexby-Cruise was an extraordinarily wealthy young man. Also, for someone of his class, he was surprisingly intelligent, one of those rare examples where generations of inbreeding had not led to vacuous imbecility, but to exceptional sharpness. He had actually read Classics at Oxford – and not on one of those closed scholarships reserved for brainless younger sons of the aristocracy. His achievement had been based on merit, and he had come away with a First Class Honours degree.

He was good-looking, too. Even Twinks, for whom the gold standard of attractiveness in a man was her brother, had to acknowledge Barrington's physical charms. Tall, languid, with floppy dark hair, he glowed with health and fitness. The only blemish on his perfect skin was a brown mole about the size of a farthing. But it was on his right forearm and thus hidden, except when he rolled his sleeve up. Which only happened when he played cricket or tennis. No, Twinks couldn't deny that Barrington Flexby-Cruise was a dashed tasty slice of redcurrant cheesecake.

Her brother gave him the pass mark too. As a rule, Blotto didn't take much notice of his sister's amorous swains. There were so many of them for a start. He seemed to have spent most of his life watching men falling for her like hoardings in a hurricane. And their moments in the sun of her pleasure were so short that it never seemed worth the effort of getting to know them.

But he approved of Barrington Flexby-Cruise. The young man was adept at adjusting his conversation to his company. When with Blotto he steered clear of the kind of intellectual badinage that went down so well with Twinks. He was sufficiently skilled and knowledgeable to discuss the minutiae of cricket and hunting in the kind of depth that Blotto favoured. He also frequently expressed his admiration for Blotto's cricket bat, something that never failed to go down well with its owner. That, along with appropriate respect for the wisdom of his hunting horse Mephistopheles and the beauty of his car (a Lagonda), could not fail to endear him to his beloved's brother.

No, Blotto reckoned, if Twinks did end up twiddling the old reef knot with Barrington Flexby-Cruise, then it was fair biddles so far as he was concerned. More than fair biddles, actually. Barrington was a thoroughly decent greengage who'd absolutely fit the available pigeonhole in the Lyminster family trophy cupboard. Which, coming from Blotto, was high praise.

Needless to say, Twinks's suitor was also a relative of the Lyminsters. If you went back far enough, most people of their acquaintance were. As has been observed, the aristocratic gene pool was a shallow one (and most of its products were pretty shallow too). But Barrington Flexby-Cruise was the exception that proved the rule. He was actually not that distant a relative. As he once joked, it would only take the death of three or four people for him to inherit the Dukedom of Tawcester. Therefore, he was, so far as the Dowager Duchess was concerned, perfect husband material.

It might have been thought that her daughter would see him in the same light, but Twinks was not so convinced. She could not deny that it was undoubtedly a pleasure – and a novelty – to speak to someone of her own class who'd read a book. It was also a relief to share conversations with a man on subjects other than hunting, cricket and what slugbuckets foreigners were.

But some aspects of Barrington's character she found less appealing. Growing up so much cleverer than all of his family and friends had engendered in him a sense of superiority, which made him undervalue – or indeed totally discount – the opinions of others. And this applied particularly when those others were women.

Now Twinks was by no means a militant suffragette. Perhaps the unquestioned dominance of the Dowager Duchess at Tawcester Towers when she was growing up had bred in her the conviction that women could do everything at least as well as men – and, in most cases, a lot better. But she didn't need to fight for a vote to prove her complete superiority. Her great enjoyment of food would never allow her to contemplate a hunger strike. And she certainly had far too much respect for horses to contemplate throwing herself in front of one.

Anyway, having a vote didn't bother her. She couldn't see any circumstances in which she would use it. Of course, she had nothing against the House of Lords. Her older brother, the Duke of Tawcester (universally known as 'Loofah'), was a member (though he very rarely put in an appearance, except for the excellent Christmas lunch). So, the Lords were very definitely their sort of people.

But the House of Commons Twinks had no time for. She was of the view that it wasn't called 'Commons' for nothing. None of its members was of the kind who would ever be allowed into her social circle. They were oikish sponge-worms from the lower classes. Some of them hadn't even been to public school ... and there were rumours that a few spoke with northern accents.

And yet, unaware of their presumption – and indeed not knowing their place – stenchers like that had the temerity to pass legislation which they insisted the rest of the country should obey. Twinks was firmly of the view that for her to use her vote would only encourage them. Thank goodness people of her breeding still had some standards. When it came to politics, she shared her mother and brother's regret for the passing of the feudal system.

The longer she spent in the company of Barrington Flexby-Cruise, however, the more aware she became of how little he respected the opinions of women. He behaved with that old-fashioned gallantry which, in many men, disguises the fact that they regard all members of the opposite sex as pea-brains. And though the brain of Twinks had been likened to many magnificent objects, it could never have been compared to a pea.

Mind you, it took her a while to realise what Barrington was really like. He was so different from the usual aristocratic numbnoddies she encountered that, at the start of their acquaintance, she did for a few weeks allow herself to believe that she might finally have met a man who was her intellectual equal. Barrington Flexby-Cruise was very definitely in with a chance of carrying off the infinitely rich prize that was Twinks . . . until he gave himself away with one fatal phrase.

They had been discussing the works of Keats. This was already an advance on the average conversation she conducted with men of her own class. The last time she had raised the subject with one at a Hunt Ball, the voidbrain had asked her what a Keat was. But Barrington not only knew the poet's name, he could also quote at length from 'To Autumn' and *The Eve of St Agnes*. Twinks was spellbound as he expatiated on the virtues and limitations of the Spenserian stanza. A not-unappealing vision opened up before her of a lifetime of breakfasts over which the two of them would discuss iambic pentameters, alexandrines and *ottava rima*. Had Barrington Flexby-Cruise asked for her hand at that moment, he might have gone straight into the Winner's Enclosure.

However, unfortunately for him – and perhaps fortunately for Twinks – the conversation took another turn. 'I'm afraid I must leave soon,' said Barrington, 'and give up the inestimable pleasure of your company.'

'Oh,' said Twinks, in a tone almost of disappointment. It was the Monday morning after a weekend house party at Tawcester Towers. She had taken pleasure in his company too, and regretted that the time to part had arrived.

'I have to go to London,' Barrington explained. 'To see my man of business.'

'Ah.'

'Just a regular monthly meeting we have. To check on how my investments are doing.'

'And what,' asked Twinks, 'is the nature of those investments?'

'Oh,' Barrington replied, 'don't you worry your pretty little head about things like that.'

It was a fatal error. Once having been said, the sentence could never be unsaid. The harm was done. Twinks's brain instantly rolled up the fantasy of breakfasts spent discussing verse forms with Barrington Flexby-Cruise and locked it in the cupboard of broken dreams. She would breakfast alone for the rest of her life. Or perhaps sometimes with Blotto, listening to his vacuous tales from the hunting field and the cricket pitch.

Barrington Flexby-Cruise would no longer feature in Twinks's life. Nobody who said 'Don't you worry your pretty little head about things like that' ever had a hope of featuring in her life.

The Dowager Duchess, unsurprisingly, took a different view of the situation. It wasn't her daughter's marital happiness she was worried about. It was the shattered vision of the Tawcester Towers plumbing being permanently fixed by generous infusions of Texan oil money. She

25

really thought that, in the form of Barrington Flexby-Cruise, she had found the solution to that perennial problem.

So, when Twinks announced that Barrington was yet another amorous swain she had no intention of ever seeing again, the temperature of her mother's permafrosted visage plummeted further. The Dowager Duchess left her daughter in no doubt about her displeasure. (Never one to hide her feelings, the old lady's craggy face would immediately register emotions ranging from dislike to loathing. And as to her finer feelings ... generosity, empathy, love ... she didn't have any of those.)

So, within Tawcester Towers there now existed a state of undeclared war between the Dowager Duchess and her daughter. Twinks herself was not happy about the situation. From the nursery onwards – perhaps because it took one to know one – she had recognised and respected her mother's deviousness. She knew she had to be on her guard. Though apparently frustrated in her first sortie, the Dowager Duchess could be relied on to make further attempts at infiltrating Barrington Flexby-Cruise into her daughter's life

So, it was a pensive Twinks who sat in her boudoir on the evening of the Peripherals match. She was too distracted to take the customary pleasure in the beauty of her surroundings. In fact, she was desperate to have a break from the oppressive atmosphere of Tawcester Towers with a resentful Dowager Duchess in residence. She even found her attention wandering from the fascinating challenge of rendering Dante's *Divine Comedy* into Urdu. She was unsettled.

Nor did she receive the usual comfort from inspecting the sequinned reticule which she always carried with her, and whose contents had proved lifesavers in so many of her adventures abroad. Though, like Blotto's, the normal setting on Twinks's emotional barometer was 'Sunny', on this occasion she felt distinctly 'Changeable'.

Therefore, it was with slight annoyance that she reacted to a tap on the door of her boudoir.

It should be mentioned at this point that Ponky Larreighffriebollaux, in common with every young man on first encounter with Twinks, had fallen for her like a Douglas fir at the mercy of loggers. And, though he had met her many times since that lightning-flash moment, in common with every young man of his breeding, he was completely incapable of putting his feelings into words. For Ponky the goggle-eyed tongue-tie was so powerful that all he could say in Twinks's presence was, 'Tiddle my pom!'

As a result, it was a very silent Ponky Larreighffriebollaux who was ushered with Blotto into the boudoir that evening. Even if Twinks hadn't been there, he would undoubtedly have been struck dumb by the alien splendour of his surroundings. Ponky had never been in a lady's boudoir before. Indeed, he did not even know that such rooms existed. And, given the slender chance of someone as inarticulate as he ever getting married, it was entirely possible that he would never visit another such inner sanctum of femininity.

Twinks greeted her guests with her customary *politesse* and suggested that their talk might be more relaxed over cups of cocoa. Ponky agreed with an enthusiastic nod of the head. (Though barely able to speak, he could drink cocoa in the presence of a woman.) He was then amazed to see that Twinks did not immediately ring for a housemaid to supply the necessary. Instead, the mistress of the boudoir became busy with kettle, tin of cocoa powder and milk, *actually making the drinks herself*. Ponky had heard rumours of a new breed of omnicompetent modern young women, but he'd never expected to see one in action.

'Right, Blotters me old bootscraper,' said Twinks once they were settled with their steaming mugs of cocoa, 'what's the bizz-buzz? Why have you pongled along here? Come on, uncage the ferrets.'

'Well, Twinks me old length of knicker elastic,' said Blotto. 'How would you fancy being twelfth man on a tour of India with the Peripherals?'

For the first time in some days, Twinks grinned. Miraculously, she had been offered the break from Tawcester Towers she so longed for. 'Larksissimo!' she responded. 'I can think of nothing I could like more. It would be pure creamy éclair!'

'Well,' said Ponky. 'Tiddle my pom!'

Mater v. Daughter

In the Antarctic there are natural ice sculptures, formed by the incessant abrasion of sub-zero winds, but none of them is as chill and forbidding as the face of a peeved Dowager Duchess of Tawcester. Actually, the expression on her face when not peeved was only a marginal improvement. Even at such public occasions as a Hunt Ball or a Royal Wedding, it was never a face that could be described as 'tender' or 'welcoming'. And that day in the Blue Morning Room, the Dowager Duchess was extremely peeved.

The cause of her peevedom sat in front of her. Twinks. Honoria Lyminster. The young woman whose name should have appeared some weeks before in the 'Forthcoming Marriages' listing in *The Times*. The young woman who should by this time be the fiancée of Barrington Flexby-Cruise, promising a union which would sort out, once and for all, the problem of the Tawcester Towers plumbing.

And yet this chit of a girl, currently facing her mother with something between defiance and insolence, had rejected the offer from Barrington Flexby-Cruise, on the fatuous grounds that *she didn't love him*. The Dowager Duchess had good reason to be peeved. Love was not a factor that had featured when her mother had made the decision that she should marry the Duke of Tawcester. Nor, indeed, had it put in even the smallest appearance during the long tedium of their marriage. This had not been a problem. Like most people of their social standing, they had kept the union going by the simple expedient of never seeing each other.

Also in attendance that day in the Blue Morning Room was the Dowager Duchess's younger son, Devereux Lyminster. He was agape and silent, shrivelled by the crossfire of venomous looks flashing between mother and sister. Following the sage advice of his chauffeur Corky Froggett, who had spent the most enjoyable years of his life in the trenches of Flanders, Blotto kept his head low.

It was, however, at his instigation that the audience with his mother had been arranged, so he felt he ought to make an attempt at breaking the ice (and there was enough ice in evidence to render the Northwest Passage unnavigable).

'Well, tickey-tockey,' he said. He had found over the years that this was a good conversation-starter in almost all circumstances. 'Actually, Mater, reason I wanted to ping a particular partridge in your direction this morning is to do with the Peripherals . . .' He still didn't seem to have engaged his mother's attention. 'The fact is, you see, not to shimmy round the shrubbery, I am a Peripheral.'

This did bring the Dowager Duchess's basilisk stare to focus on him. 'Such self-knowledge from you, Blotto, is rare. I welcome it. I realised, from an early age, that most men are peripheral, and some are more peripheral than others. Your father was peripheral to the way I ran the Tawcester Towers estate. You, as you so wisely recognise, Blotto, are completely peripheral to everything.'

He was encouraged by this rare compliment from his mother. 'That's very British of you, Mater,' he said, 'but I'm afraid you've got the wrong end of the sink-plunger. The Peripherals to which I refer is a cricket combo set up by my Old Etonian muffin-toaster, Ponky Larreighffriebollaux.'

'And in what way, Blotto, does that information have any relevance for me? The cricket season is over. Yesterday's match was the last until the end of March next year. From now on, over the winter, your main activity will be hunting. Hunting – you know? Hunting. On your horse, Mephistopheles. I know you are not the sharpest arrow in the armoury, Blotto, but I'm surprised I have to tell you this. I thought cricket and hunting were the two subjects in the world on which you were not an empty revolver.'

'Ah, no, well, you see, Mater, you are absolutely right . . . as of course you always are . . .'

'Of course,' the Dowager Duchess agreed.

'. . . but though the English cricket season has just ended, this is not the same puff in the powder box for other countries in the world.'

'And why should I care about what happens in other countries in the world?' demanded the Dowager Duchess, expressing the attitude which had sustained the aristocracy over many years – and had indeed been the guiding principle behind the British Empire. Other countries in the world existed only to provide cheap goods and even cheaper labour to keep the English upper classes in the style to which they had all too easily become accustomed.

'Because,' Blotto replied triumphantly, 'in India the cricket season continues through the winter.' Remembering what Ponky had told him, he elaborated, 'They can't have the same cricket season as us, you see, because of the mongoose.'

More crevices of puzzlement joined the fissured landscape of his mother's face.

'I think, Blotters,' said Twinks quickly, 'you mean "monsoon".'

'Who asked you?' snapped the Dowager Duchess, lest her daughter should forget just how bad the odour she was in was.

'Anyway,' said Blotto, seizing the opportunity to get his oar back in, 'not to fiddle round the fir trees, the fact is that Ponky Larreighffriebollaux has asked me to join his Peripherals combo on a tour of India.'

It was rarely that he managed to get out so much information in one sentence, and he waited in some trepidation for his mother's reaction to this new-found articulacy.

There was a long silence before the Dowager Duchess said, 'You wish to play cricket? Throughout the winter? In India?'

'That's about the size of pyjamas,' her son agreed.

'Blotto,' said his mother in tones that had, since the Norman Conquest, reduced generations of serfs to trembling wrecks, 'are you unaware of the state of the Tawcester Towers plumbing?'

'Mater,' he replied loyally, 'I am never unaware of the state of the Tawcester Towers plumbing.'

'I should hope not. Then, for that reason, even someone as brain-bereft as you should be able to work out that we cannot . . .' With years of practice, she avoided the demeaning word 'afford'. 'We cannot contemplate your undertaking a self-indulgent pleasure trip to India.'

'Ah, but, Mater, this is where the Camembert gets creamy . . . All expenses for the trip will be paid.'

'What?' He had her full attention now.

'By the Nawab of Patatah.'

'Who?'

'He was a muffin-toaster of Ponky and me at Eton. Out in India, he's an aristocrat.'

The Dowager Duchess dismissed such pretension with a 'Pooh. No other country's aristocracy has any validity when compared to our own. People with foreign titles have the equivalent status in England to bank managers, stationmasters . . . and *solicitors*!' She reserved particular contempt for these last representatives of middle-class aspiration.

'Never mind that, Mater. In his home country Patatah's quite the crystallised ginger. Jingle-jangle spilling out at every seam. And he's footing the finance for the whole Peripherals rombooley.'

'I see,' said the Dowager Duchess thoughtfully. 'And how long would this cricket tour keep you in foreign parts?'

'Round the ten-week mark,' Blotto replied.

The Dowager Duchess's 'Oh' was distinctly unenthusiastic.

Her son had, however, lived in Tawcester Towers with her long enough to know how to please his mother. 'Might be longer,' he said. 'Three months, four months . . .'

His words brought a slight thaw to her features and a shift in their tectonic plates which might have been interpreted as the beginnings of a smile. 'That would be a lot better.' Then she was struck by a moment's doubt. 'Will you be away for Christmas?'

'I could jiggle the timetable to ensure that I was,' said Blotto, with uncharacteristic cunning.

'And away for Loofah's birthday dinner?' she asked. This was in January, an event of unbelievable tedium, attended by all male members of the Lyminster family, right down to distant cousins. It was an interminable evening, which ended at midnight with fireworks set off from the Tawcester Towers battlements (though by then the guests were all too wobbulated to notice them).

Though she had never attended, it was an occasion the Dowager Duchess loathed, because it was raucous and badly behaved, in the way only dinners for rich young men with no women present can be. Blotto was one of those boddoes who inclined to treat boredom with alcohol, and his mother had, on more than one occasion, reprimanded him in the Blue Morning Room the day after one of his brother's birthday dinners.

The Dowager Duchess's expression was now almost beatific. 'Well, that would melt the chocolate perfectly,' she said. 'Blotto, of course you have my permission to go and play cricket in India.'

'Good ticket!' he said.

'And, while you're out there . . . should you happen to find the daughter of an extremely wealthy Maharajah to marry you . . . once the financial arrangements have been agreed . . . don't feel you have to come back.'

Blotto smiled, warmed by the fact that she was smiling at him. He could not recall another such overt demonstration of maternal affection. He did not allow his spirits to be dampened by the fact that the trigger of her glee was the prospect of never seeing him again.

'Toad-in-the-hole!' he said.

Now came the trickier bit, though. He checked with his sister and a flicker from Twinks's azure eyes told him that he should proceed with their prearranged plan. They had agreed that the Dowager Duchess would never consent to her daughter being twelfth man in an all-male cricket team, so they had come up with an alternative scenario.

'Mater . . .' Blotto began. 'Have you heard of "The Fishing Fleet"?'

'I am aware,' his mother condescended, 'that fish do not grow on trees, that there exists a subspecies of insalubrious common people who go out in boats to ensure that we have a sufficiency of Dover sole for dinner parties.'

'Give that pony a rosette,' murmured Blotto. 'But I was actually referring to a fleet of tubs pongling off on a regular basis to India, many of whose passengers are unmarried women looking out for some unwary subaltern whom they can trick into twiddling the old reef knot. Not much choice out there, for English boddoes, when it comes to finding a breathsapper to share your umbrella with.'

'I have heard,' the Dowager Duchess conceded, 'that such women do exist. They carry about them, I believe, that air of desperation so common among the lower classes. "Common" in every sense of the word. The younger daughter of the Marchioness of Tewkesbury did, I hear, set out on such a mission. Ended up married to a Major, whose parents were in lard.'

Blotto looked blank.

'They ran a business which grew ... or picked ... or manufactured ... or whatever it is that you do to ... lard,' his mother explained. 'The Marchioness was never seen in Society again.'

The execution of Blotto and Twinks's plan wasn't getting off to a very good start. He glanced across and received a signal from the azure eyes to press on.

'Well, the fact is, Mater,' Blotto pressed on, 'not to dally in the daffodils, we had wondered, Twinks and I, whether she might accompany me on the boat to India, in the hope of finding someone out there to ding-dong the church bells with – obviously someone with enough of the old jingle-jangle to sort out the Tawcester Towers plumbing for good.'

There was an ominous silence from the Dowager Duchess.

Blotto hastened to qualify his proposal. 'I mean, we're not talking about some tin-pot soldier here. Twinks could set the old crosshairs a bit higher than that. As I said, the Nawab of Patatah can't move for piles of gold. And I'm sure he knows lots of other Indian boddoes who are absolutely up to their ears in ruperts.'

'Ruperts?' echoed a puzzled Dowager Duchess.

'I think Blotto means "rupees",' Twinks suggested.

'Ah.'

Brother looked pleadingly at his sister, and so she took over the hopeless task. 'Mater,' she said, 'I am asking whether you will allow me to accompany Blotto to India, in the hope of finding a rich husband there.'

Another long silence. Finally, another slow shifting of the tectonic plates into something that might be interpreted as a smile. 'Twinks,' said the Dowager Duchess, 'I think that is an excellent idea.'

In a most unladylike manner, Twinks's jaw dropped. The consent had been given so easily. It seemed too good to be true.

As, of course, it was.

5

All Aboard!

There was the prospect of a sad farewell for Blotto at Southampton Docks. A second sad farewell in the same day. And neither to anything so trivial as a human being. They'd had an early start from Tawcester Towers, but not so early that he hadn't managed to fit in a visit to the stables, where dwelt one of his closest confidants, his hunter Mephistopheles.

The horse understood Blotto on a level much deeper than even his Old Etonian muffin-toasters could aspire to. The only human who showed anything like the same empathy was Twinks, and there were even times when he valued the hunter's advice over hers. The instinctive communion between man and beast did not require anything so mundane as speech. Just as, out in the field, Mephistopheles could interpret meaning in the slightest pressure of his master's thighs, so in the stables he could read and soothe the few troubles that might threaten to shadow that customary sunny disposition. Though he didn't need to talk during these sessions, Blotto quite often did, at considerable length. And Mephistopheles always understood. His master never left the stables less than energised and motivated by the horse's advice.

Their encounter that morning had been a particularly difficult one. Mephistopheles had accustomed himself over the years to fewer visits from Blotto during the summer months. He respected the necessary precedence taken at such times by cricket. But with the return of the hunting season, he very definitely required his master's full attention. So, for Blotto to tell him, as he had had to that morning, that he was forgoing the annual pleasure of chasing foxes in Tawcestershire, in favour of a cricket tour to India, was a severe equine disappointment.

Blotto still could not excise from his memory the expression of reproach he had read in Mephistopheles' eye as he left the stable.

And now, at Southampton, a parting of almost greater poignancy drew near. Next to sitting astride Mephistopheles and trampling down the crops in Tawcestershire farmers' fields, there was nothing Blotto enjoyed more than scattering the local traffic at the wheel of his magnificent blue Lagonda. He felt like a god as he roared along the county's narrow lanes at vast speed with the roof down, his blond hair straightened by the wind, forcing into the ditches an assortment of horse-drawn hay wains, nurse-pushed prams and cycling vicars.

It had been a bitter pill to swallow when Twinks, responsible for booking their passages to India (on the Nawab of Patatah's account), had broken the news that there would be no room on the RMS *Queen of the Orient* for the Lagonda. All of the vehicle space had already been booked for fleets of Rolls-Royces for various Maharajahs. After an uncharacteristic burst of petulance, during which Blotto said he wouldn't 'spoffing well go to India if he couldn't take the spoffing Lag', Twinks conceded that she'd try to see a way around the shipping line's regulations. This cheered Blotto enormously. His sister had an infinite capacity for 'seeing a way around' things. He felt quietly confident that she would arrange for his precious Lagonda to accompany them on their passage to India.

Even if the car hadn't made the cargo listing, Blotto would still have taken a chauffeur with him. Corky Froggett's usefulness extended way beyond driving. He was a self-appointed bodyguard to the Lyminsters, whose main ambition, since his disappointment at the ending of the Great War, had been to lay down his life for the young master. On many of their adventures the chauffeur had accompanied them and more than once helped them out of danger. He was, in his employer's view, 'a Grade A foundation stone'. And praise didn't come higher than that.

(Blotto also nursed the hope that under the more relaxed protocol of Indian cricket, he might be able to smuggle Corky into the Peripherals team as a wicketkeeper.)

Corky himself was more than happy to do whatever the young master requested of him. He did in fact loathe the sea and had never learned to swim, so a three-week passage to India did not fill him with glee. But the young master had asked him to take the trip and Corky Froggett had never questioned where his duty lay in relation to the Lyminsters.

But there was a chock in the cogwheel. As the day of their departure approached, Twinks had still received no confirmation from the shipping company that the Lagonda could go on board. She tried calling them but, though her telephone manner was exquisitely alluring, it was not so powerful as an appeal from Twinks in the flesh could be. The shipping company's functionary regretted that there would be no room on board for the Lagonda. Apologetic for his earlier petulance, Blotto took this news more graciously, but couldn't keep from his sister a slight disappointment, a worry that Twinks might be losing her touch. But the shipping line's diktat seemed unalterable.

It would have been too painful for Blotto to have had to say two farewells at Tawcester Towers so, having parted with Mephistopheles, he had insisted on driving the Lagonda down to Southampton. This he had done with characteristic élan, filling the ditches on both sides of the road with startled peasantry. As well as Twinks and Corky Froggett, there was a fourth passenger, another of the Tawcester Towers chauffeurs, whose task would be to drive the Lagonda back to its home garage. 'And make sure you don't take her above thirty on the way back,' Blotto had admonished the young man. 'She's a very precious piece of automotive engineering.'

A tear clouded the perfect blue of his eye as he brought the darker blue beauty of the Lagonda to a halt at dockside.

So, no Mephistopheles . . . no Lagonda . . . Blotto would have been near despair if he'd have to part from the third item in his triumvirate of favourites.

But no, he did not have to suffer that additional misery. His cricket bat was safely stored in his luggage. In one of the suitcases marked 'Wanted on Voyage'.

Wherever its owner went, Blotto's cricket bat was always wanted.

'Before we embark,' said Twinks, 'I must just go inside the office to check something.'

'Tickey-tockey,' said Blotto. He never asked for further information about such statements. He knew that 'powdering one's nose' and a whole lot of other mysterious rituals were an essential and private part of a lady's life.

So, he stayed in the car, discussing with Corky the engineering inadequacies of the row of Rolls-Royces lined up on the dockside. And how much better the Lagonda was.

Twinks was not away long. She returned with a uniformed official of the shipping company, whose bedazzled expression put him instantly in the ranks of amorous swains who had fallen for her like stumps against

40

W.G. Grace. The functionary ordered a driver to reverse one of the Rolls-Royces out of the line and gestured for the Lagonda to take its place.

'Larksissimo!' said Twinks. 'The Lag will be pongling along with us.'

Blotto knew he should never have doubted his sister.

The RMS *Queen of the Orient* was not the most opulent of vessels on the Bombay route. That enviable position had recently been usurped by P&O's RMS *Viceroy of India*, with its electric turbo-charged engines and every latest luxury, including an indoor swimming pool. But facilities on the *Queen of the Orient* were still pretty lavish.

It went without saying that Blotto and Twinks travelled first class, on the bridge deck. They had adjacent state-rooms, which were of course on the right side of the ship. 'Port Out, Starboard Home' was still reckoned to offer passengers the maximum allowance of shade for the journey in both directions. Neither Blotto nor Twinks gave any credence to the theory that in that expression lay the origin of the adjective 'posh'. They were far too posh to use such a common word.

For the first dinner on board, Blotto and Twinks were inevitably seated at the Captain's table. He was a man of rough and ready manners who rejoiced in the name of Captain Barnacle. He made rather too many references to the aptness of his name to his profession, asserting that he enjoyed 'being attached to ship's bottoms – or any other bottoms I can lay my hands on!'

His career path had been an unusual one. At first his employers had thought him far too coarse for the hosting role required by captaincy of a luxury liner, but reports from delighted passengers gave the lie to that. So rarefied by wealth were most of the people who travelled on the RMS *Queen of the Orient* that they were vastly entertained by encountering what they considered to be a 'real person'. For them, Captain Barnacle represented the salt of the earth or, as he preferred to put it (rather wittily, he thought), in another of his oft-repeated expressions, 'the salt of the salt'. He was the source of much ribald anecdotage over the dinner tables of Madras, Simla, London and the Home Counties. Aristocrats did so love affecting the accents of their inferiors. On both continents, tales of Captain Barnacle's grossnesses filled many an awkward pause between discussion of the next day's hunting prospects and the iniquities of Socialism.

For that first dinner on board, the *placement* had put Twinks to the Captain's left and next to her an Indian introduced to her as 'the Maharajah of Koorbleimee'. He was a gentleman of infinite sophistication and even more infinite wealth, at ease equally in the royal courts of Europe as in the many palaces he owned in his home country. He was tall and slender, with remarkably delicate hands.

Though most of the gentleman diners – even the Indian ones – were in conventional evening dress, the Maharajah was decked out in exotic splendour. He wore a high-necked tunic of purple silk, inwoven with gold thread. Over this were looped strings of perfect pearls, mingled with other random jewellery. His moustaches and beard were curled as by a master topiarist.

But the object which attracted all eyes in the dining room was affixed to the front of his multi-coloured silken turban. Set in silver, surrounded by lesser diamonds, was a stone the size of a duck's egg. The skill of the jeweller, who had cut it in 'brilliant' style, ensured that, reflected and refracted through many facets, the diamond seemed alive, a symbol of infinite wealth that shapeshifted with every movement of its owner's head.

It shimmered and sparkled more than ever as he made a little bow on being introduced to Twinks. She was far too well brought up to say that such an extravagant display of jewellery would be considered bad form in the circles in which she moved.

But he seemed to be ahead of her thought. In impeccable Oxford English, the Maharajah said, 'Forgive the fancy dress. I wear it only for the first night on board. Tomorrow you will see me during the day in blazer and flannels, and at night in conventional British evening dress.'

'And why do you do that?' she asked coolly.

'It gives me more choice in the company that I keep on board.'

'How so?'

'Some people, of a certain class, are so impressed by my evident wealth that they do not dare approach me. Others, of a more discerning nature, find my appearance flashy and meretricious. For that reason, they do not approach me either. In this way, I can ensure total privacy for the duration of the voyage.'

'Larksissimo!' said an admiring Twinks.

'There is also,' the Maharajah went on, 'a security aspect to my display.'

'Oh?'

'By excluding the possibility of most other passengers approaching me, I know that the only ones who do so must be jewel thieves.'

'Ah,' said Twinks. 'Give that pony a rosette.'

'Thank you.' He nodded acknowledgement of the compliment and gestured to the emerald. 'The Star of Koorbleimee is a challenge to all in that dishonourable profession.'

'I do not doubt it.'

'There have been many attempts to purloin the stone. All have failed.'

'But does not the ostentation with which you display the jewel encourage the thieving stenchers?'

'Are you suggesting that the Star might be less at risk if it were locked away?'

'That thoughtette had blipped the brain cells, yes.'

'In the ship's safe, perhaps . . . ?'

'Give that pony another rosette.'

'But what you forget,' said the Maharajah, 'Miss Honoria . . . Lady Honoria . . . ?'

'Please call me "Twinks". Everyone does.'

'Very well, Twinks . . . what you forget is that any jewel thief worthy of the name knows full well that I own the Star of Koorbleimee. Also, that I never travel without it. And, as for ship's safes . . . there is not a crew in the world that does not contain someone susceptible to bribery.' He looked sideways at Captain Barnacle. 'Such people are frequently to be found amongst the ship's officers.'

'And do you not fear that some lump of toadspawn might take the Star from you by force?'

'I am well protected against such eventualities,' the Maharajah replied complacently.

'You mean you do not travel alone?'

'Of course not. I travel with some of my wives and daughters . . . but they, of course, are not allowed out of their cabins until we reach Bombay.'

Twinks pursed her lips. Though she knew about the system of purdah (she did, after all, know about everything), an independent spirit like hers could never approve the forced segregation of members of her gender. She knew that she would have fretted considerably in the seclusion of the zenana (which, of course, she also knew was the name for the women's quarters).

'But, to make assurance doubly sure . . .' The Maharajah's long eyelashes flickered as he looked around the room '. . . my men are everywhere on the ship. Any jewel

44

thief who tried to attack me would get a lot more than he bargained for.'

'Then everything is all creamy éclair,' said Twinks.

'It is indeed.' A smug grin, a silence, then, 'When I spoke of the reactions of different people to my appearance, Twinks, you, I deduce, are of the persuasion that finds my jewellery flashy and meretricious.'

She inclined her head to show that he had guessed correctly.

'So that would provide you with the perfect excuse to have no further conversation with me?'

'You're on the right side of right there.'

'But I hope, Twinks, you will not follow that course.'

'Oh?'

'Because there is something of great importance I need to ask you.'

'And what might that be when it's got its spats on?' she asked.

The Maharajah opened his mouth to reply but was prevented from doing so. Captain Barnacle regarded interrupting the guests at his table as yet another demonstration of his salty charm. He leered at Twinks and said, 'I hope you are enjoying your dinner, Your Ladyship.'

Twinks did not censure his use of the incorrect form of address. And she was too well brought up to express her true opinion of the food. She contented herself with a simple, 'Yes, thank you.'

'Enjoy it while you can,' said the Captain with a roguish wink. 'Once we get to the Bay of Biscay, most of the passengers will only be ... *renting* their meals.'

He roared with laughter at what he considered to be a *bon mot* worthy of Noël Coward. Twinks smiled thinly and readdressed her rather tough duck. The Maharajah having recognised that she thought his appearance 'flashy and meretricious', she felt no need to indulge in further conversation with him.

But growing up with infinite wealth, power and privilege meant he was not easily daunted. He repeated, 'There is something of great importance I need to ask you.'

Twinks sighed wearily. 'All right then. Uncage the ferrets.'

'Twinks, will you marry me?'

'Maharajah, you already have a sufficiency of wives.'

'Oh,' he said, 'there is always room for one more.'

A delicate wrinkle formed on Twinks's exquisite brow. Sometimes being as beautiful as she was could be very tiresome.

6

Wanted on Voyage

Precedence in the *placement* for dinner that evening had dictated that Blotto was seated between two mature titled ladies, both returning to India after escorting six-year-old youngest sons to take up places in preparatory schools, buried deep in the Sussex countryside. The English private educational system would then see the boys through public school and university or Sandhurst, whence they might rejoin their parents to take up posts in India. Both memsahibs seemed very satisfied to have arranged this separation of fifteen years from their offspring.

Blotto entirely approved. From the nursery onward at Tawcester Towers, the Dowager Duchess could never have been accused of mollycoddling – or even tolerating – her children. What else were nursemaids, nannies and governesses invented for? And her late husband the Duke of Tawcester, on encountering the teenaged Blotto and Twinks in one of the mansion's many corridors, had to get the butler to explain to him who they were.

But, after expressions of agreement about the right way of bringing up children, Blotto found little other conversational fodder to share with his two companions. They expressed no interest in either hunting or cricket, which immediately put him at a disadvantage. Scouring his brain for other topics proved as unrewarding as scouring it for anything else had always proved.

The only subject that did raise any spark of animation between the two memsahibs was the likely order of precedence at the forthcoming ball being given by the Resident in Hyderabad. In particular, they were concerned about the allocated place of the wife of a Major in the Bengal Lancers who had committed various and continuing indiscretions with a Eurasian subaltern in Simla the previous summer.

Blotto reconciled himself to spending the rest of the evening with the two of them talking (literally) over his head.

His one further conversational foray was to ask about the sport to be enjoyed aboard the RMS *Queen of the Orient*. He had heard good reports of the fun and games organised for such voyages.

But the memsahibs told him that, this time of year, the sporting programme would not begin until they had progressed some way into the Mediterranean. And what there was would be played at a very juvenile and raucous level.

Given the unpromising conversational prospects, Blotto stiffened both his sinew and his upper lip (his collar was already stiffened). He would not be such an oikish spongeworm as to leave the table before the end of the meal. He would just have to grin and bear the evening.

His uncharacteristic gloom prevented him from observing the effect his presence was having on the large number of unattached young ladies in the first-class dining room. Though he had spoken authoritatively to the Dowager Duchess about the 'Fishing Fleet', Blotto had never witnessed them in action.

Nor did he know the speed with which their bush telegraph of girlish twitterings had registered that there was, on board the RMS *Queen of the Orient*, an extraordinarily handsome, unmarried young man of good family.

He was also unaware of the number of female hearts already nursing the fantasy of getting the matrimonial purpose of their voyage sorted out within hours of leaving Southampton.

After what seemed like an eternity, the last coffee cup had been drained, the last brandy downed, and Blotto felt he could legitimately say goodnight to the two memsahibs. 'See you tomorrow,' he said, hoping that wouldn't be the case.

From their great experience of passages to India, they supported his hope.

'You won't see anyone tomorrow,' said one memsahib.

'No,' said the other memsahib. 'Tomorrow we will be crossing the Bay of Biscay.'

Blotto woke the next morning feeling remarkably chipper. True, the *Queen of the Orient* was going through the motions of a cocktail shaker, but rather than sliding all over the floor like a lump of ice, he was determined to be the spirit (usually gin) in the mix. He was invigorated rather than nauseated by the ship's motion.

He felt full of pent-up energy. Were he back at Tawcester Towers, he'd have been down to the stables before breakfast for a gallop on Mephistopheles. Deprived of that option, he decided to take a run round the promenade deck. For the excursion, he dressed in a soft-collared shirt, flannel trousers and plimsolls.

There seemed to be nobody much else around. He passed a couple of swaying, green-faced girls on his way up to the deck, but did not notice how the sight of him allayed their seasickness for a moment.

Once out in the open, Blotto found himself up against the kind of challenge he really relished. There was no one else on deck; everything potentially movable was strapped down and the *Queen of the Orient* bucked and tossed like the most savage of stallions. Waves thundered across the wooden planks with every buck and toss. 'Hoopee-doopee!' cried a jubilant Blotto, as he began to run. 'This really is the lark's larynx!'

His route was a wave-washed obstacle course, tougher than the most testing of steeplechases. Within seconds, Blotto was drenched to the skin, shirt and trousers moulded to the contours of his body. He ran with reckless abandon, rubber soles skidding across the planks, setting up their own wake in the roiling water. It felt more like skiing than running, as he slalomed between the solid metal of the superstructure and its surrounding rails. He almost whooped with glee.

At the end of his first circuit, he noticed, by the door through which he'd come from the ship's interior, the two girls he'd seen wobbling on the stairs. The second time he came round, they had been joined by another dozen, and on his third circuit, almost the entire Fishing Fleet was there, trembling and clinging in the adverse conditions, but clearly fascinated by something. He could not think what they were looking at.

Nor could he recognise the mutual exhalation that rose from the girls each time he passed. A boddo who'd been educated at an all-male establishment like Eton would never have heard the rippling sigh of collective female lust.

As he came round for the fourth time, the *Queen of the Orient* gave a sudden lurch, more vigorous than any of its previous convulsions. Just after he had passed them, he looked back to see that the jolt had dislodged the whole group of twittering girls, who skidded across the deck to the railings. They leaned over them and were all copiously sick.

Blotto tried not to take it personally. He had no vanity, had never thought about his appearance, and only looked in a mirror when shaving. But he had never before prompted such an emetic reaction from women.

The girls had all disappeared when he finished his fifth circuit, gone back inside to groan and retch on their bunks. Blotto thought nothing more about them and went back to change into dry clothes and eat a hearty breakfast in the company of his sister.

She was not at her most relaxed. Her beauty was more compelling to the young male passengers than the imperative of seasickness, and she had to turn down three more proposals of marriage before they finished breakfast.

Corky Froggett's breakfast was consumed in less salubrious surroundings, a few levels lower into the bowels of the ship. Lower in every sense. Here it was that the servant classes and less well-heeled travellers would spend most of the voyage. It was no longer called 'steerage', its denizens were now crammed in, four to a third-class cabin, but it wasn't very *soigné*. Down below, the gyrations caused by the Bay of Biscay were even more extreme. For the passengers condemned to remain there, the sensation was not unlike that of cream being whipped in a bowl by a particularly vindictive cook/housekeeper.

Most of them gave up any attempt to move from the horizontal and remained nauseously in their bunks. Corky, though he loathed the sea, was a veteran of many troopship crossings and continual buffeting by German shells, and therefore unaffected by the turbulence.

Before going to the dining room, he went to the hold to give the Lagonda its daily polish. The great car was attached to the floor by straps and chains, to prevent the cargo from shifting. It stood at the end of a long row of inferior Rolls-Royces and, after Corky's ministrations, gleamed more dazzlingly than any of them.

That duty done, the chauffeur went to the lower decks dining room and ordered a large amount of bacon and eggs from a steward, whose dexterity handling plates on uneven surfaces could have earned him a juggling slot in Barnum & Bailey's Circus.

The chauffeur was the only person eating in the dining room. Or he was, until a rather buxom wench, spilling out of a grey uniform dress, came to sit opposite him.

Corky's moustache, always a reliable indicator of attraction to buxom wenches, bristled vigorously. The wench cast a roguish eye over his dark-blue-uniformed torso and plate of bacon and eggs. 'Looks nice,' she said.

He recognised the ambiguity in her words, but pretended she was just referring to the food. 'It is nice. Very nice. And, because there are so few people eating, the steward will bring you as much of it as you want.'

The waiter referred to came across the shifting floor to their table, demonstrating a sense of balance which might have earned him work as another Barnum & Bailey speciality act on the high wire. The buxom wench, giving him too the benefit of a roguish eye, ordered exactly the same as Corky.

It was time for introductions. He stood and gave his name.

'Pleased to meet you.' Her voice had a rough silkiness. Like his, it also had a cockney twang. 'I'm Emmeline Washboard.'

'And you are travelling all the way to Bombay?'

'I am indeed.' She volunteered that she had a cabin all to herself, which Corky thought was a good sign.

'And you, Corky . . . I may call you "Corky"?'

'Please, Emmeline.'

'My close friends,' she susurrated, 'call me "Em".'

'Then may I be so bold,' said Corky, with a smoothness born of a lifetime mixing with the upper classes, 'to include myself in your list of . . . "close friends", Em?'

'You may indeed, Corky. And you . . . are you too going all the way?'

Once again, the ambiguity of innuendo was there. 'I hope so,' he replied, 'if I play my cards right.'

'You have the look of a man, Corky, who always plays his cards right.'

'I endeavour to give satisfaction.'

'I'm sure you do,' said Em with an anticipatory grin. 'And what is the purpose of your journey, Corky?'

'I am chauffeur to Devereux Lyminster, second son of the late Duke of Tawcester.'

'Ah. And is your master's vehicle stowed in the hold?'

'It is indeed. Though the scoundrels of the shipping company wanted the Lagonda to stay in Blighty. I am actually accompanying the young master on a cricket tour to India.'

'Ah.'

'And you, Em . . . may I ask the purpose of your voyage?'

'I am to take up a position with an English family in Pondicherry. I met the father, who is a military man, in London, and he offered me the position.'

'And what position would that be?'

'A governess.'

Corky digested the information, along with a large mouthful of bacon and eggs. 'So . . . a governess, eh? I dare say you could teach me a thing or two.'

'I dare say I could,' she breathed.

'And have you always been a governess?' he asked.

'No. I originally trained as a nurse.'

'A life dedicated to caring for the needs of others.'

'I think I could take care of your needs, Corky.' And the roguishness of this smile outdid the roguishness of all her previous ones.

Corky Froggett thought he was going to enjoy his passage to India.

By the time the *Queen of the Orient* docked at Gibraltar to take on more passengers, they had left the tempestuous weather behind. Though it was late autumn, the Mediterranean still held the last rays of summer's heat. Deckchairs were much in evidence on the promenade decks and the schedule of organised games began.

There was quite a variety on offer. There were the perennial deck quoits, in which participants had to throw rings of rope to land in marked circles on the wooden floors. There was a form of tennis with a net and, again, a ring of rope rather than a ball. Lady passengers were encouraged to take part in egg-and-spoon races, though frequently with a potato taking the role of the egg. For the more vigorous young men, there were rougher sports. Tug-of-wars were popular. Another favourite was a pillow fight between two contestants facing each other astride a horizontal pole. The one who unseated the other was declared the victor.

There was even a game they had the nerve to describe as 'cricket'. But since it involved a squashy ball made of string and, if ladies joined in, gentleman playing left-handed, Blotto didn't think it worthy of the title. They even used special thin bats, which prevented him from using the famous linseed-soaked weapon which he had carried with great acclaim through Eton and Harrow matches, as well as many more dangerous adventures.

What made these games even less interesting to Blotto was the fact that, whatever handicaps were imposed on him, he still won easily at all of them. And every triumph was greeted by a purring of admiration from the girls of the Fishing Fleet, who followed his every movement with the assiduity of prison warders.

It could be said that Blotto found the organised games a disappointment.

On the bridge deck, Twinks sat in a deckchair in the autumn sunshine, once again feeling out of sorts. She had rejected another three proposals of marriage from avid young subalterns over breakfast that morning and was getting pretty fed up with it.

To enhance her anonymity, as well as having the shade of the deckchair pulled down low, she was wearing dark glasses and a silk scarf to cover the delicate blonde of her hair. Wherever she travelled, Twinks's luggage always contained a multitude of variegated silk scarves, and she was never without a spare in the sequinned reticule she always carried.

In the anonymous security of her deckchair, her plan was to spend the morning in a little light reading. For that purpose, she had brought with her from her stateroom Patanjali's *Mahabhasya*, a commentary on the *Ashtadhyayi* of Panini, a book about grammar and the philosophy of grammar. She was, needless to say, reading it in the original Sanskrit.

Though Twinks's most remarked-upon beauty lay in her face, with its alabaster skin, azure eyes, full, rosy lips and exquisitely tilted nose, her body too was a wonder of symmetry. And even though her head was covered, her neat breasts and slender waist in a dress of grey silk could not fail to attract attention. The perfection of her legs in white silk stockings added magnetic compulsion to that attention.

As a result, she had only read a few lines of morphological analysis before a young officer in blazer and flannels had stopped by her deckchair and announced, 'By Wilberforce, you're a bellbuzzer and no mistake!'

She shifted her position to turn her back on him, but the movement of her lissom form only inflamed him further.

'Strike me dead with a blueberry muffin! You're the full beach pyjama – cord and all!'

Twinks lowered the edge of her sunshade, but her new admirer was undeterred.

'Well, I'll be battered like a pudding! Listen, I'm about to rejoin my regiment, the Fifteenth Lancers, in Lucknow. Boozling social life, best polo this side of Cowdray, beezer place to bring up a family. So come on, don't shimmy round the shrubbery. Just open the tooth-trap and tell me . . .' And then the inevitable: 'Will you marry me?'

'Listen,' Twinks hissed. 'You have totally got the wrong end of the sink-plunger! You are about as welcome to me as a slug in a shower! If I spent any time with you, I'd be as bored as a frog who's off games with a strapped ankle! You're a total bucket of bilge-water and I'd rather stick needles up my nose than spend a minute in your company!'

'Is that a "yes" then?' he asked.

As Twinks took a deep breath to deliver another fusillade of scorn, she was interrupted by a calm, Indian-accented voice asking, 'Excuse me, madame, is this gentleman annoying you?'

Echoing her brother, Twinks just asked, 'Is the King German?'

The new arrival spat out some words in one of the few Indian dialects that she wasn't familiar with. They had the desired effect. Her annoyer scuttled away as if the entire Tawcester Towers pack of hounds was after him.

Twinks raised the shade of her deckchair to identify her saviour. She saw a tall Indian man dressed in a beige linen suit and a panama hat. The bits of his hair that showed were plastered close to his skull with some cosmetic preparation, and he looked at the world through spectacles of jam-jar thickness.

She was surprised by the encounter she had just witnessed. Though it was common to see an Indian being patronised by a representative of the British Empire, it was very rare to see the roles reversed. Her respect for the stranger increased.

'I fully understand,' he said, 'your desire to preserve

your privacy, so I will not introduce myself unless you give me permission to do so.'

She appreciated the charm and adroitness of his words. 'I would be very happy to be introduced to you,' she graciously conceded.

'My name,' he said with quaint formality, 'is Mr Mukerjee. I am travelling to India on business. I am what is informally – and without great respect – known as a "box-wallah".'

'I am delighted to meet you.' From underneath the shade, Twinks extended an elegantly slender hand for him to shake. 'My name is Honoria Lyminster, informally known as Twinks.'

'I am delighted to meet you . . . Twinks. If I am allowed to use that appellation.'

'Great galumphing goatherds, yes.'

'If I may be so bold as to comment, I admire your reading matter.'

'Yes. Patanjali does have a way with words, doesn't he?'

'Of course. And I think his response to the criticism of him from Katyana is both well-reasoned and graceful.'

'Mr Mukerjee, I couldn't agree more. His refutations of some of Panini's assertions are fair too.'

'And, again, gracefully expressed.'

'You're bong on the nose there. I also think it's surprising that we had to wait till the eighteenth century for Satyapriya Tirtha's commentary, *Mahabhasya Vivarana*.'

'It is strange, yes.'

'Still, you have to remember he was a peetadhipathi of Uttaradi Matha.'

'Give that pony a rosette!'

'And of course, belonging to the Dvaita school of Vedanta.'

'Larksissimo, Mr Mukerjee!' cried Twinks, who was beginning to think that her passage to India might not be so boring, after all.

7

Physical Jerks

Blotto had given up running round the decks as a fitness regime. The better weather in the Mediterranean had brought out all of the Fishing Fleet girls who'd been too prostrated by seasickness in the Bay of Biscay to watch him. And he found the oohing and aahing of the lot of them frankly embarrassing.

Also, his morning routine was making him unpopular with the other boddoes on board. It seemed there were a lot of young male *Queen of the Orient* passengers who were as keen to attract feminine attention as he was to avoid it. They seemed to share a general view – he heard this from Twinks who'd rejected proposals of marriage from most of them – that he was taking more than his fair share. In fact, his sister had heard the expression 'dog in the manger' used more than once. It was felt that he should give the other poor thimbles a chance.

The fact that Blotto had done nothing to encourage the Fishing Fleet's interest in him did not register with these other disgruntled young men. And since one of the inalienable principles which he'd grown up with at Eton was that only a stencher would queer the pitch of a fellow muffin-toaster, he decided to withdraw gracefully from the main promenade deck and work on his fitness elsewhere.

(A word should be said here about Blotto's attitude to fitness. He did not take strenuous exercise with a view to improving his skills at games like cricket. That would have gone entirely against the all-important spirit of the British amateur gentleman. It was only the more degenerate nations – like the Americans – who actually *practised* to try and get better at sport. Though he would never be so crass as to say it out loud, Blotto felt that was well on the way down the slippery slope towards cheating. He knew that for the British – and particularly the English – sporting skill was the instinctive result of breeding. So, a fitness regime for him was simply a way of expending his natural super-abundant energy. Steam was something which, in a young man's body, could build up a dangerous head. Blotto, like a boisterous puppy, had a lot of it. Exercise was a necessary means of letting some of it off.)

The new venue for his workout was below deck, a small storage space which, gathering from the equipment he found there, might have been used for the same purpose before. But not for a long time. Everything he found there was covered with dust. There were ropes which could be attached to a crossbeam, an incomplete set of Indian clubs in a variety of weights, some tarnished dumbbells and an old medicine ball, whose leather cover sagged where its contents of stuffing had become impacted over the years.

The first day he found the place, he did an exhilarating two hours of physical jerks, to work off his substantial breakfast and build up an appetite for his even more substantial lunch. The midday meal he did actually find a trial. A less formal affair than dinner, there was no *placement*, with the result that he was very much left at the mercy of the Fishing Fleet's dumbstruck adoration. He dealt with the problem by bolting his food and spending the minimum time possible in the dining room.

The second day, Blotto felt so secure in the privacy of his exercise regime that he dressed in his stateroom in plimsolls, a singlet and a pair of short footer bags. Covering the ensemble in a bathing robe, he scuttled along to his gym, confident that he was unseen by anyone.

The metal walls of the enclosed space channelled heat from the engine room and, as he worked through a sequence of squats with the medicine ball, the sweat started to pour off him and soak his minimal clothing. He felt the satisfaction of what he didn't know was 'an adrenaline rush'.

He was so caught up in the activity that he wasn't aware of the door to his sanctum being opened. Only when he turned did he find himself facing one of the more attractive vessels in the Fishing Fleet. He had seen her earlier in the corridor of the bridge deck, about to enter her stateroom. So, like him and Twinks, she was a first-class passenger. Which meant it was all right to talk to her.

'Hello,' she said, her pretty blue eyes widening at the sight of his dripping torso. 'My name's Lettice Sandwich.'

Blotto's instinctive politeness could not prevent him from saying, 'Bellhopper of a name.'

'Thank you. And you, I believe, are Leveret Demister . . . ?'

'Bit of a tangle in the tooth-trap there, I'm afraid. The labels Nanny sewed into my school shirts read: "Devereux Lyminster".'

'Oh, that's what I meant to say.'

She smiled vacuously at him. He smiled vacuously back. Vacuous smiles were one of Blotto's specialties. It was rarely that he met anyone who could match him in vacuity, though. But Lettice Sandwich, he suspected with a flicker of excitement, might be a member of that small category.

'So . . . what are you doing here, Devereux?' she asked.

'Oh, nobody ever calls me "Devereux".'

'What do they call you?'

'Well,' he replied cautiously, 'my muffin-toasters and other friends call me "Blotto".'

'Blotto?'

'Bong on the nose there.'

'But I just called you "Blotto".'

'Ye-es,' he conceded.

She beamed ecstatically. 'So, that means I'm one of your friends.'

'We-ell . . .'

'I'm so happy to be one of your friends, Blotto . . .' The big eyes blinked ingenuously. 'Because friendship can so easily develop into something else, can't it, Blotto?'

'Er-erm . . .'

'So, what is it you're pongling off to India for, Blotto?'

'Cricket tour.'

'Ah.'

'And you?'

'I'm going to stay with my brother Reuben in Chandannagar.'

'What does he do out there? Is he a military boddo?'

'No. He plants indigo.'

'Does he, by Wilberforce?'

'Yes.' A delicate pause. 'Do you know what indigo is, Blotto?'

A moment of inspiration came to him. 'Is it what boddoes shout when they jump into a swimming pool?'

'I don't think so.'

'Oh. Then I don't know what it means,' he confessed readily. 'Do you?'

'No.'

'Well, maybe your brother Reuben will give you the gin-gen when you're out there.'

'Maybe.'

'Is that sole purpose of visit? Giving the hi-ho to the old brother? Keeping the family branches glued together?'

'Well, yes . . .' Lettice was silent for a moment. 'And then

61

my parents coughed up the old jingle-jangle for the trip in the hope that I might meet someone.'

'I'm sure you will.'

'Meet someone?' Her blue eyes were now bigger than ever.

'Oh yes,' Blotto replied confidently. 'There are lots of people in India. Most of them Indian, but that's only to be expected. I'm sure you'll meet some people.'

'Yes.' Lettice dared another look at his sweat-drenched torso. 'What is that you are holding in your hands, Blotto?'

'It's a medicine ball.'

'To make people feel better?'

'Yes, using it will make people feel better.'

'They must be very unusual people.'

'Sorry? Not on the same page?'

'Well, if they can get a pill that size into their mouths.'

Blotto looked at Lettice with renewed interest. She seemed definitely to be confirming her credentials as one of those few people who was stupider than he was. He always treated such rarities with empathy and respect. He felt it would be rude for him to correct her impression that people swallowed medicine balls like aspirin.

She, meanwhile, was interested in the rest of his fitness apparatus. 'And what is that?' She pointed.

'Indian club.'

'Oh yes. My brother Reuben belongs to one of those in Chandannagar.'

'Does he, by Denzil!'

She pointed once again. 'And that?'

'Dumbbell.'

Lettice Sandwich smiled prettily. 'Yes,' she said. 'People often call me that.'

One of the perennial dangers of life on a long sea voyage is the *placement* for dinner. Cautionary tales abound of passengers seated, the first evening, next to fellow travellers with whom they had exhausted their meagre supply of small talk before finishing their soup. And then having to sit with the same company and the same conversation, every dinner, for the next three weeks. Though some cynics have claimed this to be good training for the social life they were likely to experience among the expatriate community in India, it was not an enviable prospect.

And certainly not one that Twinks was going to put up with. The problem didn't arise for the second night's dinner. The Bay of Biscay experience had decimated the numbers of passengers. Many were still prone and moaning on their bunks, so the *placement* went out of the window.

But the third night, as Twinks approached the dining table and saw that the name cards were in exactly the same positions as the first, she immediately took the issue up with Captain Barnacle. 'This will have to be changed,' she announced, in a voice chillingly reminiscent of her mother's.

'This is the way it's always been done aboard the *Queen of the Orient*,' said the Captain, with one of his trademark roguish winks. 'And it's got things moving like a dose of senna pods. You wouldn't believe it if I were to tell you how many extramarital affairs have started at this table – out of sheer boredom. If you can't talk to people, well, there's only one other thing you can do with them, eh? Besides, the table plan's given you the best seat, right next to me.'

'That,' Twinks responded with icy *hauteur*, 'is arguable. Sitting next to you again would absolutely be the flea's armpit. This evening I wish to sit next to . . .' She looked around the dining room and was rewarded by the sight of Ponky Larreighffriebollaux, looking goggle-eyed and lost.

'That gentleman on my right. And on my left . . . someone different. Pass me the list of passengers who joined us at Marseille.'

Transfixed by the basilisk stare that she had definitely inherited from the Dowager Duchess, Captain Barnacle found himself handing across the demanded document. Twinks ran her azure eye down the names and announced, 'I wish to have on my left . . . M. le Vicomte Xavier Douce.'

'Are you already acquainted with the gentleman?' asked the Captain, cowed into politeness.

'No, but his name interests me. I think we might enjoy sharing a little chittle-chattle. Arrange it, Captain.'

As Twinks swept imperiously off to corral Ponky, Captain Barnacle summoned stewards and gave them instructions as to the changed *placement*. He was learning, as many had before, that it didn't do to cross the Lyminster women.

'Ponky!' cried Twinks, taking him by the arm, 'you are to sit next to me for dinner.'

The Old Etonian looked as if all his birthdays had come on the same day. 'Well, tiddle my pom!' he said, somewhat predictably.

M. le Vicomte Xavier Douce had the manners of a real aristocrat, though of course Twinks knew he wasn't one. Her upbringing had taught her that only Britain had a true aristocracy, and by that really she meant England. Scottish and Irish peerages were distinctly inferior. And as for other countries . . . well, there the titles were virtually made up – rather like the musical comedy uniforms they invented for their royal personages.

People from France who claimed to have titles were particularly suspect. Any family who might have ever been taken seriously as aristocrats had been very effectively purged by the guillotine.

M. le Vicomte Xavier Douce was probably in his sixties. Tall and well-upholstered, he wore immaculate evening dress though, in a rather foppish French way, the jacket was made of velvet. Twinks thought wearing spats for dinner was way beyond the barbed wire, but no doubt they had different standards in France about such niceties. She recognised that his cufflinks and the studs on his shirtfront were fine diamonds. The signet ring he wore on his right little finger also featured a substantial sparkler. It came as no surprise when he told her his business was the diamond trade. 'India is the source of some of the finest stones in the world,' he said. 'I travel there with some frequency. Is this your first trip to the fabled East, Lady Lyminster?'

He too clearly had done his homework on the passenger list, but she had to correct him on his choice of title. 'Doesn't matter a tuppenny butterscotch to me, Vicomte old strawberry, but you have the air of a boddo who likes to pot the black with no chalk on his gloves. So, I will tell you that, technically, I should be called "Lady Honoria Lyminster" or "Lady Honoria". But everyone calls me "Twinks".'

'Ah. "Twinks". This is, I think, what you English call a "knockname".'

'"Nickname" is more usual.'

'"Nickname", yes. As ever, your language has no logic to it.'

'Unlike French?'

'Unlike French,' he confirmed. 'In France there is a rule for every eventuality.'

'In England we've never donned our worry-boots too much about rules. Generally, we just trust our instincts. Except when it comes to games, of course. Only downright stenchers and oikish sponge-worms cheat when it comes to games.'

'And what, Twinks, do you think about people who cheat at the Game of Life?'

'They're four-faced filchers too.'

The Vicomte smiled a knowing smile. 'Four-faced filchers perhaps, but frequently very wealthy four-faced filchers.'

'Maybe. But getting wealth by any other means than inheritance has always been a bit beyond the barbed wire.' Twinks was once again practising her patrician *froideur* – with a healthy dollop of *hauteur*. And the way she did it, she was no *amateur*.

Ponky Larreighffriebollaux thought maybe it was time that he contributed to the conversation. 'Tiddle my pom!' he said.

As they left the dining table, Twinks found herself confronted by the Maharajah of Koorbleimee, dressed once again in his full regalia. She remembered their conversation about why he wore such splendour, to frighten off potential acquaintances who were either too cowed or who considered the display 'flashy and meretricious'.

'I thought,' she said to him, 'you only dollied yourself up for the first night of a voyage.'

'Ah. You misunderstood. It is after each stop at a port where we take on new passengers. It is to see whether such people are worthy of my attention.'

'Ah,' said Twinks, 'in that case we should crack out the calling cards.' She gestured towards the Frenchman in her wake. 'M. le Vicomte Xavier Douce – the Maharajah of Koorbleimee.'

The two gentlemen smiled and shook hands. Twinks watched for signs of the Maharajah assessing his new acquaintance. The Vicomte did not look cowed. Nor did he seem put off by the meretriciousness or flashiness of the Maharajah's costume.

66

But he was transfixed by the Star of Koorbleimee at the centre of the Indian's turban.

Professional interest, thought Twinks, from someone involved in the jewellery business.

Or possibly, she wondered, remembering something else the Maharajah had said, criminal interest.

8

Naval Engagements

There was very little communication between the decks where Blotto and Twinks were being pampered and those where the lower orders subsisted. So Corky Froggett, though ready to leap into action at the smallest summons, didn't see much of the young master, as the *Queen of the Orient* traversed the Mediterranean.

He cannot have been said to have minded. His governess, Emmeline Washboard, proved not only to be a schoolmistress and a mistress of verbal innuendo, but a mistress in every other sense of the word. Her straightforward carnality struck a chord with his. She had boasted that she had a cabin to herself, but Corky Froggett saw to it that she was not alone in it for long. He looked forward to his passage to India.

But sadly, a fly buzzed into their particular ointment of joy when the *Queen of the Orient* docked at Marseille. It buzzed into it in the form of a tiny Scottish missionary lady called Miss McQueeg, who invariably dressed in clerical grey. She had booked the voyage to Bombay and been allocated to share with Emmeline Washboard.

When they first met, the latter had suggested some form of slot-sharing arrangement, whereby Miss McQueeg would guarantee to be out of the cabin at certain times

8

(thus enabling the entertainment of Corky). But the missionary lady could not see the necessity for such a system. Her luggage was mostly Bibles, crated in the hold, which she planned to scatter lavishly among the heathen of India, with a view to leading them on to the Right Path. Her intention was to spend most of the voyage inside the cabin, rereading the sacred text. 'There are so many bonnie riches in the Bible,' she said. 'Every time I read the Good Book, I find another wee insight that the Lord wishes to share with me.'

It was the view of both Corky and Emmeline that the permanent presence of a Bible-reading Miss McQueeg between the bunks might put a bit of a candle-snuffer on their carnal intentions.

Miss McQueeg herself had not been shocked by Emmeline Washboard's suggestion of a time-sharing arrangement, because she could not understand why anyone should need such a thing. She combined all the most annoying personality traits of the innocent – ignorance, an unfailing belief in her own righteousness and, even more irritating, an unfailing belief in her own rightness. No argument would divert her from her chosen path.

Miss McQueeg had not always been religious. She was a convert, with all the aggravating qualities that usually entails. Her father had been a jeweller and, once she had left school, she had worked for him for many years. But after her father's death, she needed to fill the void, and found God. Miss McQueeg was delighted about finding Him. God's opinion of the matter of being found is not recorded. She decided to dedicate the considerable fortune she had inherited to missionary work, taking as her guiding text the lines from Matthew chapter 6: 'Lay not up for yourself treasure upon earth, where moth and rust doth corrupt' (though jewels were pretty well impervious to moth and rust), 'and where thieves break through and steal' (a much more common risk with jewellery).

Miss McQueeg spent all of her inheritance on Bibles, which she intended to thrust upon the heathen, regardless of what the heathen felt about it.

Her belief system also centred on the concept of Sin, which she imagined to be all around her. Though her practical knowledge and experience of Sin was minimal, she still reckoned everyone in the world lived in its shadow. Except for herself. She glowed with the confidence that, when the Almighty got round to sorting things out, she alone would be saved, while the rest of humanity were consumed in the fires of hell. The only way of evading that fate was to accept one of the Bibles which she scattered around with such random magnanimity.

And even that might not work. Most people, in her view, would slip up one way or the other, ending up in the fires of hell, anyway. And she would go and sit, very smugly, at the right hand of God.

In spite of her constant reference to Sin, Miss McQueeg also conducted herself at a level of prudishness which Emmeline Washboard had never before encountered. Miss McQueeg arranged to have a sheet draped across the cabin between their two bunks, lest either should be shocked or corrupted by the sight of the other dressing or undressing. For Em who, in the brief time since she had met Corky, had taken to lounging round the cabin in her smalls (or even her tinies), this was an unwarranted inconvenience.

But it took more than puritanism from a daughter of the manse to cool the middle-aged ardour sparked between Corky Froggett and Emmeline Washboard. They just had to be more inventive in where they met to enjoy each other's company.

It is safe to say that, over the ensuing days, few nooks and crannies within the hull of RMS *Queen of the Orient* remained unexplored.

* * *

70

Blotto too had a companion. He found himself spending an increasing amount of time with Lettice Sandwich. The initial attraction, to her stupidity, did not diminish. Indeed, it only increased as he discovered that she might be even more stupid than he'd first thought.

The other advantage of being in Lettice's company was that it kept him safe from the attentions of the rest of the Fishing Fleet. He was blithely unaware of the levels of back-biting and bitchiness that had been engendered by his choosing to spend time with Lettice.

And Blotto was far too stupid to realise the assumptions people might make from their spending time together. Or from the assumptions Lettice herself might be making from the amount of time they spent together.

So, Blotto, quite as innocent in his own way as Miss McQueeg, just relaxed in enjoyment of Lettice's conversation. They would sit in adjacent deckchairs on the sundeck, sublimely unaware of the miasma of seething jealousy and cattiness that arose from the promenade of Fishing Fleet girls who kept walking past them.

And they would talk. To be accurate, it was Lettice who carried the main burden of the talking. It was often Blotto who set the ball rolling, though.

'I was thinking, Lettice,' he said one morning, 'about your first name . . .'

'Lettice?'

'That's the Johnnie.'

'What about it?'

'I've suddenly realised . . . it sounds like a vegetable.'

'I'd never thought of that.'

'Well, it does, by Denzil!'

'Does it?' A long silence. 'What vegetable?'

'Can't you guess?'

Her delicate lids wrinkled around her big blue eyes. 'No.'

'Can you bring the brainbox to bear on a girl's name that

sounds like a vegetable ...?' That appeared to be too tricky for her. 'Something you put in a salad ...?'

Still tough but she was there. A beam irradiated her face as she announced, 'Olive.'

Blotto felt strange and disoriented. He had a feeling he had never encountered before, and which he could not identify. It was intellectual superiority.

He found it weirdly empowering. And it made him feel very protective of Lettice Sandwich.

Things were not getting any less complicated for Twinks. The vehemence of her brush-offs had reduced the number of proposals from the *Queen of the Orient*'s young subalterns. This process had been helped by her custom of planting Ponky Larreighffriebollaux in the deckchair next to her. The presence of this giraffe-limbed, goggle-eyed Old Etonian, reading the cricketing records in *Wisden* (while his companion delved into weightier tomes), seemed to act as a deterrent to oikish sponge-worms from lesser public schools.

But the Maharajah of Koorbleimee seemed as enthusiastic as ever to enrol Twinks in his stable of wives. And she could not be quite so rude to him as she could to the subalterns. Though foreign titles didn't count for much, there still obtained a code of required behaviour between aristocrats of different nations.

It was the day by whose evening they were due to arrive in Port Said. There, while the huge coal stores of the RMS *Queen of the Orient* would be replenished by teams of local labourers, the passengers were required to leave the vessel and spend the night in the city where Africa and Asia join. Already the temperature was mounting and Europe felt long left behind.

Late that morning, the Maharajah found Twinks on deck, hiding behind a floppy straw hat and sunglasses, trying to concentrate on reading Nietzsche's *The Birth of Tragedy from the Spirit of Music* (in the original German, of course). He was dressed in a gold-buttoned navy blazer and white flannel trousers. He had abandoned a tie for a brightly coloured paisley silk cravat. 'Flashy and meretricious' was Twinks's immediate thought when he hove into view. Back in Blighty, only the socially insecure wore cravats.

'Good morning, Twinks,' he said. 'You are looking lovelier than ever this morning.'

'Don't talk such meringue,' she said languidly.

'Tiddle my pom!' said Ponky, wishing to assert that he too was present.

The Maharajah ignored him and took the empty deckchair on the other side of Twinks. 'You will not be surprised,' he said, 'that I return to you with the same question which I put to you when we last met.'

'I am as unsurprised as a turkey being told he won't see Christmas.'

'So, then . . . Twinks . . . will you marry me?'

'You will be equally unsurprised – or you certainly should be – to hear that my answer has been no more changed than a fishmonger's socks.'

'But why? I can offer you wealth beyond the dreams of avarice.'

'Yes, but it never was for money that I enrolled in this "being alive" business.'

'I could smother you in jewels.'

'I have no desire to be smothered – in jewels or in anything else.'

'I would even let you, on special occasions, wear the Star of Koorbleimee.'

'Look, when will you get it through your thick turban that I have no more interest in money than a tiger does in cucumber sandwiches. I am not interested in money!'

'No . . . perhaps not.' A silence. 'But your mother might have different views on that subject . . . ?'

She looked at him sharply through her dark glasses. It sounded as though the Maharajah had been doing some homework.

His next words confirmed that indeed he had. 'I have reason to believe that the Dowager Duchess would welcome an inexhaustible supply of money . . . to deal in perpetuity with the Tawcester Towers plumbing!'

A complacent smile emerged from the foliage of his luxuriant moustaches. Twinks wondered how he'd found out the family secret. It wouldn't have been too difficult. The Maharajah could afford to pay for the best sort of private detective. And around a grand estate like Tawcester Towers there was always to be found some disgruntled and recently dismissed maid or groom, ready to dish the dirt for the right amount of the old jingle-jangle.

But Twinks passed no comment on the quality of his research. She merely said, 'At the risk of sounding like a phonograph with a coffinated needle, if nothing else to put me off becoming your wife – and there are as many reasons as a golf ball has dimples – there is the fact that I would be one of many with that esteemed title. In the English aristocracy, though a peer can enrol as many mistresses as he wishes – and I know many who are vying to create the world record in that particular competition – only one woman can have the glacé cherry on the trifle of being called a "wife".'

'If you were to marry me, Twinks, I can assure you that you would be my favourite wife . . .'

'Thanks for a Manx cat's tail!'

'. . . at least initially,' the Maharajah continued with commendable honesty.

Twinks shrank into her deckchair and returned pointedly to reading Nietzsche.

* * *

74

She had hardly re-engaged with the intellectual dichotomy between the Dionysian and the Apollonian before she was distracted by another interruption. Gliding along the deck in unhurried elegance, dressed in an immaculate pale blue linen suit – and again with spats – M. le Vicomte Xavier Douce appeared. The Mediterranean sun twinkled on his monocle and refracted through the diamond of his signet ring.

'Mademoiselle Twinks,' he enthused. 'How enchanting it is to see you this beautiful Mediterranean morning.'

A French aristocrat whose ancestors somehow dodged the guillotine did not command the same level of *politesse* as a Maharajah, so Twinks just pretended she hadn't heard him. But the Vicomte was not to be deterred by a turned back. With a stately motion, he lowered himself into the deckchair next to her.

'Tiddle my pom!' said Ponky Larreighffriebollaux. He was again ignored.

'Mademoiselle Twinks,' the Vicomte repeated, adjusting his monocle and completely unfazed by her lack of reaction, 'I have something of great importance to say to you.' The back was unmoving. 'I may not have mentioned to you that I am a widower. My late wife was a woman of great elegance, *toujours chic*, and it was always my pleasure to cover her with diamonds. She looked wonderful, of course, *très belle*, and wherever she went, she was a wonderful advertisement for the business, particularly in the early years when I was building up my clientele. It was a great sadness to me when she died, caught in the crossfire during an attempted theft at my shop on the Champs-Elysées.

'The burglarious attempt, I am glad to say, failed. I lost nothing from it . . . except of course the aforementioned wife. And by then my European clientele was well established and so the necessity of having a model to show off my wares was diminished. It had not entered my thoughts that I would ever need to marry again.

'That situation obtained until very recently, when opportunities emerged for me to develop my business in the United States of America. There, though I have many valuable contacts, I do not yet have the level of recognition that I would wish for. To put it in simple terms, what I need is someone to accompany me on my forthcoming business trip to America, someone who will be as effective a model for my jewellery as my late wife was.

'I wondered, when I first met you only a few days ago, Twinks, whether you might be the right person for my purposes. And after considering the matter, I have decided that you would be an ideal fit. You will be flattered to know that you are beautiful enough for my purposes. The sight of you at social occasions in New York, smothered with jewels, could be extremely useful.'

For the love of strawberries, thought Twinks, why does everyone want to smother me with jewels?

'It would enhance the reputation of my business and build up my clientele the other side of the Pond. So, Twinks, we get to the question that I am sure you have been waiting for . . . Will you marry me?'

M. le Vicomte Xavier Douce was not a man to take no – or even 'non' – for an answer. Twinks didn't know how she was going to get rid of him. Ponky Larreighffriebollaux was an empty revolver when it came to the business of protecting her. If the Vicomte wasn't frightened off by one 'Tiddle my pom!', he wasn't going to budge however many times the expression was repeated.

Salvation finally arrived in the form of Mr Mukerjee. 'Monsieur le Vicomte,' he said, 'I can tell from the lady's posture in her deckchair that you are causing her annoyance. Will you please desist and leave her to read her book on her own?'

'Pouf!' said the Vicomte, as only a Frenchman can say 'Pouf!' 'I am not in the habit of taking orders from untitled Indian businessmen.'

'Perhaps not. But you might be more inclined to do as I say, were I to tell you that I know what went on two years ago in the honeymoon suite of the Hotel de Luxe in Monaco.'

It worked. Instantly. With a cry of *'Zapristi!'*, the diamond merchant's considerable bulk took off vertically from his deckchair and disappeared with indecent haste into the ship's interior.

'Splendissimo!' said Twinks. 'You're a Grade A foundation stone, Mr Mukerjee.'

He acknowledged the compliment with a small bow of the head. 'It is natural for a gentleman to come to the aid of a damsel who is so clearly in distress.'

'I appreciate it as much as a whale does krill.'

'Ah.' He looked at her book. 'Nietzsche, I see.'

'Yes. A girl needs a little light reading on shipboard.'

'Certainly. Do you mind if I sit, Twinks?'

'Nada problemo, Mr Mukerjee.'

He placed himself sedately in the deckchair the Vicomte had vacated. 'I see you have the original 1872 edition. *Die Geburt der Tragödie aus dem Geiste der Musik.* I personally prefer the 1886 reissue, *Die Geburt der Tragödie, Oder: Griechentum und Pessimismus.*'

'His ideas about the Dionysian and the Apollonian are better developed in the later work, I agree,' said Twinks. 'But in the 1872 one, there's greater clarity about the inevitability of human existence's ecstasy and suffering conjoining.'

'I concur completely. Nor can one ignore the commentary on the first book which occurs in the second under the title "An Attempt at Self-Criticism".

Twinks's azure eyes sparkled as she warmed to the dialogue. 'And one can already recognise the nascent thoughts he was to develop in *Menschliches, Allzumenschliches . . .*'

And so the conversation continued. After the morning's earlier annoyances, Twinks luxuriated in discussion with someone who approached her own intellectual level. What a relief to be with a man who was totally uninterested in her physical attractions. She couldn't wait to get on to a proper deconstruction of *Die Fröhliche Wissenschaft*, and was disappointed to see the sundeck emptying as the passengers made their way towards lunch.

'Oh, your brainbox is just perfectino, Mr Mukerjee,' she said, as she rose from her deckchair. 'I could talk to you forever.'

'I too could talk to you forever, Twinks.'

'Larksissimo!'

'So, let us do that.'

'Sorry? Not on the same page?'

'Let us talk together forever.'

'Still not with you. Come on, uncage the ferrets.'

And then Mr Mukerjee went and spoiled it all by saying, 'Twinks, will you marry me?'

She'd had enough. Extreme measures were called for. Ponky Larreighffriebollaux was unwinding himself from his deckchair. She grabbed him by the hand, 'Ponky, you're up for a whizzo lark, aren't you?'

She took his 'Tiddle my pom!' as an expression of assent and turned to her Indian suitor. 'I'm sorry. I cannot marry you, Mr Mukerjee. Because I am engaged to be married. This gentleman is my spoffing fiancé!'

Ponky looked as if not only all his birthdays, but all his Christmases, saints' days and bank holidays had come at once.

There was a new depth of feeling – and of meaning – in the way he said, 'Tiddle my pom!'

9

Disembarkation in Port Said

'First-class innings from Ponky, wasn't it, Blotters?' said Twinks. 'To rescue me like the cavalry coming up the canyon.'

They were in her stateroom, both suitably dressed for the shore visit to Port Said. Their overnight bags had been packed and would be taken by ship's stewards to their accommodation, a place near the harbour called the Savoy Hotel. As an habitué of the London establishment which shared the name, Blotto was looking forward to the same level of luxury that he found at the 'Savvers' on the Strand. Twinks was more sceptical about what they might be letting themselves in for.

'Sorry?' said her brother. 'Hit me with the headlines about what Ponky's done.'

'He's agreed to play charades. Larksissimo! Ponky is a Wellington of the first water.'

'Twinks, me old cushion cover, I'm afraid my touchpaper hasn't ignited yet. What has that poor droplet Ponky agreed to do for you?'

'He's agreed, for as long as we're aboard the *Queen of the Orient* – and possibly after we dock in Bombay if required – that he will put the crud in the crumpets of all these horracious sponge-worms who keep asking me to marry them.'

'And how's he going to win the raffle on that?'

'He'll pretend that he and I are going to twiddle the old reef knot.'

'Toad-in-the-hole!'

'Yes, so far as anyone else on the *Queen of the Orient* is concerned, I'm going to ding the church bells with Ponky. I am going to become Mrs Larreighffriebollaux!'

'By Denzil! Are you really?'

'No, of course I'm not really, you chump-faced wibbler! I couldn't begin to become Mrs Larreighffriebollaux. Apart from anything else, with a name like that, imagine how long it would take to write a cheque. No, Ponky, the goggle-eyed Galahad, has agreed to *pretend* that we're taking on the marital manacles.'

'Are you sure he knows that, Twinks me old nutmeg-grinder?'

'Well, of course he does, Blotto me old eiderdown. When I had yet another proposal of marriage this morning – from Mr Mukerjee, would you believe – I told him that Ponky and I were engaged.'

'And what did Ponky say?'

'Need you ask?'

'No, I suppose I don't, really. But what I want to wipe the dust off is whether Ponky Larreighffriebollaux knew that you were jiggling his kneecap, that you weren't really suggesting the two of you were taking a double ticket on the marital motorbus.'

'Oh, for the love of strawberries, Blotters! I told him. I asked him if he was up for a whizzo lark. He said "Tiddle my pom!" in a way that said he certainly was – and there we were. The table was laid for frolics and fun. His brain-box can't have latched on to the notion that I meant we really were in marital manacles. Ponky was never going to believe that in a million Mondays, was he?'

80

'I'm rather afraid he was. For a long time, Ponky has thought you were the crystallised ginger.'

'Has he? Well, why hasn't he ever said anything? Except "Tiddle my pom!", that is?'

'It's because that's the effect your presence has on him. In conversation with other people, he says a lot of different things.'

'Does he, by Cheddar!'

'Yes, he and I can burn down the midnight candles chuntering on about cricket.'

'Oh, I've never heard him do that, Blotto me old pastry fork.'

'What you have to bang into your brain cells, Twinks me old rhubarb-slicer, is that the first time he clapped his peepers on your lovely visage, Ponky fell like for you like a guardsman in a heatwave.'

'Oh, lawkins!' said Twinks. 'I have made a gumbo of things, haven't I?'

'Yes,' said Blotto. 'I'm afraid you have.'

'How am I going to get out of the gluepot?'

The only reason Blotto wouldn't have thought that his sister asking him for advice was 'unprecedented' was that he didn't know what the word meant. But he did think it was very unusual for the sock to be on the other sole.

There was a rare note of self-righteousness in his voice as he responded, 'It's your own glue, I'm afraid, sis, and it's down to you to reset the clock on this ... before the announcement is printed in *The Times*.'

'Oh, Blotters, you really have brought me out in crimps now,' said Twinks.

Corky Froggett had also made plans for his night of shore leave. Some of them involved the estimable Emmeline Washboard. And some of them didn't. Having spent a long time in the trenches during the last little dust-up with the

Hun, he had heard a lot of soldiers' talk. In particular, he'd heard about a few of the things that Port Said had a reputation for.

The place was universally described as a 'fleshpot'. And though some of Corky's fleshly needs were being catered for more than adequately by the compliant Emmeline Washboard, there were others he wished to access from the fleshpots of Port Said.

The departure of all the passengers from a vessel the size of the *Queen of the Orient* was a lengthy process. The lower orders had to bide their time while their betters were allowed off first. This great movement of people did of course open up new areas of the *Queen of the Orient* in which the chauffeur could enjoy the delights of his governess. So, he suggested climbing aboard her one more time before they disembarked.

Blotto's customary sunny outlook was a little shadowed as he queued to take the gangplank on to the docks of Port Said. The real sun was beating down with a vengeance but not shedding its warmth on his thoughts. Nor was the prospect of going on shore in a new city, a new country, bringing him any glow of excitement. The air was loud with shouts in many tongues but he hardly saw the eager souvenir-sellers being held at bay on the docks by the ship's stewards. He was unaware of the restaurateurs and hoteliers proclaiming the quality of their facilities to the passengers. He just did not see or hear the shrill cries of small brown-skinned boys diving for the pennies that a few bored tourists threw into the oily water for them. He was preoccupied.

Almost never in their long relationship had Blotto felt the slightest impulse to criticise his sister, but her behaviour towards Ponky Larreighffriebollaux had seemed, on reflection, a bit beyond the barbed wire.

He knew exactly why she had done as she had. Having grown up from birth with her beauty and brilliance, she was totally unaware of them. Not unaware that they had an effect on the opposite sex, but not realising quite how powerful that effect could be. Unwittingly, over the years, she had left indelible scars on the hearts of many unattached young men, and prompted in the married variety enduring detrimental comparisons between herself and their frumpy wives. Twinks had cut a swathe through a whole generation of young men, rather in the manner of the last little dust-up with the Hun.

Blotto had never before thought of his sister as a dangerous weapon, but now he realised that she could be one.

'May the Lord be with you.' A Scottish voice shook him out of his mournful reverie.

'Which Lord would that be?' Blotto was personally acquainted with quite a few members of the House of Lords through the current Duke of Tawcester, his older brother Loofah.

'The Lord whom we will all face on the Day of Judgement. The Lord who will condemn most of humanity to the fires of hell.'

'Not sure I know the boddo,' said Blotto.

He squinted against the bright sunlight and looked down at the tiny grey figure of Miss McQueeg. One shoulder was lower than the other, weighed down by a bag of Bibles. She held one out towards him. 'I refer to the Lord who is the inspiration and guiding light of this book.'

'Ah.' Blotto understood. 'Religious flipmadoodles, is it? I'm afraid I don't have much to do with religion. Which is another way of saying that I'm Church of England.'

'The Lord is everywhere. He is all around us.'

'Is he, by Denzil?' Blotto looked rather nervously from side to side.

'Think of the ways in which the Lord appeared to Elijah.'

'Elijah? Sorry, don't know the poor old thimble.'

'The Lord created a mighty wind and an earthquake and a fire and then a still small voice.'

'Toad-in-the-hole!' said Blotto. 'Bit of a Victor Ludorum, wasn't he? Fortunately, we don't have any of those here. Or at least there could be a still small voice, but no one would hear it above all this bimbambong.'

'But the Lord can create a wind whenever he wants to.'

'No wind here, me old fruitcake. Could do with a bit, actually. Air's as still as yesterday's porridge.'

'I agree. So, young man, it must be a wind that God has created that's causing that.' She pointed above their heads to where one of the ship's lifeboats was rocking from side, as though at the mercy of a mistral.

Blotto looked down to where he'd last seen the missionary lady, but had to look even lower. She was now on her knees, crying out, 'The Lord be thanked! It's a miracle!'

Fortunately, Miss McQueeg had moved nearer the gangplank and didn't see when, a few moments later, there emerged from under the lifeboat's tarpaulin a rather red-faced Corky Froggett and Emmeline Washboard. Which was perhaps just as well. Otherwise, she would have had more reasons to think they were destined to the fires of hell.

Blotto hadn't read any books of etiquette. Proper behaviour came instinctively to someone of his breeding. But he'd have bet a guinea to a groat that there wasn't an etiquette book in the world that spelled out the correct procedure for a boddo explaining to another boddo that when his – the first boddo's – sister said she was going to marry the second boddo, she had been joking.

Blotto's mood improved only partially when he saw Ponky Larreighffriebollaux sitting at a table in front of a harbourside café. Here he was, being presented on a plate the perfect opportunity to put things straight with his old muffin-toaster. How doing that was actually achieved was less clear to him.

Though it was only a matter of hours since the two of them had last met, they went instinctively into one of their Old Etonian greeting rituals. 'Ratteley-Baa-Baa!' said Blotto.

'Ritteley-Boo-Boo!' his friend responded.

'How're you pongling, me old fruit bat?' asked Blotto.

'Knobby as a chest of drawers. And are your suspenders tight, Blotters me old shrimping net?'

'Tight as a hippo's hawser, Ponky me old boot-blackener.'

'Ra-ra!' said Ponky.

'Ra-ra-ra!' said Blotto.

These ancestral formalities concluded, Blotto sat down beside his friend. 'What are you drinking, me old swordfish-sharpener?'

Ponky looked dubiously at the small cup in front of him. 'Well, I asked the waiter Johnnie for coffee, but all he seems to have brought me is coffee grounds. Tastes like sand.'

'It might *be* sand,' said Blotto shrewdly. 'They seem to have plenty of the stuff around.'

'You're bong on the nose there, Blotters.' Ponky stretched out his gangling limbs in the Mediterranean sunshine. 'You know, I don't think I've felt in such zing-zing condition since I hit that century for Cambridge in the Oxford Parks.'

Blotto quailed inwardly. He'd never in his life expected to hear his old muffin-toaster make such a momentous comparison. And he knew the only thing that could have so fizzulated Ponky was the fact of being engaged to

Twinks. The size of the task ahead of him swelled up like a barrage balloon.

The terrible moment was put off, however, by the arrival of the waiter, who extolled the high quality and availability of the extensive menu, the adjacent hotel . . . and his sister.

Deterred by Ponky's experience with the coffee, Blotto asked if he could have 'freshly squeezed lemon juice with ice and sugar'.

'Ah,' said the waiter. 'A *citron pressé*.'

'No,' said Blotto patiently, 'I'd rather have freshly squeezed lemon juice with ice and sugar.'

Shaking his head at the eternal idiocy of foreigners, the waiter went off to fulfil the order.

There was an awkward pause. Well, that is to say, it felt awkward for Blotto. Ponky still smiled the serene smile of a man into whose custard no one would ever put lumps. It didn't make his friend's task any easier.

'Ponky, me old fruit salad . . .' Blotto began uncontroversially.

'Yes, Blotto me old chinstrap?'

'About you and Twinks . . .'

'Larksissimo, isn't it? As she would say. I mean, I think you already know that, from the first moment I saw your sister, I thought she was the absolute panda's panties.'

'Yes, that impression did kind of take up lodgings in a brain cell of mine.'

'But it never in a million millennia occurred to me that she might have the wiggles for me too!'

'No. Well, it's about that that I had a thoughtette I wanted to share with you . . .'

'Today's the best day since they lifted the Siege of Mafeking!'

'Good ticket,' said Blotto uncertainly. 'Erm . . . Ponky . . . did the idea ever thread its way into your think-box that Twinks might have been joking . . . ?'

'Yes, of course it did, Blotters.'

'Thank Disraeli for that!' Blotto sat back in his seat with considerable relief.

'And that just made me even happier,' Ponky went on. 'To think that I would be twiddling the old reef knot – and spending the rest of my bornies – with such a merry soul. Everyone says humour is the absolute bedrock of a marriage.'

This wasn't going according to Blotto's plan. Not at all according to his plan. It went against his nature, but he knew he was going to have to take a more brutal approach. 'Listen, Ponky me old crystal set, what would you say if I told you Twinks doesn't love you at all – and has no intention of marrying you?'

A beam settled below Ponky Larreighffriebollaux's goggle eyes and beaky nose. 'I'd say I'm the luckiest Labrador in the litter! To be joining a family where my brother-in-law has the same sense of humour as my wife.'

'Listen, Ponky. This couldn't be clearer if I painted it on a banner and hung it from Nelson's Column. Twinks doesn't love you!'

Ponky was now laughing so much that tears were running from the goggle eyes over the beaky nose. 'Blotto, you are a caution!' he managed to say.

Before there was time for a response, a third person joined them. It was M. le Vicomte Xavier Douce, dressed in a light linen suit and the inevitable spats. 'Monsieur Larreighffriebollaux, are you ready to leave?'

'Ready as a ship's bucket in the Bay of Biscay!'

'Excellent. Then shall we be on our way?'

'Where in the name of snitchrags are you going?' asked Blotto.

The Frenchman smiled serenely and adjusted his monocle. 'Monsieur Larreighffriebollaux wishes to take advantage of my expertise and knowledge of the diamond merchants in Port Said.'

'That's the Johnnie!' cried Ponky. 'I'm going to see to it that my gorgelicious Twinks gets the best engagement ring this side of the Milky Way!' Which, of course, with his wealth he could afford and still have change.

Blotto watched as the two men walked away. Then, out loud, he said, 'Oh, broken biscuits!'

Which was a measure of the depth of the gluepot he now found himself in.

10

Peril in Port Said!

The day ends quickly in the Eastern Mediterranean. The sun drops below the horizon and suddenly it's night. The bright bustle of Port Said changes in a twinkling to something darker and more sinister. The more sedate passengers from the *Queen of the Orient* settled for the evening into their hotels or restaurants close to their hotels. The more adventurous set out to explore the night life – or perhaps the expression should be 'fleshpots' – of the city.

Corky Froggett was one of the latter group. After he and Em had checked into a hotel as squalid as their lowly status deserved, they had a meal in a café whose hygiene standards demanded a stiff upper lip and closed eyes. Corky found the local method of cooking perverse. Why thread lumps of beef on a stick and dish it up with rice, when the natural way to serve it was in slices with potatoes, vegetables, gravy and English mustard? It was bizarre how far out of their way foreigners would go to avoid the obvious.

The meal concluded, the chauffeur returned his governess to their hotel and, assuring her that he wouldn't be long, set off into the maze of half-lit alleyways that was Port Said. He had not confided in her the purpose of his mission but he had impressed her with its importance. It

of a rum baba, isn't it? You'd have thought every boddo in the world knew that custard came out of a tin!'

'Do you mean, Blotto,' asked an awestruck Lettice, 'that you've actually been in a kitchen and watched custard being made?'

'Well, no . . .' he conceded, 'I've never been in a kitchen in my life. Boddoes of my . . . well, I mean, for boddoes like me to go into kitchens would be way the wrong side of the running rail. But my chauffeur Corky Froggett told me about how they dibble up the custard.'

'Does he cook as well as chauff?'

'No, but he had a, er . . . a wodjermabit with a, er . . . that is he was a close friend of one of the kitchen maids at Tawcester Towers and she opened his eyes to what went on.'

'Why had he got his eyes closed?' asked Lettice.

'Well, erm, let's let that one go into the net, shall we? Another thing Corky told me was that in some abroad countries, they haven't got a mouse-squeak of an idea how to cook vegetables properly.'

'Really?'

'Yes, you'd have thought that wasn't the hardest double on the board, but in some countries apparently they cook vegetables for less than an hour!'

'Good gracious!' said a deeply shocked Lettice.

'So, if you want my advice, when running the peepers through a menu in a foreign country, dab the digit on something as simple as a moneylender's greed. Then you'll always be on the right side of right. You take my word for it.'

'I take your word for everything, Blotto,' said Lettice. 'I know you are wise in the ways of the world.'

He still got a charge from her saying things like that to him. The experience of having his intellect admired was so novel that he couldn't get enough of it.

'So, Lettice, not wishing to jump the start-shot, would it

tickle your mustard if I were to do the ordering for both of us?'

'I'd love you to do it, Blotto.'

'Hoopee-doopee!' He snapped his fingers and immediately at their tableside appeared a white-jacketed waiter.

'Good evening, sir,' he said with an excellent accent.

'By Wilberforce!' said Blotto. 'How the chitterlings did you know I was English?'

'You were talking louder than anyone else in the restaurant, sir?'

'Well, I'll be jugged like a hare! And that told you I was English?'

'That and the fact that you were talking louder than anyone else *in* English.'

'Ah, good ticket. Right, me old moustache-waxer . . .' Blotto pointed to the menu. 'We'd like two "biftecks".'

'No *mezes*, sir?'

'No, we don't want any of your foreign messes, thank you. And no sauces on the bifteck, thank you.'

'No sauces on the bifteck? But sauces are our chef's speciality and he will be—'

'No sauces on the bifteck,' Blotto repeated implacably.

'Very good, sir,' said the waiter, clearly keeping his views of such gastronomic sacrilege to himself. 'No sauces on the bifteck. Would you like something to drink, sir?'

'A bottle of burgundy.'

'Very good, sir.'

'French burgundy, mind.'

'Very good, sir.'

As the waiter retreated, Blotto beamed towards the admiring face of Lettice Sandwich.

'Oh, Blotto,' she breathed, 'you are just so masterful.'

He looked out across the harbour. The gently rippling sea between the many vessels winked back the light from strings of hanging oil lamps. The *Queen of the Orient* appropriately queened it over the lesser craft, pleasure

93

steamers, feluccas, dhows, fishing vessels, colliers and small rowing boats.

All of the doors and portholes of the *Queen* were closed and sealed. On a gangplank – not the elegant one by which Blotto and the other passengers had recently come ashore, but a filthy, blackened structure, moved an antlike stream of men. On the right-hand side, they were bowed under the burdens on their backs; those returning on the left were upright, holding their empty sacks, returning to the depot to refill them. The stream was continuous and endless. Most of the men were bare-footed, wearing little more than loincloths, once white but darkened by the persistent dust. Light from lit torches reflected off the blackness of their bodies. They worked to the rhythm of some alien chant.

'What're they doing, Blotto?' asked Lettice.

'They're "coaling",' he replied, proud that Twinks had given him the correct name for the activity.

'What does that mean?' she asked, giving him another opportunity to flex his intellectual prowess.

'It means,' Blotto said masterfully, 'putting coal into the boat.'

'Oh,' said Lettice. 'They're putting quite a lot of it in, aren't they?'

'They are, by Denzil,' he agreed.

'Which is strange,' she said.

'Why strange?'

'Well, I haven't got a fireplace in my cabin.'

'Toad-in-the-hole!' said Blotto.

'Have you got a fireplace in your cabin?'

Blotto confessed that he hadn't.

They both agreed that it was a bit of a rum baba to be putting so much coal into a ship that didn't have any fireplaces.

Then, remembering something else Twinks had told him, Blotto said, 'Actually, Lettice, I think we may have got the wrong end of the sink-plunger here.' He was far too much of a gentleman to say 'you' rather than 'we'. 'I think the reason all these poor thimbles are stuffing the ship as full of coal as a pheasant is full of lead is that coal is what makes the engine go.'

'Go where?' asked Lettice.

'No, you're shinnying up the wrong drainpipe. When I say "what makes the engine go", I mean "what gives the engine power". Coal is what will give the *Queen of the Orient* the zoomph to take us all the way to India. Coal,' he concluded triumphantly, 'is a fuel!'

She looked at him uncertainly.

'You do know what "a fuel" is, don't you, Lettice?'

'Yes, of course I do.' Her blue eyes widened. 'It's a stupid person.'

Blotto experienced once again the unfamiliar glow of intellectual superiority. He even allowed himself a modest smile, which he shared with Lettice Sandwich. And he didn't hear the massed sighs of jealousy that arose from a bunch of Fishing Fleet girls who happened to be passing in front of the Savy Htel.

Behind an upturned fishing boat on the dockside opposite the restaurant terrace, two men crouched. They were Port Said locals, dressed in black djellabas with black *kufi* caps on their heads. A tall man, carrying a leather shoulder bag, approached through the shadows and crouched down beside them.

No greetings were exchanged. He reached into the bag and pulled out two bundles of bank notes. He handed one to each man. 'You get the second half when the job is done,' he said.

'Do we get to know his name?' asked one, in halting English.

'It is Lyminster. But that is not important to you. Kill him as if he was a rabid dog.'

He reached back inside the bag and produced two service revolvers of German manufacture. 'You make sure he is dead, then you throw these into the harbour. If either of you tries to keep the guns, we will know, and you will not get the second half of the money.'

The two men nodded grimly. 'And where is the target?' asked the one who had spoken before.

The man with the leather bag raised a long thin hand and pointed towards the Savoy Hotel terrace restaurant. Directly at Blotto.

With no idea of the fate that had been planned for him, Blotto was feeling spoffing good. Adulation, like that he constantly received from Lettice Sandwich, did something for a boddo.

After the meal – whose bifteck had had the texture of some by-product of the tractor tyre industry – he saw his companion back to her hotel (even more squalid than his) and walked back towards the Savoy, feeling in zing-zing condition.

Unaware, of course, of the two men in black sidling from shadow to shadow in pursuit.

Corky Froggett was pleased with the deal he had done with the salesman in a dingy backroom. He'd beaten the man down by about 50 per cent and his precious possessions were now stuffed in the front of his tightly buttoned uniform jacket. He was also pleased with the other object he had bought from a tiny cave-like emporium hung with metal lamps, that wouldn't have looked out of place in a performance of *Aladdin*. Corky knew how to treat a lady.

His mood was improved further when . . . who should he see walking towards him than the young master, looking equally pleased with life.

Corky was about to call out a cheery greeting when he saw the two men behind Blotto. Both had stopped and their raised pistols were focusing on the back of their intended victim.

With a fierce cry of 'Run for it, milord!', Corky Froggett rushed forward to interpose himself between the assassins and their target.

The last thing he heard was the reassuring noise of Blotto's frantic footsteps receding into the labyrinth of backstreets, as he felt the impact of the two bullets in his chest. The chauffeur fell backwards on to the ground and everything went black.

But beneath his bristling moustache was a smile of contentment.

It had always been Corky Froggett's ambition to give up his life for the young master. And his last thought before the blackness overwhelmed him was that he had achieved his aim.

11

Coaling

His armed pursuers had the advantage of Blotto. The pair had spent their entire lives in the seedy backstreets of Port Said. He was encountering them for the first time. And, though in a straight flat race he would have lost them in short order, he was now negotiating narrow streets full of passers-by, stumbling into donkeys, getting hooked up in hookahs, tripping over tradesmen's wares spread out over the ground.

Some of the locals also made it their business to impede his progress. Given a white man in a linen suit running away from two Arabs, they knew whose side they were on. Port Said was a thoroughly cosmopolitan city. Outsiders were greeted warmly so long as they were spending money. When they weren't, their welcome was very much thinner.

Suddenly, Blotto found himself in more space. He was in a square in front of a mosque, lit by flaming torches. Round the edges were a collection of small cafés and tiny cave-like shops. Everyone seemed to be looking at him.

Apart from the way by which he had entered, there were two exits from the square. He dashed towards one, but before he could make his escape, a group of six men in black djellabas suddenly materialised to block his way.

They looked like his pursuers but wore black turbans rather than *kufi* caps. On a command from their leader, they all drew pistols from the folds of their garments.

Blotto looked back the way he'd come, to see his two original enemies enter the square. Eight to one. Those were the kind of odds Blotto – or any boddo who'd been through the English public school system – relished. He only wished his trusty cricket bat wasn't currently stuck in the stateroom in his 'Wanted on Voyage' trunk. With the bat, he'd be more than a match for eight armed Arabs. Without it, things might be a cuckoo-spit trickier.

He heard an incomprehensible shout from behind him and turned to see that the ringleader of the six had just issued an order. He and his henchmen all raised their pistols.

Reckoning at that moment discretion might be the better part of valour, Blotto dropped to the ground. Over his head, bullets fizzed. After a moment, he realised that none of them were going near him. He seemed to have stumbled into a local gangland turf war. Raising a cautious head, he saw that the six were actually firing at the two. And winning. He couldn't see whether any of the bullets had actually reached their targets, but they'd had the desired effect of chasing his pursuers out of the square.

Blotto turned back to face his saviours, relieved to see them lower their weapons. He strode towards their leader, seized him by the hand and said, 'You know what you are, chumbo? You're a Grade A foundation stone!'

The man said something that sounded like 'suit'.

'Yes, you and your men *shoot* very well,' Blotto agreed. 'Saw off those four-faced filchers like a dose of Benskin's Powder, eh?'

'Suit!' the man repeated.

'Good ticket,' said Blotto. 'Good shooting. Got rid of the lumps of toadspawn. Give that pony a rosette!'

'Suit!' the man said again, and the word now had an

ugly edge to it. Responding to his tone, the five henchmen once again produced their pistols and focused them on Blotto.

It took a while, and some fairly rough mime – to get the point across that what they wanted from him was his suit.

In no position to argue – again desperately wishing he had his cricket bat with him – Blotto started to remove his linen jacket, waistcoat and trousers. Taking these off involved removing his handmade brogues, which the Arab gang-leader insisted on keeping too. It was in vain that Blotto explained that they had been made on a special last by his bootmaker in Jermyn Street and wouldn't fit anyone else properly.

He was now dressed in shirt, undershirt, drawers, Argyll socks and sock suspenders. And, of course, tie.

The Arab gangster gestured to him to remove the latter.

'Sorry, me dear old greengage,' said Blotto. 'No biddles to you in taking that. You see, the point is . . . that tie's the Old Etonian Johnnie. Can only be worn by someone who spent his muffin-toasting days back at the old place. And, I may be guessing here, but I don't think you went to Eton, did you? Which, I mean, could tip you into all kinds of gluepots. You know, if you were to turn up with that tie round the old collar stud at – I don't know – Henley . . . Ascot . . . Lords . . . well, quick as two ferrets in a rabbit warren, someone's going to finger you as leadpenny.'

In spite of the undeniable force of these arguments, they did not exert much traction with the gang-leader. The answer Blotto got came in the form of having the tie torn off from around his neck. Then his shirt was removed – including the gold studs and cufflinks engraved with the Lyminster crest. And his undershirt.

Perhaps out of some respect for decency, the gang did not remove his drawers.

Then they decamped, leaving him in the middle of the square in front of the mosque, surrounded by avid locals, whose general view seemed to be that the sight of an almost naked Englishman was an amusing one.

Blotto tried to trace his way back to the dockside, but without marked success. His sense of direction wasn't great at the best of times, and this was far from the best of times. Remarkably, the locals – and those of other nationalities – whom he approached seemed to have little understanding of the words 'Savoy Hotel'. Which seemed to him bizarre beyond words. Surely everyone in the world had heard of the 'Savvers'? A problem of translation, perhaps?

One thing he did discover, though, was that a sense of humour transcends mere language. It wasn't just the people in the square by the mosque. Everyone he passed by found the sight of a barefoot Englishman in his smalls equally uproarious.

He seemed to be making some kind of headway with one tall Berber figure, who stood by a cart filled with watermelons. Blotto was using his hands to mimic the motion of waves, in the hope that he would be pointed towards the sea. The man seemed to understand, even to the point of saying, in heavily accented English, 'I understand.' He mimicked the waving hand movements, then, gesturing towards a voluptuous figure in the shadows behind him, said, 'You want my sister, yes?'

Blotto realised that his mime skills didn't quite wing the partridge.

But he had at least made contact with someone who had a bit of English, and would have tried further elucidation, had he not been interrupted by the sound of a bullet taking a sizable chunk out of a pillar by his head.

He turned to see his two original pursuers, the men in the black *kufi* caps, coming towards him with pistols raised. Instinctively, he overturned the melon cart, sending an avalanche of squelchy fruit towards them. His enemies' momentary distraction was long enough for him to leap sideways and hightail it along another narrow alley.

Though impeded by his lack of shoes, Blotto was cannier than he had been in the earlier chase. He'd got more sense of the terrain and the likely obstacles in his path; he was better at making use of the intermittent light from torches and oil lamps. He was relieved to see that superior fitness was leaving his pursuers almost out of sight. He was losing them! The dockyard smells of salt and fish and engine oil were getting stronger. He was going to make it!

Hardly had this thought taken up residence in the soft tissue of his brain than he turned a corner and found himself in a dead end. A high wall blocked the route ahead. To one side a vine had been trained over a metal arch to provide shade for a small restaurant. Hearing the triumphant shouts of his pursuers – one of whom shouted, 'There is no escape for you now, Lyminster!' – Blotto leapt forward, shinned up the vine's thick stem and hurled himself over the wall ahead. He heard two bullets dig into the brickwork where his bare feet had been nanoseconds before, as he launched himself into the void.

It was not a comfortable landing. There was no light on the other side of the wall, so Blotto could only feel a hard slope of small stones, like gravel but with sharper edges, on to which he bounced. His semi-naked body tumbled through the darkness in a shower of shingle, picking up cuts and scratches on the way, until the surface levelled out and he came to an untidy, painful halt.

Blotto lay still, trying to regain the rhythm of his breathing and work out where, by Wilberforce, he was. He assessed his situation. The only good thing about it was that he heard no more gunshots or sounds of pursuit. But, though he didn't know where he was, his pursuers probably did, so the danger was not over. He was sure that, if he tried to get back to the *Queen of the Orient*, the men in black would be waiting for him on the dockside.

The gritty feel of the dust on his fingers and the smell of the stuff both gave him the same message. What he had landed on was coal.

Blotto sat up and now, peering through the darkness, he was aware of a source of light. Gingerly picking himself up, he started to move towards it. His progress was slow. The light was too feeble to reach the pathway in front of him and he kept tripping over unseen obstacles. Each time he rolled in the dust and had difficulty scrambling back to the vertical. The pain on the soles of his feet wasn't getting any better either.

But he staggered on and, slowly, as the light drew nearer, he was able to pick a path of greater safety. Also, able to see what lay ahead.

He was in a huge open-air coal store. Through the arched entrance, tantalisingly, he could see the huge white flank of the *Queen of the Orient*. Inside the store, dust-covered half-naked workers continuously filled sacks with coal. As they put them down, the full sacks were picked up by more dust-covered porters, who hoisted them on their shoulders and made their way towards the blackened gangplank which led into the British ship. This was the ant-run of coal-carriers which Blotto and Lettice had observed from the terrace of the Savoy Hotel.

Under the arch of the coal store, a flaming torch burning above his head, a wizened clerk perched behind a tall desk, noting in a ledger the number of sacks of coal going to the vessel. Somehow, in spite of the ambient dust, the over-seer's robe retained its gleaming whiteness.

Blotto looked over the man's shoulder. As he feared, between the coal store and the gangplank which was cur-rently the only means of access to the *Queen of the Orient*, stood two men in black djellabas and *kufi* caps. Their right hands were ostentatiously hidden in the folds of their robes. They watched the arched entrance intently, knowing the coal store only had one exit.

Blotto couldn't decide what to do. Obviously, he was not afraid of making a dash for it, in the hopes of getting to the ship before they shot him. Putting his life on the line had always been one of his favourite pastimes. But he really didn't want to die, not at that particular moment. Not until he'd sorted out the business of his sister's non-engagement to Ponky Larreighffriebollaux. He couldn't leave an old muffin-toaster in the gumbo.

Preoccupied by thought (never his strongest suit), Blotto must have wandered too far into the light, because he was suddenly aware of being shouted at in some incomprehensible language. He turned to see the voice came from the white-clad checkout clerk. The man seemed quite aerated, spitting out what was clearly abuse and making lifting gestures.

Blotto looked down at his arms, his legs, his chest, his stomach. Normally, the skin of his body, never aired in public, remained a very pale pink, except for his face, forearms and a little v at his neck exposed by his cricket kit. Now, though, every inch of skin was black with coal dust. His pristine white drawers were so marked with coal that they looked for all the world like a grubby loincloth.

Obedient to the angry clerk's gesturing, Blotto picked up a sack of coal, heaved it on to his shoulders and joined the ant-line of workers crossing the gangplank on to the *Queen of the Orient*.

He walked between the two men in black, so close that, if his hands hadn't been occupied with the sack of coal, he could have pickpocketed the pistols from the pair of them. They showed no signs of recognition. For them, he was just another coal-carrier in the endless line.

Once inside, having emptied his sack into the void below, Blotto did not follow his fellow workers back to the coal store.

Instead, he slipped through a door and made his way to his stateroom on the bridge deck.

12

Curtains for Corky

Not a drum was heard, not a funeral note, as Corky Froggett's body was brought back on to the *Queen of the Orient*. The previous evening, Emmeline Washboard had started to worry about his late return from his mission of 'man's work'. Being a woman of remarkable pluck, she had set out into the hazardous night-time of Port Said to find him.

Being also a woman of considerable intelligence, before she left the hotel, she had torn from a magazine an advertisement for a Bentley motor car. It was not the vehicle itself which was relevant but, beside it, opening the passenger door with a beaming smile, was a chauffeur. He didn't look anything like Corky, but the dark-blue uniform could provide a useful point of reference.

Em's strategy worked. The strutting figure of Corky had attracted attention on his promenade earlier in the evening, and many of the locals she approached nodded in recognition at the photograph she thrust towards them.

Her search took a long time, but Port Said was not the kind of city that ever shut down completely, so there were still people in the narrow alleyways to direct her. Her route was mazy, not as straight as the one Corky had taken.

Eventually, Em found the salesman from whom Corky had made his purchases.

The emporium was like a narrow cave, his wares spread out in low trays, covered with black cloth. There was a strong electric light for those who wanted to check out the quality of their purchases. Probably because of the nationality of many of his customers, the shopkeeper had more than a smattering of English.

And he was certainly surprised by the arrival of Emmeline Washboard. 'But you are woman,' he said, his voice quavery with shock. 'No women come here. You come here to buy for your man?' He didn't sound as if he approved of the idea.

'No. I've come looking for my man.'

'Ah.' That seemed more acceptable.

She showed him the chauffeur picture.

'Yes, yes,' the man said. 'I do not forget him.'

'Why not?'

'He is the best customer I ever have. No one buy more of my goods than this man.'

'And do you know where he went?'

'Sorry? I do not understand.'

'After he left here, which way did he go?'

The man shrugged and gestured back the way she had come. 'Back to the dockside. They all go back to the dockside.'

Em hesitated, then looked at the covered trays. 'Could you tell me, please, what it is that you sell?'

'You do not wish to know this,' said the shopkeeper.

'I do wish to know,' she said firmly. 'That is why I asked.'

'I cannot tell you. I cannot tell a woman,' he said.

'But they are objects of great value?'

'Of great value, yes. And I have the best selection of any merchant in Port Said.'

107

'Because I was wondering, if my ... friend ... if he had bought so many of these ... objects, is it likely that he might have been robbed between here and the docks?'

The dealer supposed it was possible, but he did not think it was likely. 'My goods are goods for specialists,' he said.

Still showing the magazine picture, as she followed the more direct route back to the docks, at last Em found someone who had witnessed the events of earlier in the evening. He was a seller of oil lamps, looking for all the world like a character from the pantomime of *Aladdin* she had seen the previous Christmas.

He told her what had happened. She asked where Corky had been taken.

'To the city morgue. That is where all the unclaimed corpses in Port Said are taken. He will be buried at first light.'

Ship's stewards reclaimed Corky Froggett from the morgue, an insalubrious, foul-smelling cellar, and brought the body on a stretcher to the *Queen of the Orient*, just as the coaling had been completed and the ship's doors and portholes were being reopened.

Em was on board ahead of the stewards' cortège. Ignoring protocol, she went straight to the bridge deck, hoping to find someone who might know where Blotto had spent the night. The young master must be informed of the sad news as soon as possible.

Rather surprisingly, she found no staff in either of the first-class dining rooms or in the corridor between the first-class cabins. So, since Corky had mentioned to her which one his employer was in, she knocked on the door, with no expectation of its being opened.

Blotto had just got out of his third bath, which had

removed most of the residual coal dust (though the inside of his ears still felt a bit gritty) and put a robe around himself when he heard the summons. He opened the cabin door and was confronted by a rather voluptuous woman he had never seen before in his life. (Passengers from the lower decks rarely encountered those in first class.)

'Toad-in-the-hole!' said Blotto. 'What in the name of strawberries are you doing here?'

'It's about Corky,' the woman replied, a tear glinting at the corner of her eye.

'Corky? Are you talking about my chauffeur boddo?'

'Yes.'

'He's a Grade A foundation stone.'

'Was.'

'Where?' Blotto frantically flapped his hands about his head.

'*Was*,' Em insisted.

'Oh. Sorry, wasn't on the same page. Thought you said "Wasp". So, what are you saying? Come on, uncage the ferrets.'

'I was saying that Corky has . . . gone to the other side.'

'Has he, by Denzil! Port, would that be? Or starboard?'

'No. He's . . . gone the way of all flesh.'

'Yes. He has been putting on a bit of weight recently.'

'No, milord. Corky has . . . bitten the dust.'

'Don't talk to me about spoffing dust.' Blotto poked a finger in his ear and circled it around. 'Can't get rid of the fumacious stuff.'

'No! What I'm saying is . . . Corky has gone to a better place.'

'Yes, well, he always liked a flutter on the horses.'

'No, milord. What I am trying to tell you is . . .'

Emmeline Washboard might have continued with her thesaurus of euphemisms for some time, had she not been interrupted by the arrival of the ship's stewards with their doleful burden.

'Well, I'll be kippered like a herring!' cried Blotto. 'Corky, me old fruit bat, where have you been pongling? Come on, decant the haricots!'

'I think,' said Em mournfully, 'his last haricots have already been decanted.'

Finally, an edge of understanding forced its way through the density of Blotto's skull. 'Surely you're not telling me Corky's taken the quick route to the Pearlies?' Em nodded. 'You mean he's been coffinated?'

Another nod.

'Oh, biscuits smashed into a hundred thousand crumbs!' said Blotto. Which was a measure of how badly he took the news. He gestured to the stewards to place the inert body on his own bed. As it was laid out, Twinks appeared in the doorway.

'What filth-fingering's been going on here?' she asked. 'Corky coffinated?'

'Yes. More's the moping.'

The stewards stood back to let Twinks into the room, then withdrew discreetly to the corridor.

'Sorry, haven't got your name-tag,' said Twinks to Em.

'Emmeline Washboard, milady.'

'Call me Twinks. Everyone does.'

'Very good, Twinks.' The governess looked embarrassed. 'I'm, er, a friend of Corky.'

'Splendissimo. He was always good at making friends.'

Both women looked at the prone figure on the bed.

'I can't believe it,' said Twinks. 'I always thought Corky was as tough as a boulder-breaker's boot.'

'I only met him here on the boat,' said Em, 'but he seemed as strong as an ox.' She corrected herself wistfully. 'Or perhaps I should say "as a stallion".'

'Who coffinated him, Blotters? What lump of toadspawn would pull a trick like that?'

'I haven't got a blind bezonger of an idea.'

'Did you see him out in the town?'

'Well, I thought I heard his voice, but maybe the old lug-sockets were playing tricks on me.'

'When did you hear him, Blotters? And what was he saying?'

'I thought I heard him say: "Run for it, milord!".'

'And when was this?'

'Just when the two stenchers were about to coffinate me.'

'What "two stenchers"? And why did they want to coffinate you?'

'Do you know, Twinks me old omelette pan, I hadn't thought of that. Why *did* they want to coffinate me?'

'Blotto, me old button-hook,' his sister asked patiently, 'who were they?'

'Just two out-of-bounders with pistols, who seemed pretty determined I was the partridge they wanted to pop.'

'Tell me exactly what happened, Blotters. Come on, uncage the ferrets.'

While Blotto went through the events of the night in detail, Emmeline Washboard moved across to look at the bodily shell which had once contained Corky Froggett.

'So,' asked Twinks, when Blotto had laboriously reached the end of his narrative, 'did you actually clap your peepers on Corky before the two four-faced filchers fired?'

'Can't do a hand-on-heart on that, I'm afraid. But it was definitely his voice that shouted, "Run for it, milord!".'

'Just a minute,' said Em from the bedside. 'There's something strange here.'

'With Corky?' asked Blotto.

'Yes.' The governess pointed at the uniformed chest. 'Look where the bullets went in.'

The two holes were symmetrically spaced either side of the neatly buttoned opening of his jacket. 'Don't you see there's something missing?'

'No,' said Blotto. 'Oh, rein in the roans a moment there.' He looked more closely at the chauffeur's front and announced proudly, 'I think I've pinged the partridge here all right! Corky's not wearing his wartime service medals! By Wilberforce, that must be why the stenchers shot him? To filch the medals of a decorated war hero? What lumps of toadspawn!'

'You rein in the roans for a moment there, Blotters,' Twinks intervened. 'Was Corky actually wearing his medals when you last saw him?'

Blotto had to shake his head. His sister turned to the governess. 'Did Corky say anything about medals to you, Em?'

'Yes, he did, Twinks. He told me all about them. You bet he did. Otherwise, I wouldn't have known he'd won the last little dust-up with the Hun single-handed. But he said he'd left all his medals back at Tawcester Towers, because he didn't want to risk them being trousered by any foreign filchers.'

'So, I'm afraid that puts the candle-snuffer on your theory of the crime, Blotters,' said Twinks.

'Tough Gorgonzola,' said Blotto ruefully.

Twinks moved towards the body on the bed. 'But I think I may have won the coconut on what you were asking about, Em; what's missing round the bullet holes.'

'Yes?' the governess asked.

'Blood,' said Twinks.

'Exactly. Two bullets point-blank at the chest and no blood. What does that tell you?'

'That maybe something else caused his coffination . . . ?'

'Just what I was thinking.' Showing her nursing training, Em slipped her hands under Corky's neck and lifted his head to reveal a large bruise at the nape. 'My suggestion would be that the impact of the bullets knocked him backwards and he got this when his head hit the roadway.'

'So, it was the boff on the brainbox that did the actual coffinating?' asked Blotto.

'Maybe,' Em replied. 'There's still something odd here, though . . .'

'No sign of rigor mortis?' Twinks suggested.

'Exactly. Of course, we don't know the precise time he was shot, but rigor mortis tends to develop pretty quickly in a hot climate. Yet there's no sign of it . . .'

'Suggesting . . . ?' asked Twinks, instinctively recognising Em's superior medical experience.

'Suggesting . . . I don't know . . . Do you know what I mean by the word "catatonia"?'

'Yes,' Blotto replied eagerly. 'It's that noise cats make when they—'

'Stuff a pillow in it, Blotters!' snapped an uncharacteristically harsh Twinks. She turned back to Em. 'Are you saying Corky might not have booked a berth on the burial boat?'

'I wish I could say that. He doesn't seem to be showing any vital signs, but . . . It's like his body's in shock. And maybe a countershock might—'

She was interrupted by a loud voice from the doorway. 'Another stiff on the steamer, do I hear?'

Twinks did not have to turn round to recognise the tone – and the tact – of Captain Barnacle.

He strode into the stateroom and looked at the body on the bed. 'He shouldn't be in here! He's not a first-class passenger!'

'There are no classes in death,' said Twinks, rather piously. Though she knew as she said the words that they were complete puddledash. No member of the Lyminster family would dream of going to a heaven where their breeding was not respected. In the Bible, Jesus said that in His Father's house there were many mansions, and Twinks had never doubted that the best of them would be reserved for the aristocracy. That was how things worked everywhere else. Why should heaven be an exception?

'Nothing to worry about,' the Captain went on. 'The stiff won't be lying here long.'

'What do you mean?' asked Em.

'We have procedures for this kind of thing, you know. Happens quite often. We'll wait till we're through the Suez Canal. They don't like you clogging that up. And I'm never keen on doing it in the Red Sea. Once we're past Aden, though . . . miles of empty ocean. We'll do it there.'

'Who'll do what there?'

'I will.' The Captain made a mock-bow. 'All part of the service. The service is part of the service.' He chuckled at another of his well-oiled witticisms. 'Do marriages, and all. They're not legal, marriages conducted by a ship's captain, but a lot of people think they are. And, anyway, it gives the bloke a get-out if he thinks better of it. As many men do after a few months.'

'I'm sorry,' said Blotto, 'but what, in the name of strawberries, are you chuntering on about?'

'What I'm saying,' Captain Barnacle replied, 'is that I will see to it that matey here gets a good burial at sea.'

'"Burial at sea"?' a voice boomed from the prone figure on the bed. 'I have loathed the sea all my life! If you think I'm going to be buried in it, you've got another think coming!'

Corky Froggett sat bolt upright. The threat of being buried at sea had provided the countershock that Emmeline Washboard had been hoping for.

Corky wasn't well. The deathlike state he'd been in for the last few hours – not to mention the blow to the back of his head – had taken its toll. Everyone agreed that it might be dangerous to move him and that, given her nursing training, Emmeline Washboard should stay to 'minister to his needs'. The fact that Corky did not chortle when these words were spoken was a measure of his debilitated state.

While all these decisions were being made, the *Queen of the Orient* slipped away from the harbour of Port Said, past the statue of Ferdinand de Lesseps and out into the Suez

Canal. According to regulations, the liner could only go at six miles an hour in the canal, but it speeded up when they reached the open sea. For the rest of their passage to India, the crew wore their white duck uniforms and, as the heat increased, increasing number of passengers started sleeping on the decks.

Inside Blotto's stateroom, Corky was unwilling for Em to open his jacket and reveal what had prevented the assassins' bullets from piercing his chest, but he was too enfeebled to put up much resistance.

She undid the buttons and out slipped a mountain of rectangular pieces of cardboard. Being a woman of the world, Em immediately recognised what they were. And, of course, she knew that the number Corky had bought represented the salesman's best-ever day's trading.

She held one card up for him to look at. He squinted against the sunlight which came through a high window in the stateroom. And he saw that the thugs' bullets had made holes where nature had never intended them to be.

'Thank goodness you bought so many of them, Corky,' said Em. 'They saved your life.'

'Yes,' he agreed, not sounding particularly pleased about the outcome. 'But they're not going to be much use now as dirty postcards, are they?'

He reached inside his jacket, saying, 'Anyway, it wasn't the postcards that actually saved me.' Producing and handing across a neat velvet bag, he announced, 'It was this. I bought it for you.'

From the bag, Em extracted a small silver scent bottle, only about four inches long. The fine decorative chasing on its surface had been further embellished by large dents at either end, dents where it had taken the impact of two bullets.

'Oh, Corky! And you say it's for me?'

'That's right,' said the chauffeur. He knew how to treat a lady.

'Bless you.' She removed his dark-blue jacket and looked at its punctured front. 'I'll get this washed and invisibly mended . . . unless there's anything else you'd like me to do . . . ?'

'Well . . .' said Corky Froggett.

Blotto and Twinks had adjourned to her stateroom. She wanted to know more about the attempted assassination. 'You'd never clapped your peepers on them before, had you?'

'Oh, bite the reality rhubarb, Twinks. I don't know a single boddo in Port Said. So how could I recognise that pair of four-faced filchers?'

'And you hadn't spotted their fizzogs on board ship, had you?'

'No. I'm sure they were manufactured locally. They knew their way around the backstreets like beagles on a boar-hunt.'

'And you say they knew your name-tag?'

'They definitely called me "Lyminster".'

'Hm.' Twinks looked serious. 'That does make me don my worry-boots a bit.'

'Why, sis?'

'Well, it means you had a target on your back.'

'Sorry? Not on the same page?'

'They were actually trying to coffinate *you* – Devereux Lyminster – not just some random tourist.'

'Toad-in-the-hole!'

'And since you've got no one from Port Said in your address book, and you hadn't been in Port Said long enough to put lumps in anyone's custard, it must mean the attack was organised by someone on this ship who wants to kill you.'

'Must it?'

'Is the King German?'

116

'So, Twinks, are they likely to have another pop at the partridge?'

'I think they might. Probably not while we're on board. Too many people around. But once we get to Bombay ... you'd better keep the peepers peeled.'

'Good ticket.'

'And the next question, of course, is a very basic one.'

'Oh?'

'Why would anyone want to coffinate you?'

'Over the years, I've often bunged that one in the brain-box to try and work it out. But I never can. Mind you, in our various adventures, Jereboams-full of people have tried to coffinate me, haven't they?'

'You're bong on the nose there.'

'Maybe I'm just an accident prune.'

'I think "accident-prone" is the expression you're looking for, Blotters.'

'Ah.'

There might have been further discussion about why so many people wanted to kill Blotto, had they not been interrupted by a discreet knock at the door.

Twinks moved across the stateroom to admit Em.

'I'm sorry to bother you, but the sunlight's shining right on Corky's face where he's lying on the bed. I wondered if you'd got any cloth or something we could string across the windows ... ?'

'Of course! Larksissimo!' cried Twinks. 'I've got more scarves than a swordfish has scales!'

She produced a selection. Em took a few and crossed to the other stateroom to make curtains for Corky.

13

Terms of Engagement

There are people who, knowing that they were travelling on the same ship as someone who wanted to murder them, might have been worried by the fact. But they were people more reflective than Blotto. Throughout his life, he had benefited from the incalculable blessing of having absolutely no imagination.

His sister, by contrast – and in any discussion of the two siblings, the word 'contrast' always played a large part – was fully aware of the danger to him. But she was still of the view that a potential murderer would not take the risk of doing the deed in the crowded setting of the *Queen of the Orient*, where everyone's every move was scrutinised by everyone else. She reckoned it was when they arrived in Bombay that Blotto would need once again to be on his guard.

In the meantime, between rereading the *Five Classics* of the traditional Confucian canon (in the original Chinese, of course), she applied her skills of observation and deduction to the question of who might want Blotto dead.

And she also puzzled over the problem of how, without causing pain to the other party concerned, she could get out of her engagement to Ponky Larreighffriebollaux.

* * *

That particular gluepot did not get any less gluey when, the evening of their departure from Port Said, Twinks was lying on her deckchair, enjoying the last of the sunshine. Also enjoying solitude. That was an advantage – the only one – of her supposed engagement. Had her fiancé not been on board, there were plenty of amorous swains who might have flirted with her or tried to go further. But the presence of Ponky Larreighffriebollaux did at least save her from that, and the news of their engagement had spread to every deck of the *Queen of the Orient* at the speed of influenza. Once they knew about it, despite the unlikelihood of a female of Twinks's beauty and accomplishments allying herself to such an inarticulate stringbean, the male passengers showed proper respect for her affianced status.

But that evening her attention was drawn away from the familiar charm of *Spring and Autumn Annals*, the history of Confucius's native state of Lu from 722 to 481 BC, by the appearance of her intended (or perhaps 'unintended' would be a better word), in the company of M. le Vicomte Xavier Douce.

Inevitably, it was the latter who did the talking. An engaged Ponky Larreighffriebollaux turned out to be no more articulate than an unengaged one. Twinks dismally contemplated an endless sequence of marital breakfasts enlivened only by the occasional 'Tiddle my pom!'

Apparently having forgotten their earlier conversation, after adjusting his monocle, the diamond merchant again greeted her with the wrong honorific. 'Good evening, Lady Lyminster.'

Twinks didn't have the energy to correct him.

'I am honoured that your fiancé has entrusted me – on very short acquaintance – with the delicate task of choosing an engagement ring for you.'

'Oh, larksissimo,' said Twinks feebly. Never in her life had she felt less larksissimo. 'Drabissimo' would better describe her current mood.

'He made a very wise choice,' the Vicomte went on. 'I am acquainted with the best diamond merchants in every city in the world – that is, outside the United States of America – and so I knew exactly who to go to in Port Said to source the most magnificent stones. You are fortunate, Lady Lyminster, to be marrying a man of exceptional generosity. Though I have frequently done the same service for other young men desirous of procuring the best engagement ring for their bride-to-be, they usually give me an upper limit for the amount they wish to outlay on such a purchase. And I am pleased to be able to tell you that, though it is a frequent occurrence in my dealings with Indian Maharajahs, your fiancé is the first Englishman I have ever encountered who set no such upper limit. You are indeed blessed, Lady Lyminster.'

Oh, put a jumping cracker under it, thought Twinks. But she was far too well brought up to voice the words.

'So, anyway . . .' The Vicomte turned to his client. 'It is now over to you, Monsieur.'

Ponky had clearly done his homework. He uncoiled and arranged his long limbs into a kneeling posture. Then, reaching into the pocket of his jacket, he produced a small box. He clicked it open and held it out to his beloved, doing a passable impression of a Wise Man going manger-wards in a stable.

Twinks did not dislike jewellery, but her main require-ment was that, like furniture, it should be inherited. There was something irredeemably vulgar about buying stuff like that new. Even having it purpose-made by the finest craftsmen was a bit beyond the barbed wire. She reminded herself that, though Ponky Larreighffriebollaux was extraordinarily wealthy, he wasn't actually a member of the aristocracy. It was little things like buying new jewellery or furniture that gave that away.

But she couldn't deny the splendour of the engagement ring that she was being offered. A single huge diamond, surrounded by a cluster of lesser satellite diamonds, it caught the dying sunshine and redirected it through a thousand facets.

Twinks was caught on the prongs of a dilemma. Here, surely, was her opportunity to explain to Ponky how seriously he'd got the wrong end of the sink-plunger. She would never get a better opportunity to put the candle-snuffer on his illusions. And yet . . . And yet . . .

The appeal in his goggle eyes was so strong that to end his dreams would have felt like drowning a kitten.

Involuntarily, Twinks found her left hand stretching forwards and found herself allowing him to slip the ring on the relevant finger. She found her lips forming the words, 'Thank you so much, Ponky. It's a real bellbuzzer with three veg and gravy.'

And she found she wasn't at all surprised when her fiancé said, 'Tiddle my pom!'

'I'm very sorry, milord,' said the bridge deck chief steward. 'This voyage is packed tighter than an acrobat's drawers. Every stateroom's chocker. Anyway, milord, would it not be more appropriate that, since we're only talking about a chauffeur here, the patient should be accommodated in the ship's sick bay?'

'We are not "only talking about a chauffeur here",' insisted Blotto. 'We are talking about Corky Froggett.'

'Very good, milord,' said the chief steward, long habituated to obsequiousness. What he actually thought was another matter. 'But I'm afraid, if we were talking about the Father, the Son and the Holy Ghost, there still wouldn't be a spare stateroom.'

'Tickey-tockey,' said Blotto with dignity. 'I will make arrangements.'

What he always meant when he used that expression

was: 'I will go and tell my sister the problem and she will make arrangements.'

But when he knocked on Twinks's stateroom door, there was no reply. Instead, he went back into his own to check up on the invalid.

Twinks's scarves were in position to shade Corky from the sun. He looked almost as pale as the Egyptian cotton pillows on which he lay. His bullet-pierced chauffeur's uniform had been removed and he was dressed in one of Blotto's nightshirts. If nothing else defined how ill he was, that did. The idea of his plebeian body being clad in anything belonging to the young master would deeply offend Corky Froggett's sense of priorities. He must have been unconscious when the change of clothes was effected, or he would never have allowed it.

His state of health was reflected in the anxiety written on Emmeline Washboard's face. Corky Froggett may have been as durable as the cladding of a Mark IV tank, but his near-death experience had knocked the stuffing out of him.

'Not in the zing-zing condition we know and love?' asked Blotto, respectful of nursing skills when he saw them.

'At least he's breathing,' Em replied, 'which he appeared not to be for some time. He's very weak, though. Look, even his moustache isn't bristling.'

Blotto's eye followed her pointing finger and saw the truth of her words. The moustache, normally as upright as a thistle, lay on Corky's upper lip like overboiled cabbage.

'Has the ship's sawbones clapped his peepers on him?' Blotto asked.

'Yes. He was a gloomy git. Like that bloody Captain. Said we should make preparations for a burial at sea.'

'Toad-in-the-hole!'

'But ships' doctors always do that.'

'Do they, by Denzil?'

122

'Yes, don't want their incompetence shown up. All doctors bury their mistakes. The disadvantage of that is that most of them can still be dug up again. Ships' doctors have it easy. Body over the side, no questions asked.'

'Great galumphing goatherds! I hadn't thought of that.' Blotto looked down at the prone body. 'But you can kindle something from Corky's embers, can't you?'

'I can do my damnedest, yes. He couldn't be in better hands than mine.'

'Good ticket.'

'He actually said that to me. He said, "Em, I've never been in better hands than yours."'

Blotto, who had enough difficulty understanding a single meaning, and had never got near to a double one, said, 'You're a Grade A foundation stone, Em.'

'But, milord,' she said, 'surely we must move Corky from here? This is your stateroom. We can't keep you out of it all the way to Bombay.'

'Of course you can, by Wilberforce! I wouldn't be such a hippo on a houseboat as to give him the shoehorn. No, you stay here, girded about with your ministering angel togs, and I'll pongle off elsewhere.'

'But where, milord? I hear the chief steward say that all the staterooms were full. Will you be all right?'

'Tickey-tockey,' said Blotto once again with dignity. 'I will make arrangements.'

And once again, when he left his own stateroom, he knocked on his sister's. And this time Twinks was there to let him in.

Left alone with the unresponsive Corky, Emmeline Washboard placed a gentle hand on his forehead. In spite of the ambient heat, the skin felt very cold. Slowly, she moved her hand down his body, slipping under the light sheet. The flesh, beneath the thin material of the nightshirt, was still cold. As her hand roamed further, she felt an ominous shudder run through his frame.

123

Fearful, Emmeline Washboard looked at his face. 'My goodness!' she said. 'Your moustache is bristling!'

'It's not just my moustache,' said Corky Froggett.

'I think the solution . . .' Blotto always loved it when his sister started sentences like that. It always happened when he had come to her with a problem which he found insoluble. And since he found insoluble every problem that didn't involve cricket, hunting or fighting off stenchers, he heard her saying it quite a lot.

'I think the solution,' Twinks repeated, 'is that you should move into this stateroom and I should pongle off elsewhere.'

'Give that pony a rosette!' he cried, delighted that, once again, his sister had achieved an instant fix on the problem. 'So where is this "elsewhere" you might pongle off to?'

'Another stateroom.'

'Good ticket,' said Blotto. 'The trouble is, according to that oikish sponge-worm the chief steward, all the other staterooms are occupied.'

'Then I will have to share with someone, won't I?'

'What a bellbuzzer of an idea! Why didn't I think of that?'

'Let's let that one go into the net,' said Twinks, as ever unwilling to answer questions that might be hurtful to her brother.

'Just blipped the brain cells, though, Twinks me old orange-peeler,' said Blotto, 'that most of the staterooms on this deck are occupied by . . . well . . .'

'By what?'

'Well, by boddoes who're . . . boddoes. That is to say, they're . . . well, think about it. Who've we got parking their jim-jams along this corridor? There's Ponky, of course . . . and that Froggy diamond merchant, that Mr Mukerjee greengage, and the Maharajah . . . and, well, they're all boddoes. I mean, none of them are of the gentler gender. And I know you're very modern and all that, Twinks – you make your own cocoa, for the love of strawberries! But I still don't think it would be in the rulebook for you to share a stateroom with a . . . with a . . . with a man.'

'I'm not—'

'Oh, Lordie in a kitchen coop! You're not . . . I've heard of these modern Jezebels who think being engaged gives them the right to move under the same umbrella as their fiancés and act like the reef knot had already been twiddled and—'

'Blotto!' It was one of those very scary moments when Twinks sounded exactly like their mother, the Dowager Duchess. Blotto quailed appropriately. 'If you think I, Honoria Lyminster, would consider living in sin with Ponky Larreighffriebollaux, then—'

'No, no, of course I didn't mean that, Twinks me old tea-strainer!'

'I should hope not! And let me assure you, Blotto, when I do choose to live in sin with someone – a choice which, as an emancipated woman of the 1920s, I absolutely have the right to make – it will not be with Ponky Larreighffriebollaux!'

Blotto was steeped in apology. 'No. On the same page with you now, Twinks me old sand-blotter.'

'So, obviously, I will share a stateroom with someone of my own gender.'

'Good ticket, yes, bong on the nose. So, what, will you be chummying up with some of the Maharajah's wives?'

'Not on your nuthatch, Blotters! Apart from anything else, they're all in purdah.'

'Ah.' Blotto nodded sagely, as if he had a bat-squeak of an idea what she was talking about. Clearly, it was one of those . . . women's things. 'Would that be face purdah? Or talcum purdah?' Another thought. 'Surely not gunpurdah?'

'No, purdah is the seclusion of women in ... Do you know what a "zenana" is?'

Blotto considered the question seriously. 'A kind of fruit . . . ?' he hazarded.

Twinks was as exasperated as she ever could be with her brother and decided to move the conversation on. 'Blotto,' she said patiently, 'don't worry about it. I have already made the arrangements. I will be sharing a stateroom with your admirer.'

'My admirer? I don't think I've got any admirers, have I?'

'Lettice Sandwich.'

'Oh. Ah. Well. Yes. I suppose, in a way . . .'

Twinks just about managed to keep the disbelief out of her voice as she said, 'Lettice Sandwich is in awe of your intellect.'

Blotto beamed. 'Well, jolly good solution all round. Nothing now to stop us from lighting the fireworks of fun all the way to Bombay. That is, I'm assuming that you've managed to break the news to Ponky that . . .'

His words trickled away, as Twinks thrust forward her left hand, with its huge sparkler on the wedding finger.

'Oh, rats in a sandwich!' said Blotto.

14

A Life on the Indian Ocean Wave

Lettice Sandwich had no objections to sharing her state-room with Twinks. In fact, she thought it was all creamy éclair. To be in the same accommodation as his sister guaranteed the prospect of seeing a lot of Blotto. And Lettice could not imagine the moment when she would not want to see a lot of Blotto. Also, having Twinks around might cut down the number of catty visits she received from other, disappointed members of the Fishing Fleet.

Twinks herself also saw advantages in the new arrange-ment. Though she was protected now by the rock on her finger, there were still amorous swains who, at the end of an evening's drinking, might try their luck at invading her single stateroom. Twinks did not doubt her ability to see off such unwelcome advances – it was a skill she had honed over the years – but encounters of that kind could still cause social awkwardness. Sharing with Lettice Sandwich would rule out the risk completely.

The stateroom had been designed for double occupancy, so there was plenty of space for both women's extensive wardrobes. There was also shelving to accommodate Twinks's library of books. Those, along with the rest of her possessions, had been moved from her original room by the *Queen of the Orient*'s staff of chambermaids.

As she reorganised the volumes into the orders in which she liked them (alphabetically, according to language groups – Sino-Tibetan, Tor-Kwerba, Yuki-Wappo and so on), she said to Lettice, 'If you do want to borrow a book, this is Liberty Hall.'

'No, it isn't,' said Lettice. 'It's a stateroom on the *Queen of the Orient*.'

'Ye-es,' said Twinks. 'What I actually meant was: feel free to help yourself to a book.'

'That's all right,' said Lettice. 'I've got one.'

'Oh, what is it?' asked Twinks, always intrigued by other people's reading tastes.

'I haven't got it with me,' Lettice replied. 'I left it at home.'

'Why?'

'Because I'd read it.'

'Oh, well, then you're probably ready for another one.'

'No,' said Lettice. 'I'm still thinking about that one.'

'Ah,' said Twinks.

'Tell me, Twinks, what was it like growing up in the company of someone brilliant?'

'Not to shimmy round the shrubbery, I never gave it the tiniest thoughtette. Things always came easily to me. I was lucky fate turned an ace with the brainbox I was born with.'

'I wasn't talking about you, Twinks. I was talking about Blotto.'

Ah, thought Twinks, there are no coconuts being awarded here.

The further they advanced into the Indian Ocean, the hotter it got. Though the women could get away with light summer frocks, dressing for dinner was a nightly, sweat-inducing ordeal for the first-class male passengers. And it was even worse for the old India hands who still wore woollen cholera belts under their shirts. But social decencies had to be observed.

Blotto spent an increasing amount of time with his sister's roommate, still revelling in the unfamiliar glow of having his intellect admired, while Twinks continued her programme of Confucian rereading. She quickly moved on through the *Five Classics*, leaving the historical delights of the *Ch'un Ch'iu* (*Spring and Autumn Annals*) for the court ceremonies of the *Book of Rites* (*Liji*).

Twinks saw little of the Maharajah of Koorbleimee. And even less of the Star of Koorbleimee. The Maharajah seemed to spend most of his time closeted in his stateroom, possibly with some of his wives, possibly not. There was no way of knowing. And when he did appear for dinner in the first-class dining room, he wore conventional Western evening dress. Though the diamonds on his cufflinks and studs were of the highest quality, they did not attract attention on the level of the famous Star.

Nor was M. le Vicomte Xavier Douce much in evidence during the remainder of the voyage. Presumably, there is little for a diamond merchant to do on board ship. Having had the unexpected demand for his professional services from Ponky Larreighffriebollaux in Port Said, the rest of his time must have been occupied with planning for the commercial dealings he would undertake once he reached India. Twinks wondered whether he had investments in diamond mines there. She knew there was quite a history over the centuries of Western businessmen cheating the locals out of mineral rights (just as they'd cheated them out of practically everything else).

Being the fiancée of Ponky Larreighffriebollaux was not an onerous role either. He made very few demands on her time – or anything else of hers. The satisfaction of having put a ring on her finger seemed to be all that he required of the arrangement. Certainly, his new status had not made him any more articulate. He could sit beside her on a deckchair all morning without saying anything more than a couple of 'Tiddle my poms'. And the protection he gave her from other amorous swains was not to be taken lightly. Twinks knew that at some point she had to shatter his illusions, but the urgency did not now seem to be so great. A problemette to be sorted out once they actually set foot on the subcontinent.

Maybe it was the enervating heat that made everything seem less important. Twinks found she was also spending less time trying to identify the stencher who wanted her brother dead.

One thing she did appreciate was the intellectual stimulus of Mr Mukerjee's company. Since his offer of marriage had been turned down, and since he had seen her apparently become engaged to someone else, he accepted the situation with equanimity. Theirs was a meeting of minds, never destined to be anything else.

It goes without saying that he was also an expert on Confucianism. Many a conversation in their deckchairs on the bridge deck went along the lines of this one:

MR MUKERJEE: Of course, the unanswered question in any discussion of the subject is whether Confucianism is a system of ethics or a religion.

TWINKS: You're bong on the nose there, Muckers! But that's not a kink in the flyline for me. It's never blipped my brain cells that the two are mutually exclusive.

MR MUKERJEE: You mean that Confucian principles depend on the unity of the individual self and God?

TWINKS: Give that pony a pink rosette! And that very unity biffs two budgerigars with the same boomerang. In the same way

	as the Christian God slipped into the jim-jams of a human boddo, the divine and the corporeal are linked in Confucianism as closely as a baby and its bottle.
MR MUKERJEE:	Which was why it was always going to be at odds with the Legalism or *Faija* which became prevalent under the Qin Dynasty.
TWINKS:	Larksissimo, Muckers! And I'd put my last shred of laddered silk stocking on the fact that you're about to compare Legalism with the Western Machiavellianism.
MR MUKERJEE:	I was about to, yes. You're very percipient, Twinks.
TWINKS:	Just the way the gene-pool ripples. But I think that spoffing religion/system of ethics dichotomy bears closer comparison with the way that fruity crumb Huang-Lao developed from a school of syncretism to proto-Taoism and all that rombooley.
MR MUKERJEE:	As ever, Twinks, you've put your finger on it.
TWINKS:	I always do my bounciest. And I think, to take the thing down to its frilly drawers, it's forty thou to a fishbone that Confucianism retains both an ethical and a religious dimension.
MR MUKERJEE:	Spot on. Don't you agree, Mr Larreigh-ffriebollaux?

PONKY [WHO IS SITTING IN A DECKCHAIR THE OTHER SIDE OF TWINKS]: Well, er . . . Tiddle my pom!

Not for the first time, Twinks reflected that her perfect

fiancé would combine Ponky's wealth with Mr Mukerjee's intellect. Oh, and of course be an aristocrat as well.

Once he was fit enough to express opinions (very quickly, under the expert ministrations of Emmeline Washboard), Corky Froggett took a lot of persuading that he had a right to stay in Blotto's stateroom. Loyalty to the young master ran through him like 'Brighton' through a stick of seaside rock. And he regarded usurping anything that belonged to Blotto as a form of *lèse-majesté*.

So, in spite of Em's blandishments (and she was very handy with a blandishment), he demanded to be moved, unless he actually had permission given face-to-face by the young master.

This Blotto was more than happy to provide. When informed of the situation by Em, he instantly abandoned a rather desultory game of deck quoits to attend the recumbent chauffeur.

'Listen, Corky me old tank-trap,' he began, 'you probably wouldn't know this, because you weren't one of my muffin-toasters at Eton, but while I was grinding the old brainbox at the place, one of the beaks kept trying to cram poetry into our lug-sockets. Most of it slipped through the old memory-filter like cocoa through a colander, but one bit I remember was a poem about some poor little greengage called "Dunga-Gin".'

'Might it have been "Gunga-Din"?' Emmeline Washboard suggested.

'Could have been. Yes, that does blip the brain cells a tidge. "Gunga-Din", tickey-tockey. Anyway, I haven't a bat-squeak of an idea which boddo wrote the thing . . . if writing's what you do to a poem . . .'

'Kipling,' said Em, who had read a lot of his stuff in preparation for being a governess in India. 'Do you like Kipling?'

'I don't know,' said Blotto. 'I've never kippled.'

'No, I meant . . .'

Em didn't bother continuing, as Blotto went on, 'This Gunga-Din greengage, anyway, was the absolute dregs of the servant classes . . .'

'Rather as I am, milord?' the chauffeur humbly suggested.

'Good ticket! You've pinged the partridge there and no mistake! But the point about it is, not to fiddle round the fir trees, this poor old thimble Gunga-Din, who does something pretty murdy for the military.'

'He's a water-carrier,' Em supplied.

'You've potted the black there! Anyway, the soldiers reckon that, when it comes to water-carrying, this Gunga-Din droplet's about as much use as a trouser press in a convent, and they keep telling him so; saying what an oikish sponge-worm he is, you know, the whole clang-dumble.'

'Just as people of my class should be treated,' said a subservient Corky.

'Tickey-tockey. Then the boddo who's uncaging the ferrets about Gunga-Din gets shot, and old G.D. himself gets coffinated and the poet laces up his thinking boots and decides that Gunga-Din's not such a lump of toadspawn, after all. And, in fact, he's a better boddo than the other boddo.

'And that's how I feel about you, Corky,' were the words with which Blotto concluded this triumph of diplomacy and demonstration of his common touch.

'Very British of you, milord,' said the devoted chauffeur.

'And what this means,' the young master went on, 'is that you can park your jim-jams here for as long as you fancy the fishing.'

'Talking of jim-jams, milord . . .' Corky's hand crept guiltily down to touch the fine cotton of his nightshirt. 'I'm afraid I seem to be dressed in togs of yours. I would like

133

to assure you, milord, that I did not take the garment. Someone must have put it on me while I—'

'Don't don your worry-boots about that, Corky. Take what you want from my wardrobe. I'll get the stewards to ferry my flipmadoodles – including the old cricket bat, of course – to the other stateroom, but . . .' He turned to the governess '. . . if there's anything Corky needs from my toggings, can I rely on you to pick them for him, Miss Washboard?'

'Of course you can, milord.'

'Hoopee-doopee! All clear as a nun's conscience, are we?'

'Yes. Just one thing, milord . . .' said Em.

'Ask and it shall be granted.'

'I just thought, milord, given Corky's debilitated state, he's going to need intensive nursing.'

'Tickey-tockey.'

'Twenty-four-hour nursing.'

'That'll fit the pigeonhole.'

'But I would hate it if, in such a gossipy place as the *Queen of the Orient*, anyone should get the wrong impression.'

'Which wrong impression's that when it's got its spats on?'

'The impression that I should be in a stateroom with Corky for any other reason than nursing him.'

Blotto's patrician brow furrowed. 'Sorry? Not on the same page . . . ?'

'Some people might suffer from the delusion that I might be here . . . for immoral purposes.'

'Ah.' This didn't seem to clarify things much for Blotto.

'Some people might think that we might be sharing the same accommodation so that we could . . . behave like a married couple.'

'What, you mean bicker at each other all the time? No, I don't think Corky's ever been much of a bickerer.'

Emmeline Washboard was beginning to find this rather an uphill task. 'Some people might think that Corky and I would be sleeping in the same bed.'

'Oh, I don't think you'd want to do that, not in this hot weather. And if it does get a bit nippy round the knees, just ask the stewards to rattle up some extra blankets.'

'No, milord. What I meant was . . . people might think we were . . .' She leaned close to the splendid thatch of blond hair and whispered.

Blotto recoiled in horror. 'Toad-in-the-hole! Are there stenchers out there who'd be so oikish as to think that?'

'I'm afraid there are, milord.'

'Well, they should wash their minds out with soap and water.'

'So, milord,' said Em, 'if you do hear any rumours like that going around on board, will you quash them?'

'Quash? I'll take my cricket bat to them, by Cheddar!'

'Thank you so much, milord.'

'So, is that your little problemette de-ticked?'

'It is, milord.'

'Hoopee-doopee! Right. So, Corky, these are your quarters till we pongle into Bombay. And the only thingette I ask you to do in return is to get yourself back into zing-zing condition as quick as a doctor's bill. We all want to have Corky firing on all cylinders, don't we?'

'I certainly do,' said Em. 'And don't you worry. I'll get his cylinders firing in no time.'

'Beezer!'

'And in the meantime,' she said, picking up Corky's perforated uniform jacket, 'I will get this cleaned and invisibly mended, milord.'

'Tickey-tockey!' said Blotto. 'I knew you'd come up with the silverware. So, Corky, I'll leave you in Miss Washboard's capable hands.'

With that, stemming the effusion of chauffeurly thanks, Blotto swept out of the stateroom.

Emmeline Washboard grinned at the invalid and placed herself lasciviously on the bed beside him.

'Now, Corky,' she said, 'where were we?'

'Well, I know where we were,' he replied. Picking up one of the unperforated postcards, he went on, 'But I thought we could try *this*.'

Miss McQueeg's demands in life were simple. All she required was one copy of the Bible to read exhaustively and a large number of other copies to press on people who might well not know what to do with them. Her belief was that once a heathen had a copy of the Good Book in their possession, her job was done. She could leave the follow-through to the Almighty.

Before setting her sights on India, Miss McQueeg had done extensive missionary work in Africa. Measured by the number of Bibles she had handed out, she regarded her sorties there as completely successful. But she had relied perhaps too much on the Almighty to tell the proud recipients of her gifts what to do with them. Many of Miss McQueeg's Bibles had been used as pillows, others to prop up uneven chair legs, and in Nyasaland there was an entire dog kennel built of them.

Miss McQueeg was very interested in Sin. She did not believe in the doctrine of Original Sin, because that would mean that she too shared a part of the flaw in all human-ity. She reckoned her devout Bible-reading absolved her from that. There was no Sin in her, but she was fascinated by Sin in other people.

She already had suspicions of her cabin-mate. She had seen Emmeline Washboard in the company of Corky Froggett more often than she considered seemly for a governess. It was her view that the teaching of small children demanded a level of purity and sobriety not very different from that of a missionary.

And in a small cabin divided from the other bunk only by a suspended sheet, Miss McQueeg could not help noticing the night-time absences of her cabin-mate. Inside her small, tight-laced mind, insalubrious thoughts jostled for space with remembered quotations from the Good Book. And the more she tried to concentrate on the quotations, the more space – cuckoo-fashion – the insalubrious thoughts occupied.

She knew it was only a matter of time before she investigated. Managing to contain her curiosity for a couple of days, the next morning she finally succumbed to the temptation. Though she didn't think of it as a temptation. She thought of it as part of her vocational mission on behalf of a vengeful God.

Miss McQueeg had found over the years that carrying a supply of Bibles gave her instant access to anywhere. The sight of a pile of Good Books perhaps made people fearful that their bearer was about to engage them in theological argument or, even worse, try to convert them. For this, or perhaps some other reason, a Bible-carrying Miss McQueeg was rarely engaged in conversation by anyone. People just let her pass.

So, despite her lack of first-class status, she had no problem in accessing the bridge deck and its corridor between the staterooms. Consultation with the passenger list had identified which one Blotto had occupied *and* the fact that he'd vacated it for Corky's intensive care and recuperation.

Miss McQueeg knocked on the door. Receiving no reply, she pushed it open.

And saw a sight which gave her an instant crash-course in the nature of Sin.

15

The Fires of Hell!

Bibles scattered to either side of her as Miss McQueeg ran along the corridor of the bridge deck. 'I have seen the fires of hell!' she cried. 'I have seen the fires of hell! All will be engulfed in the mighty flames!'

'Where did you see them?' asked a steward who stood in her way.

'In one of the staterooms!'

He didn't wait for further information. Like every member of the crew, he knew the dangers of fire on shipboard and rushed to tell the chief steward. Within moments, all of the crew had been apprised of the emergency. And no one had noticed that, in the bridge deck corridor, Miss McQueeg, from sheer shock, had dropped to the floor in a dead faint.

Soon sirens wailed and instructions were bellowed through megaphones for all passengers to evacuate their cabins and assemble at their muster stations on the various decks. Sailors were quickly in position by the davits to lower the *Queen of the Orient*'s lifeboats. Others were busy getting lifejackets out of storage. Yet more, dressed in full firemen's kit and carrying axes, trailed hoses into the interior of the bridge deck.

Though all of the passengers had been instructed about

emergency procedures before embarkation, few had taken much notice at the time or thought about the details much since. So, there was a considerable amount of confusion and misdirection as the voyagers tried to find the muster assembly points on the various lifeboat decks.

As with everything else on board, money counted, and the drill was easier for those in first class. There were fewer of them, for a start. Then, it being late morning, many were already on deck rather than in their staterooms, so it did not take them long to assemble at the muster point.

Blotto, who'd been on a deckchair sharing vacuities with Lettice Sandwich, saw to it that they were among the first into position.

'Are we going to drown?' asked Lettice timorously.

'Great Wilberforce, no!'

'Thank heavens for that.'

She looked relieved, as he went on, 'If there's a conflagration on board ship, you're more likely to be frizzled to a fag-end before you even get a leg into a lifeboat.'

The look on her face suggested this might not have been entirely the right thing to say, so Blotto quickly asserted, 'You'll be safe with me, though.'

'Do you mean you're not flammable?'

'Me? Don't don your worry-boots about that. I'm spoffing well inflammable!' He looked confused for a moment. 'Something's just blipped the brain cells. You know what it means, Lettice me old Chelsea bun, when someone says that you're "competent" ...?'

'No.'

'Why not, in the name of strawberries?'

'Because no one's ever said it to me.'

'Ah. Right. Good ticket. Actually, it hasn't been said to me as often as the second hand comes round. But the point I'm dabbing the digit on is that, if you can come up with the silverware on something, boddoes say you're "competent". And if you can't, they say you're "incompetent".'

'Oh, people have said that to me quite often,' said Lettice, relieved.

'And yet it's different when you set things on fire.'

'Sorry?'

'Well, "flammable" and "inflammable" mean exactly the same thing.'

'So they do.'

'Bit of a rum baba, isn't it?' said Blotto.

They might have delved deeper into semantic philosophy, had they not at that point been joined by Twinks, her head still deep in the work of Confucius that she was currently reading. She had moved on to the *Shu Ching* (*Book of Historical Legends*), and was so absorbed that she hardly responded to her brother's greeting.

The seamen manning the davits had now lowered the lifeboats to embarkation level and one of the ship's officers was about to start a roll call of the first-class passengers. Not all were demonstrating the same insouciance as Blotto and Twinks. There was much frightened chattering from all of the Maharajah of Koorbleimee's womenfolk. They were heavily veiled, and it was hard to tell whether they were more upset by the prospect of being burned to death, being drowned or being out of the purdah of their staterooms. The Maharajah's detached posture gave out the firm message: 'They're nothing to do with me.'

Blotto looked around the passengers to see if any familiar faces were missing. Just as he became aware of the absence of Mr Mukerjee, the gentleman himself appeared, hurrying out of the door from the first-class staterooms.

Through the same door then appeared Corky Froggett and Emmeline Washboard, the former buttoning up his newly repaired jacket in a flustered manner. The governess's face was red, though with recent exertion rather than shame. Shame was not an emotion she had ever felt. She and Corky scuttled past the first-class passengers down to their proper level.

Seconds after the roll call had begun, out of the doors to the staterooms issued M. le Vicomte Xavier Douce. The diamond merchant moved with his customary unruffled ease towards the muster, arriving just in time to answer to his name.

They had to wait a long time on the lifeboat deck. Captain Barnacle's social skills may have lacked for something, but he knew how to keep the *Queen of the Orient* safe. He would not allow the passengers to return to their cabins or leisure pursuits until every last space on the ship had been checked for evidence of the reported fire. It took over two hours before the 'all-clear' was finally sounded

During all that time, an unworried Twinks continued to read Confucius.

'It's a very serious accusation,' said Captain Barnacle.

'Yes, but it's spoffing well not true!' Blotto protested.

'Are you suggesting I should doubt the word of a devout missionary lady?'

'If that devout missionary lady is shinning up the wrong drainpipe, then yes.'

Blotto had been summoned to the Captain's private office. Twinks had elected to go with him, just in case her brother plunged himself deeper into the gluepot.

And she intervened at this point. 'Listen, Captain, even if Miss McQueeg was shinning up the right drainpipe, and she did see Mr Froggett and Miss Washboard doing some . . . under-the-counterpane jiggling . . .' The expression on her brother's face suggested he could not imagine such a thing '. . . surely it wouldn't be the first time that's happened on the *Queen of the Orient*?'

'Well—'

'I know a lot of flappers and filchers who reckon the sole purpose of a sea voyage is stuffing their toes in other people's socks.'

'Yes, but—'

'Indeed, Captain, at the first evening's dinner, you were running up the flag yourself about the number of extra-marital affairs that had started, out of sheer boredom, at your table.'

'Yes, but that's entirely different.'

'Why, in the name of snitchrags, is it different?'

'Because that kind of thing tends to happen between two people who're both first-class passengers.'

'Don't talk such meringue! Are you telling me there hasn't been some boddo – male boddo, obviously – who's pounced on a juicy chambermaid or lured one of the more available Fishing Fleet up to his stateroom?'

'Of course it's happened. Indeed, I'd be worried if there was a voyage under my command on which it didn't happen. And I agree, the possibility of a holiday romance is one of the big attractions of travel. But in every case on board the *Queen of the Orient*, it's been the person who had actually booked the stateroom who was rumping the pump there.'

Twinks looked suitably shocked as the import of this sank in. 'Whereas in this case, neither the Party of the First Part nor the Party of the Second Part was a first-class passenger . . .'

'Exactly.' The Captain wiped his brow nervously. 'If news of this was to get out . . . If the management of the shipping company was to hear about it . . . Well, I don't know how much longer I'd be in a job.'

'I wish someone would hit me with the headlines on this,' said Blotto plaintively. 'Corky Froggett got nearly coffinated by those slugbuckets in Port Said and Emmeline Washboard, who's a governess who's also stocked up some savvy on the nursing front, was caring for him. We decided he'd be on camomile lawns with her personal attention, rather than being in the ship's sick bay. What is there in that to put lumps in anyone's custard?'

Twinks and Captain Barnacle exchanged looks, the result of which was an unspoken agreement that she should tackle the explanation.

'It really comes down, Blotto me old kettle-glove,' she began confidently, 'to the nature of the "personal attention" that Corky received from Emmeline Washboard.'

'He was the patient. She was the nurse. Surely that's not too tough a rusk to chew?'

'I think there may have been a bit more on the dessert menu than that, Blotters.' She leaned closer. The two heads, hers silver blonde, his the colour of wheat, almost touched as she whispered into her brother's ear.

He jumped away, as though jump-leads had just been attached to a particularly tender part of his body. 'Well, I'll be kippered like a herring!' he exploded. 'Corky? It is Corky you're cluntering on about here? Corky's a Grade A foundation stone. He wouldn't get involved in any kind of sneaky backdoor-sidling!'

'Well, I'm afraid in the present circs he has been,' said Twinks, who had been just as aware of all Corky Froggett's previous carnal encounters as her brother had been unaware of them.

'Twinks, me old front collar stud, if that's true, then I'm an Apache Dancer!'

Rather than shattering her brother's illusions by a confirmation of the chauffeur's misdemeanours, Twinks took a gentler approach. 'Whether it's true or not, that pot-brained pineapple Miss McQueeg thinks it's true and, if she starts scattering the story round the ship like confetti, a lot of other boddoes are going to think it's true too.'

'And if that happens,' said Captain Barnacle grimly, 'it's "bye-bye, job" for me.'

'So where is the murdy missionary now?' asked Blotto.

'She's in the sick bay. Apparently, just after she'd set off the fire alarm, she went into a dead faint. Shock, the ship's doctor says.'

'So, Captain,' suggested Twinks, 'since we're only a couple of days out from Bombay, can't we see to it that Miss McQueeg stays in the sick bay until everyone has disembarked?'

Captain Barnacle thrust out a dubious lower lip. 'According to the ship's doctor, she's coming round.'

'Well, then,' said Twinks in her mother's voice, the voice of a Dowager Duchess who cannot be disobeyed, 'the ship's doctor must examine the old Bible-basher and find that she has developed a tropical disease which requires her to remain in quarantine.'

'I'm not sure that he—'

'I have in my sequinned reticule a list of suitable infections,' Twinks steamrollered on, 'from which he may select the most virulent.'

'I'm still not—'

'In the meantime,' she continued majestically, 'Blotto, you will get the semaphore to Corky and his . . . friend . . . that they are not, under pain of purgatory, to venture again on to the bridge deck until we've docked in Bombay.'

'Tickey-tockey.'

'And you will also return to your stateroom and make sure that you remove any item or object that could possibly be traced to Corky Froggett or Emmeline Washboard!'

'Will do, sis,' said a beaming Blotto. He found life very comforting when his sister made all the decisions for him.

It felt rather daring for him to go down into the lower decks. As he had demonstrated when he talked to Corky about letting the chauffeur convalesce in his stateroom, Blotto rather prided himself on his common touch. After all, he never had any complaints from the staff at Tawcester Towers. They treated him with proper deference, and he treated them in a manner appropriate to their peasant status. It never occurred to him that their civility might be

144

in some way related to the fact they owed their jobs to Lyminster generosity.

(The success of Blotto's common touch was not so marked with the local shopkeepers. They entertained the rather bizarre notion that the honour of supplying Tawcester Towers with goods was insufficient recompense for their services, and they wanted to be paid as well.)

He was amazed how cramped conditions were in the bowels of the ship. The heat and the engine noise also seemed to increase the lower he descended. To ascertain Corky's whereabouts, he consulted a steward, though the man was considerably less smart and obsequious than his colleagues on the bridge deck. And when Blotto knocked on the relevant door, he was surprised to be let into a tiny space crammed with four bunks. One of the three oikish sponge-worms who were accommodated there confirmed that it was Corky Froggett's billet, 'but he's never here. He's off with his bit of skirt.'

Blotto laughed. 'I don't think you'll ever find a fighting machine like Corky wearing a skirt. He's not Scottish, you know.'

The man tried a few more expressions like 'fancy woman', 'floozie', 'bit of stuff' and 'crumpet', but without success. It was only when he said, 'Bit on the side' that he got a reaction.

'Port or starboard?' asked Blotto.

The man gave up and pointed out directions to Emmeline Washboard's cabin.

Blotto found them both there. Em was taking down the sheet that Miss McQueeg had put up to divide the space. 'The Bible-basher's in the sick bay,' she announced, 'so she won't be around to stop us getting on with things.'

'Things like you nursing Corky back to health?' said Blotto. 'Getting him back to zing-zing condition, eh?'

'Exactly,' Em confirmed. 'Firing on all cylinders.' She grinned at Corky. 'On one in particular.'

145

'Hoopee-doopee!' said Blotto. 'Do you know, I was just talking to some people, and they were telling me some globbins about you two actually being up to . . .'

But, looking at the two honest, innocent faces in front of him, he just couldn't continue. He passed on Twinks's instructions about removing all traces of their occupancy from his stateroom and left them to their own devices.

'Shall we go straight up there and do that?' asked Em.

'Do what?'

'Remove all traces of our occupancy from the stateroom.'

'We'll do that in a minute.' Corky shuffled his deck of postcards and produced one. 'I thought we might try this one first.'

Blotto planned to go and report to Twinks but, as he entered the bridge deck corridor, he was diverted by the irruption of the Maharajah of Koorbleimee from his stateroom.

'The Star of Koorbleimee!' the dignitary shouted in distress. 'The Star of Koorbleimee has been stolen!'

16

Daylight Robbery!

Tact had never been Captain Barnacle's strongest suit. And it didn't feature at all in the announcement he made in the first-class dining room that evening, in the interval between the main and the dessert course.

'All right, ladies and gents,' he said, 'we've had a right day of it and no mistake. First, the report of a fire on the bridge deck, which turned out to be a false alarm. And now a very serious burglary. We on the *Queen of the Orient* pride ourselves on the security of our passengers, and so when something like this happens, we regard it as a right cock-up and something that we will sort out sharpish. We dock in Bombay tomorrow and by then I want this crime solved. In fact, no one will be allowed to disembark until it has been solved.'

A groan of annoyance rumbled through the assembled diners.

'No, that's the way it's going to be. Once a ship gets a reputation for not being a safe place for your valuables it does untold harm, not only to the crew of that particular vessel but also to the shipping line that runs it.'

Almost as much harm, thought Twinks, as a ship having a reputation for allowing non-first-class passengers to jiggle the counterpane in first-class staterooms. That evening the *placement* made her a victim of M. le Vicomte Xavier Douce's rather elaborate French charm. But at least the ring on her finger, which he had helped Ponky to purchase, had stopped him from proposing marriage, with a view to expanding his American diamond business. So that was some compensation.

'And I'm going to see to it,' the Captain went on, 'that the *Queen of the Orient* does not get that kind of reputation. So, the first thing that will happen, starting this evening, is that I and the other ship's officers will be interviewing all first-class passengers – and if necessary searching their staterooms – until we find the missing Star of Koorbleimee.'

'And presumably,' Blotto called out, 'you're asking the first-class boddoes first because we are always first in line for whatever's on the trolley? And then you'll move on to the poor thimbles on the lower decks?'

'No,' Captain Barnacle replied. 'I am starting with the first-class passengers because it is amongst them that I think it is likely that we will find the Star of Koorbleimee.'

This prompted another rumble from the assembled diners, this time of agreement rather than dissent. They knew the kind of people they were.

'So,' the Captain concluded, clearly enjoying every moment of his power over them, 'be prepared for a visit from us. And I'm sure I don't need to point out that if anyone refuses to be interviewed or makes a fuss about having their accommodation searched, we will regard that as very suspicious behaviour. So . . . enjoy the rest of your dinner, ladies and gents. Or perhaps I should say, "Enjoy the rest of your dinner, all but one of you." The waiters will be looking out for a passenger who is too nervous to eat because of the robbery he or she has just committed.'

Everyone regarded this as a joke and laughed. But at the same time, they looked at their neighbours, to see if any of

them was too nervous to laugh because of the robbery he
or she had just committed.

As the dessert course was served, M. le Vicomte Xavier
Douce said to Twinks, 'I could not help noticing that
extremely attractive reticule that you always carry on
your arm.'

'Don't know why it tickles your mustard. No diamonds
on that little baublette. Only sequins.'

'I do know enough about jewellery to recognise that,
Lady Honoria. But it is still very *chic*.' He looked at the
huge engagement ring. 'It is not always the value of
something that is of primary importance. Paste and
counterfeit jewellery can also have a *je ne sais quoi*.'

'I hope you're not suggesting that my engagement ring
is leadpenny?' asked Twinks in mock-affront. Though,
when she came to think of it, the engagement itself was.

'If I were to agree to your suggestion, I would be
denigrating my own professional skills. Was it not I who
selected the stone for your fiancé Punky?'

'Ponky,' said Twinks.

'So,' the Frenchman asked casually, 'when the Capitaine
and his acolytes come to question you about the dis-
appearance of the Star of Koorbleimee, you will of course
allow them to examine the contents of your sequinned
reticule?'

'Like sausages I will! No snoopnose ever has the right to
examine the spoffing contents of a lady's reticule! It's way
beyond the barbed wire!'

'But did you not hear what the Capitaine said? Anyone
who is reluctant to have their accommodation searched
will immediately make themselves look guilty.'

'Any boddo who wishes to may search my accommodation. My stateroom. But might I point out to you that
this . . .' She pointed to the sequinned reticule '. . . is not
my accommodation. I do not live in a sequinned reticule.
And only the worst kind of four-faced filcher would dream

of asking a lady to disclose the contents of her sequinned reticule. It would be as fumacious as asking her age.'

'So, if the Capitaine and his ship's officers ask you to reveal its contents, you will refuse?'

'Is the King German?' asked Twinks.

'And if they try to persuade you . . . ?'

'I am not persuadable.'

'Do you think they will accept that?'

Twinks went into full Dowager Duchess mode. 'Would they dare not to?' she demanded, channelling the bellicose spirit that had seen the Lyminsters through the Norman Conquest, Magna Carta, the Reformation, the Civil War and many Hunt Balls.

The Vicomte argued no more.

At that moment, Twinks looked across the room towards her brother. 'I'm afraid I must pongle over there for a momentette,' she said. 'Blotto's honour is being threatened by members of the Fishing Fleet.' And she swept away, leaving the sequinned reticule on the table.

And leaving a very satisfied smile on the face of M. le Vicomte Xavier Douce.

The questioning of the first-class passengers began straight after dinner. It followed the principle of 'Ladies First', as was the British way in most things, including lifeboats (though not including financial affairs and only very recently including votes). And, again in the British way, it was done in order of precedence. This meant they started with Twinks, who was, after all, the daughter of a Duke. (There was no thought that any of the Maharajah's wives might go first, because of course British aristocracy trumped that from any other nation, particularly on a British-owned liner.)

Having assumed, rightly, that she would be top of the list,

Twinks sat in her own stateroom (the change with Blotto had been quickly reversed), awaiting her interrogators.

Once they'd arrived, it was no surprise that she did most of the interrogating. 'Well, you can scratch me from the runners straight away,' she began formidably.

'And why should we do that?' asked Captain Barnacle.

'I'm assuming that the gemmo was filched during the false alarm fire drill.'

'What makes you think that?'

'Oh, come on, Captain, put a jumping cracker under it! With the Maharajah's womenfolk having been in purdah throughout the voyage, they haven't left their spoffing staterooms. So, a jewel thief has had about as much chance of filching the gemmo as I have of joining the Athenaeum Club. Until, that is, everyone was evacuated for the lead-penny fire alarm.'

'All right,' Captain Barnacle conceded. 'We had been beginning to think along those lines, yes.'

'Give that pony a rosette! So, I'm out of the frame for the filching.'

'Why?'

'Oh, do get on the same bus, Captain! I hadn't been near the staterooms since I left after brekkers. I spent the morning in a deckchair on the bridge deck reading the *Shu Ching* of Confucius. Don't know if you've read it . . . ?'

'I don't believe I have,' said Captain Barnacle, whose reading rarely went beyond the *Regulations for His Majesty's Mail and Passenger Ships* (1919).

'It's absolutely plumpilicious!' Twinks looked up at the clock on the wall. 'Don't let me detain you, Captain. I'm sure you have to interview lots of other passengers who might actually have played the diddler's hand with the Star of Koorbleimee.'

Captain Barnacle stood up, as if to leave, then hesitated. His customary raucousness seemed subdued. Twinks's frostiness had daunted him. 'The fact is, milady,' he began humbly, 'that because you have been sharing a stateroom with Miss Sandwich . . .'

'Yes? What? Come on, uncage the ferrets!'

'. . . I do have to consider the possibility that the person who purloined the Star of Koorbleimee might have hidden it after the theft in another stateroom . . .'

'So, are you suggesting that you should be allowed to search this room?'

Though the Captain's cap remained on his head, his posture was undoubtedly cap in hand. He had been totally cowed by Twinks's performance as her mother.

'It would be as unreasonable for me to refuse that request,' she replied, 'as it would for a Shetland pony to run at Ascot. Would you wish me to stay here while my guilty secret is exposed?'

'That will not be necessary, milady.'

'Jollissimo! In that case, I will go and partake of coffee in the lounge. And it would really hit the bull's eye, were you to inform me when I may return.'

'Of course, milady,' said an obsequious Captain Barnacle, as Twinks picked up her sequinned reticule and swanned out.

Some half-hour later, a steward gave her the all-clear and, while the Captain moved on to his next first-class suspect, she returned to her empty stateroom.

Twinks was relieved that she had avoided having her sequinned reticule examined. This was not just the prudery of a lady trying to keep the contents of her handbag private, lest it reveal secrets of the aids required to maintain her beauty. Twinks had no need of such aids, anyway. Her beauty was entirely natural.

No, what she didn't want Captain Barnacle – or indeed anyone else – to see was the amount of weaponry her sequinned reticule contained.

* * *

Blotto was informed over breakfast (a modest affair of porridge, bacon and eggs) that he would be questioned by the Captain later in the morning, so when he'd finished eating, he went straight back to his stateroom. He searched the space assiduously, still worried that some evidence might have been left of Corky and Em's occupancy. Though he had no thoughts the wrong side of the running rail about what might have gone on, he knew that there were others on board whose minds would undoubtedly need washing out with soap and water.

Blotto heard a lot of commotion and a look through his open porthole told him that the *Queen of the Orient* was about to dock in Bombay. Tugs were pulling the great ship towards its designated berth. Their passage to India was over. The noise level from the busy port was tremendous and Blotto's stateroom was invaded by a mixture of aromas, some exotic and redolent of the mysterious East, and some frankly disgusting.

Of course, he reminded himself, if Captain Barnacle stuck to his plan, no one would be allowed to disembark until the thief of the Star of Koorbleimee had been unmasked.

The knock on his door came about eleven o'clock. He composed his face into an expression of innocence. Which wasn't difficult. Blotto always wore an expression of innocence. Had Tennyson ever had the good fortune to meet the young Devereux Lyminster, he would have agreed that his strength was as the strength of ten because, like Galahad's, his heart was pure. And, besides, Blotto wasn't clever enough to be devious.

He was also pathologically truthful. Lying didn't come naturally to him. Which was a good thing. Effective lying demands a level of consistency to which he couldn't aspire. The only occasions when he had been known to lie were when someone else's honour had been at stake and a well-placed untruth might let the other party off the hook. Unfortunately, Blotto's untruths were rarely well-placed.

The visitor to his stateroom that morning was not, as expected, an accusatory Captain Barnacle. Instead, in bounced an extremely cheerful-looking Ponky Larreigh-ffriebollaux. He'd looked pretty cheerful since he had become 'engaged' to Twinks, but clearly something else had happened to get him positively rolling on camomile lawns.

'So, what's put the icing on your Swiss bun, Ponky?' asked Blotto.

His old muffin-toaster waved a telegram at him. 'Just been given this by one of the radio officers. From the Nawab of Patatah! He's set up the first match of the tour! And it's only going to take place in the Princely State of Koorbleimee!'

'Where the boddo who's short of a hat-gemmo comes from?'

'You're bong on the nose there, Blotters! And, to add a cherry to the cheesecake, it turns out that the Nawab and the Maharajah are great chumboes, so we've an offer of transport to the Princely State of Koorbleimee in the Maharajah's Special Train.'

'Toad-in-the-hole!' said Blotto.

'And from what some of the boddoes were saying about the Special Train, it sounds like the Savoy Hotel on rails!'

'You are dabbing the digit at the Savvers in London, aren't you, Ponky? Not the one in Port Said?' Though he had spent very little time in the latter, Blotto's memories of the place were not fond.

'Oh, definitely the London branch. I think we could be in for a splendiferous time, Blotters! Pampering, luxury and cricket too! Isn't that just the panda's panties?'

It should be remarked that Ponky Larreighffriebollaux was considerably more communicative to her brother than he was to his fiancée. Not a single 'Tiddle my pom!' so far.

At that moment, however, there was a knock on the door, and Twinks entered.

Ponky Larreighffriebollaux's confidence and vocabulary were instantly minimised. 'Tiddle my pom!' he said.

But Twinks hardly seemed to notice her fiancé. She walked straight across to her brother and said, 'Blotto me old nitcomb, I thought I'd sit in on your chittle-chattle with the Captain.'

'Good ticket,' he said. Then, after a moment, 'Why?'

'Oh,' his sister replied airily. 'Just to see there are no chocks in the cogwheel about our disembarkation.'

Blotto didn't ask what kind of chocks she had in mind, or whether she thought he might be the one who inserted them into the cogwheel. He trusted Twinks's instincts on that kind of thing and felt safer with her present.

Almost immediately, there was another knock at the door. This time it was Captain Barnacle on his mission of investigation. He looked slightly taken aback at Twinks's presence. He felt he'd been patronised sufficiently the previous evening. But he made no comment. Having been offered a chair, he sat down.

'Well, milord,' he began, 'I don't need to tell you why I'm here this morning, do I?'

Blotto looked confused and glanced towards his sister. She gave a slight shake of her head and he said, 'No. No, by Wilberforce, you spoffing well don't.'

'The fact is that the Star of Koorbleimee has been stolen and our belief is that the jewel has not left the bridge deck. What we think most likely is that whoever stole it had no wish to be caught with the loot in his or her possession and for that reason hid it in one of the staterooms, with a view to collecting it when the hue and cry had subsided. That is why we are currently restricting our search to this deck.'

During this speech, Blotto was looking nervously around the stateroom. And he saw something underneath the chair the Captain was sitting in which caused him grave disquiet.

'So, I would like to ask you, milord, whether you—?'

The movement was so quick that they hardly saw it. Blotto leapt across the room, snatched the object from under the Captain's chair and, in one smooth move, threw it out of the open porthole. He turned, red-faced, to face his inquisitor.

'What was that you threw out of the porthole?' demanded Captain Barnacle.

'Erm . . .'

'Was it the Star of Koorbleimee?'

'Yes,' said Blotto, looking almost relieved. 'Yes, it was.'

'And did you steal it?'

'Yes,' said Blotto. 'Yes, I did.'

17

Meet and Cheat

Now he had found the thief who had stolen the Maharajah's jewel, Captain Barnacle immediately author-ised disembarkation of the passengers from the *Queen of the Orient*. Needless to say, as in everything else, first class took precedence.

One of the first-class passengers, however, was not allowed to leave. Immediately after his confession, the Captain issued the order 'Clap him in irons!', and Blotto had been seized by ship's officers. He was taken out of his stateroom before Twinks or Ponky had the opportunity to react. The last thing he saw were expressions of total astonishment on both of their faces.

The shock was so great that Ponky actually said some-thing different in the presence of his fiancé. 'Well,' he announced, 'my pom is well and truly tiddled!'

The noise and chaos of the dockside was intense. After the comparative serenity of the sea voyage, the new arrivals found all their senses assaulted at once. Bright colours on banners and saris, ferocious smells and a cacophony of voices shouting in a myriad languages.

The passengers were hustled towards the sheds where

immigration and medical checks had to be gone through, but already many had been greeted by family, friends and employers. There was much high-pitched squeaking from the girls of the Fishing Fleet. Porters swirled around the crowd, together with street-sellers, hoteliers touting for business, beggars and a few pickpockets. As in Port Said, the harbour wall was crowded with semi-naked boys, encouraging the disembarking passengers to throw coins for them to dive for.

It was towards these that M. le Vicomte Xavier Douce directed his fastidious footsteps in his fastidious spats. To the sparkle-eyed excitement of the boys, he produced a handful of coins from his trouser pocket. But he made no attempt to cast them into the oily water. Instead, with a little knowledge of the local dialect and a lot of Mediterranean gesturing, he indicated that there was something else he wanted them to dive for.

Lettice Sandwich was disappointed not to have seen Blotto to say goodbye, but in the chaos of disembarkation it was difficult to find anyone. She hoped maybe that she'd bump into him the other side of the immigration control. He had told her his Tawcester Towers address, so she could write to him, but she'd rather see him again while he was still in India.

Such thoughts were banished, though, by the excitement of being greeted, the moment she stepped off the gang-plank, by her brother, Reuben Sandwich. She hadn't seen him for five years and, though she had no difficulty recognising him, his body had filled out, his skin was tanned to leather and he sported a very authoritative-looking moustache.

Lettice flung her arms around her brother, and only when the embrace had ended did she take in the other man who was with him. About the same age, clean-shaven and dressed in military uniform, introduced by Reuben as: 'Major Biskett. Known to everyone in the chummery as "Ginger"!'

'Very pleased to meet you, Ginger,' said Lettice, stretching out her hand. He shook it with the vigour of a bell ringer.

'Topping to meet you too,' he said.

'And am I right, Reuben?' asked Lettice. 'A "chummery" is a house where a group of single men share accommodation?'

'You're bong on the nose, Lettice.'

'So, that means, Ginger,' she said, interest kindling, 'that you're not married?'

'No, I'm not, by Jove,' the Major replied. 'How did you work that out? Your sis is a bit of a brainbox, isn't she, Reuben?'

Ginger smiled at Lettice. Lettice smiled at Ginger. Vacuity called to vacuity.

A fleet of Rolls-Royces, with liveried chauffeurs and other servants, awaited the Maharajah of Koorbleimee and his entourage. The route to the railway station, the Victoria Terminus, was relatively short, but the Maharajah always travelled in style. It seemed that his family did not have to bother with immigration.

Twinks was determined to speak to the Maharajah, to intercede for her brother, to plead for his release. She knew that, if only she could communicate with Blotto, she would quickly find out the reason for his inexplicable behaviour. Never in a million years would she actually believe that he had anything to do with the theft of the Star of Koorbleimee.

So, with her bewildered fiancé in tow, Twinks rushed up to the line of Rolls-Royces and approached the most over-dressed of the flunkeys to speak to the Maharajah.

The man looked down at her haughtily and told her that his master was still on the ship. 'The Maharajah is with the jewel thief, arranging his punishment,' he added.

'But the boddo you call "the jewel thief" is actually my brother,' Twinks insisted.

'That is not something for you to be proud of.'

'I'm not proud of it,' said Twinks. 'Because it's not spoffing well true. My brother has never played anyone a diddler's hand in his life.'

The flunkey shrugged. 'As I say, the Maharajah is still on the *Queen of the Orient.*'

Twinks, with Ponky still in tow, returned to the ship. But no amount of blandishments – and Twinks's blandishments were definitely world class – would persuade the crew members guarding the gangplanks to allow her back on board.

Exasperated, she turned to her 'fiancé'. 'Oh, for the love of strawberries, what are we going to do?'

'Tiddle my pom!' said Ponky mournfully.

Blotto was maybe not 'clapped in irons' but he was handcuffed and held in Captain Barnacle's office. The two ship's officers who had escorted him from his stateroom stayed as guards, watching his every move. The Captain was there too, and a very angry Maharajah.

'This,' he was saying, 'is the entire history of the British in India writ large! From the very start you have been stealing from us. The East India Company was set up as a vehicle for organised robbery and, since those days, nothing has changed. My forefathers were right never to trust the British. And now one more sneak-thief has been caught in the act!'

Blotto had made the decision, fairly soon after his arrest, that the best way to deal with this particular gluepot was to say nothing. Words, he knew, were dangerous things.

He'd often found that words he'd said to extricate himself from some quagmire had ended up embedding him even deeper in. So, silence was the policy he would abide by.

At this point there was a rather apologetic knock at the door of the office. The Captain had said something about summoning a representative of 'His Majesty's Government in India', and that's who the newcomer turned out to be.

Arnold Wembley-Dither's title was Resident of Koorbleimee. In spite of the heat, he was dressed in a black jacket and waistcoat above pin-striped trousers (he never wore anything less formal than that). His dark old school tie was pulled around his stiff wing collar at strangulation tension. (As an Old Etonian, Blotto was amazed that the poor greengage had the nerve to wear the tie. Surely no one would want to advertise the fact that they'd gone to an oikish minor public school like Charterhouse?)

Wembley-Dither was the classic example of an upper middle-class Englishman who, having shown no competence for anything in the home country, had been sent out to the Colonies to prove that he was equally incompetent there. He was one of those people who had been meek all his life and, having read his Bible, went on waiting quietly for the day when he would inherit the earth. So far, in his case, that had showed no signs of happening. The meek, by being just a bit too meek, have always had that problem.

The Resident's manner, like his hairline, was receding, apologetic and slightly scruffy. He had the furtive look of a schoolboy whose smoking behind the cycle sheds had been witnessed by a beak. He was in a blue funk. He knew retribution would come, in the form of a summons to the headmaster's study, but he wasn't quite sure when. Though he would never admit it (he had to uphold his nation's sovereignty, after all), at the core of his being Wembley-Dither felt that the British had got away with exploiting India and the Indians for far too long. And it was only a matter of time before they would be unceremoniously booted out of the subcontinent.

'So, got a bit of a diplomatic incident here, have we, Captain Barnacle?' Clearly, he knew the *Queen of the Orient*'s commanding officer.

Before the Captain could respond, the Maharajah did. 'Not a "diplomatic incident", Wembley-Dither. A simple case of crime, committed by a common criminal – by this representative of the indolent British upper classes who thinks the world owes him a living and who, when that living is not handed to him on a plate, has no scruple about helping himself to other people's property.'

The temptation was strong for Blotto to say, 'Now rein in the roans there for a minute!', but he resisted it. He had decided his course of action and he wasn't going to deviate from it.

'I'm sure things are not as bad as they seem,' said a palliative Wembley-Dither. 'Wires got crossed somewhere, I dare say.' He turned to the accused. 'Where did you go to school?'

Blotto didn't think it would be incriminating, so he replied, 'Eton.'

'Well, there you are, Maharajah,' said the Resident of Koorbleimee, relieved to have had the worrying wrinkle so quickly ironed out. 'If he went to Eton . . . obviously, a case of mistaken identity.'

It was clear that Wembley-Dither had had many previous dealings with the Maharajah. It was also instantly clear who wielded the whip-hand in the relationship.

'"Mistaken identity",' said the Maharajah, 'will not wash when the criminal has actually confessed to the crime.'

'Oh.' Wembley-Dither looked crestfallen as he turned back to the accused. 'Did you, actually . . . confess?'

Blotto nodded.

'Well,' said the Resident, 'the prisoner was clearly not in his right mind. Sunstroke?' he suggested hopefully.

'I witnessed his confession,' said Captain Barnacle, 'and when he spoke, he was as sane as I am.'

Wembley-Dither had the look of a man who would like to observe, 'That's not saying much', but was too well brought up to do so. He turned again to Blotto. 'Listen, Mr Lyminster . . . as one public school man to another . . .'

Blotto resisted commenting on the kind of person who boasted about having been to Charterhouse and maintained his silence.

'. . . I'm sure we can sort out this unfortunate concatenation of events. What I would suggest in these circumstances is that I, as a representative of His Majesty's Government and representative of the British justice system, should take Mr Devereux Lyminster into my own custody, so that I can question him in detail about the circumstances of the theft of the Star of Koorbleimee.'

'Before letting him go scot-free?' suggested the Maharajah.

'No. We will of course go through the full process of British law.'

'And then you'll let him go scot-free?'

'Maharajah, you don't seem to have a very high opinion of the British legal system.'

'That is certainly true, Mr Wembley-Dither. It is a system created by the British to protect British interests all over the world. Tell me, in your much-vaunted Empire, when there is a dispute between an official of His Majesty's Government and an indigenous person, and the case gets to court, how often does the indigenous person win?'

'Well, erm . . .' This put the Resident rather on the spot. 'It does just frequently turn out to be the case . . . that the indigenous person . . . is guilty.'

'Nonsense!' boomed the Maharajah. 'The system is as dodgy as a loaded dice. And in this case, Mr Wembley-Dither, the crime is a completely Indian affair. Mr Lyminster has confessed to stealing a part of the princely

163

regalia of Koorbleimee. This is a matter that will be dealt with by the judicial system of Koorbleimee!'

'But, as a representative of His Majesty's Government, I must protest. A Princely State is a vassal state in a subsidiary alliance with the British Raj. And I, as the Resident of Koorbleimee, must be in control of—'

'Take the prisoner to the Victoria Terminus!' The Maharajah snapped his fingers at the two ship's officers, who immediately raised Blotto from his chair and frog-marched him out of the office.

The Maharajah reached into his blazer pocket and produced a small cloth bag which clinked reassuringly of gold sovereigns. As he handed it across, he said, 'And I can rely on your discretion, Captain Barnacle . . . ?'

'As ever,' said the Captain, trousering his pay-off.

'Look, I'm sorry,' protested Arnold Wembley-Dither, 'but this is absolutely the wrong way to go about things. As a representative of His Majesty's Government, I must make clear that in judicial matters, all decisions must be . . .'

But his words trickled away into the steamy air of the Captain's office. The Maharajah had left the room.

When the small boy handed over to M. le Vicomte Xavier Douce what he had retrieved from the bottom of the harbour, his eyes sparkled in anticipation. And when he saw what the tall Frenchman had put into his grubby palm, he reacted as if he'd been handed a fortune.

A fortune it may have been for the boy. For the diamond merchant, it was small change. As he placed the retrieved object in his jacket pocket and moved away from the dockside, there was a smile of satisfaction on the face of M. le Vicomte Xavier Douce. He was reflecting on the large fortune he was about to make.

18

A Passage Across India

The Maharajah of Koorbleimee's Special Train was as luxurious as it had been built up to be. And it was to be found in a different part of Bombay's Victoria Terminus from the regular services. The Maharajah, his family and guests were driven the short distance from the docks in his fleet of Rolls-Royces. They drove into the cathedral-like Italian Gothic edifice and parked right on the concourse, so that the travellers had only a few yards to walk to the train. The cars would in time go back to their garages in the city. They were the Maharajah's Bombay fleet of Rolls-Royces. The passengers would be met at their destination by his Koorbleimee fleet of Rolls-Royces.

Twinks was given a compartment to herself, with a lockable door which led to her fiancé's. Whatever issues the Maharajah had with her brother, he made sure that she and Ponky would get the full experience of Koorbleimean hospitality.

Her accommodation was more like a Victorian sitting room than a railway compartment. There were armchairs and a private bathroom, and servants in the Maharajah's livery were instantly on hand to fulfil requests for iced water, tea, champagne, or whatever took her fancy.

Twinks could not enjoy any of these amenities, however,

because she was so worried about Blotto. She had heard from one of the Maharajah's men that a representative of His Majesty's Government was going to sort things out with Captain Barnacle. Twinks had assumed that she'd soon see her brother bouncing along to the Special Train with his customary insouciance and a merry cry of 'Hoopee-doopee!'

But there was no sign of him. And none of the Maharajah's staff knew – or were prepared to tell her – whether her brother was on the train or not.

She shared her anxieties with Ponky Larreighffrie-bollaux. After all, if you couldn't share your anxieties with him, what was a fiancé for? Particularly if it was a fiancé you had no intention of marrying. Though you hadn't yet actually told him that you weren't going to marry him. Life, thought Twinks miserably, is sometimes a tough rusk to chew.

'The thing is, Ponky,' she began, 'I've known Blotters since I was in nursery naps, and you've known him since you shared the same toasted muffins at Eton, and we both know he hasn't got an evil cell in his bloodstream. And yet we both heard him swear on the Lyminster lineage that he stole the spoffing Star of Koorbleimee from the Maharajah. Well, I'd put my last shred of laddered silk stocking on the fact that he didn't do it. So, the questionette we must put to ourselves is . . . why should someone who's as honest as a shrimping net suddenly come up with a colossal lie? It's as out of character as a skeleton playing skittles, isn't it?'

Ponky nodded. Which was actually a conversational advance in their relationship. Did she dare hope it might lead to his opening up with more actual words?

'The only explanation I can see for this problemette is that Blotters was behaving like a pot-brained pineapple because he wanted to keep someone else's soles out of the slush. So, he would only put his hand up to stealing the Star of Koorbleimee to protect the boddo who he thought had stolen it. Which must mean Blotters thought Corky Froggett had done the deed. Which is as unlikely as Blotto himself being the four-faced filcher. Corky's a Grade A foundation stone, but my brother must've got a buzz in his brainbox that he was the jewel-jiggler. Don't you agree, Ponky? Tell me you agree!'

But the encouragement given by Ponky's earlier nod came to nothing, as he said, once again, 'Tiddle my pom!' The prospects for a lifetime of marital breakfasts with him did not look alluring. Twinks would have to search elsewhere for her treasured discussions of Sanskrit texts, Nietzsche, and Confucianism. She had to find a way out of the engagement.

But, more urgently, she had to find Blotto. She couldn't forget about the men who'd tried to coffinate him in Port Said. Or the likelihood that, now he was on Indian soil, there might be another attempt on his life.

Corky Froggett had to wait around the dockyards of Bombay for some time until the Lagonda was craned out of the hold, along with its retinue of Rolls-Royces. He did not stand out in his invisibly repaired dark-blue uniform because there were plenty of other chauffeurs waiting to escort the wealthy into the Indian interior.

Through the *Queen of the Orient*'s onboard grapevine, the message had reached him that he was to drive to the palace of the Maharajah of Koorbleimee. He was told that the young master would be transported there by train, but not the circumstances in which he would be travelling. Corky knew nothing about what had transpired in Blotto's stateroom earlier that morning.

The young mistress, he was informed, would be going on the Maharajah's Special Train – presumably with her brother – for the two-day journey.

He had also consulted Emmeline Washboard about her

plans. The family to whom she would be a governess were in Pondicherry, the other side of India, and she had instructions to travel there by train. She could see no reason, however, not to take a detour via Koorbleimee, even though it was in almost completely the wrong direction. 'It's my nursing training,' she told Corky. 'I never like to leave a patient until I'm absolutely sure that he's ready to be up and about.'

'And what is your diagnosis in this case, nurse?'

'I think the patient needs a little more hands-on care.'

'Yes, I think you're probably right,' Corky agreed.

They were sitting, side by side, in the front of the Lagonda. The roof was down. Although it had only been out of the hold for a matter of minutes, the Indian sun had already made the metalwork too hot to touch. Corky and Em had retrieved their bags, which were now stowed in the dickey. The car was swamped by a rabble of locals, offering them all kinds of services, few of which, because of the language barrier, they could understand.

Corky pressed the self-starter and the mighty engine roared into life. 'I think it's time we were off,' he said.

'An excellent idea, but are you quite sure where you are going?'

The precise, slightly accented voice made them turn round to see a tall, well-dressed figure approaching the Lagonda. Though dressed in Western style, he was clearly Indian. Having not met before, they did not recognise Mr Mukerjee. 'Do you even know,' he asked, 'which side of the road you drive in India?'

'In England,' the chauffeur replied haughtily, 'we drive down the middle. Particularly when the young master is at the wheel.'

Mr Mukerjee tutted. 'That is a dangerous thing to do in India. There may be cows in the middle of the road. If you were to hit one of those, Mr Froggett, you would be in very serious trouble.'

Corky didn't think to question how the stranger knew his name. 'How do you know all this?' he asked.

'I have travelled extensively in India for my business. My name is Mukerjee, by the way.' The tall man smiled. 'But you, I think, have not been to India before?'

'No. But don't worry, I've travelled over most of Europe, you know. And America. And I came through that last little dust-up with the Hun. I can find my way around.'

'I am sure you can, Mr Froggett, but may I ask how you plan to find your way from Bombay to Koorbleimee?'

'I've got a very good sense of direction,' came the defensive reply. 'And, if I lose my way, I'll ask a policeman.'

'The friendly bobby on the beat? I think you have a lot to learn about India, Mr Froggett. But I have a suggestion which will make things much easier for you.'

'And what is that?' asked Corky suspiciously.

'I know the way to Koorbleimee. As a box-wallah, I have done the journey many times. You give me a lift in this splendid Lagonda, and I will show you the way.'

The chauffeur hesitated, but Emmeline Washboard, who had enough experience of men to know how unlikely they were ever to ask for directions, said quickly, 'Thank you very much, Mr Mukerjee. We have pleasure in accepting your offer.'

M. le Vicomte Xavier Douce also went by rail to Koorbleimee, but not on the Maharajah's Special Train. The Maharajah had had few dealings with the diamond merchant during the voyage on the *Queen of the Orient*, so his name was not on the extensive invitation list. The Vicomte was unworried by his exclusion. He knew he had something in his pocket that would make him an extremely welcome guest in Koorbleimee. And he had planned exactly when the precious object would be revealed.

There was a look in his eyes which went beyond the sun-dried earth and dusty trees his train passed by. It was as if he were gazing upon a distant horizon. That look always appeared on his face when the diamond merchant was about to realise a large profit.

Miss McQueeg was travelling on the same train, though the two passengers were unaware of each other. The Vicomte's only contact with her on the voyage had been stepping over her prone body after she had fainted and caused the false fire alarm.

Like him, she travelled first class on the journey to Koorbleimee. Though she had bought a more economical ticket for the *Queen of the Orient*, she had heard enough about Indian trains not to take the same risk on one of them.

She found herself in a Ladies compartment with the two memsahibs whom Blotto had encountered at dinner on the *Queen of the Orient*. Still glowing with the satisfaction of having transplanted their boys back to England for the rest of their childhood, the ladies appeared to be in no hurry to return to their homes and husbands. 'Stuck in Madras,' one confided to Miss McQueeg, 'one sees so little of India.'

'It's the same in Poona,' her friend agreed. 'Just an endless round of dinners and balls with other British people.'

'So, we thought this was a rare opportunity to do a little sightseeing,' said the other one. 'Now we don't have to worry about our boys.' She didn't speak the words 'ever again', but they were implied. 'And people say there is much to see in the Princely State of Koorbleimee.'

'What,' asked Miss McQueeg, 'is particularly note-worthy to see in the Princely State of Koorbleimee?'

'Well, there are the Milkibar Caves,' replied the first memsahib. 'Very famous.'

'And what is special about them?'

'Apparently, the walls are as smooth as glass,' said the second memsahib. 'And there's a very splendid echo.'

'Also, of course,' added the first, 'a lot of local superstitions have grown up around the caves.'

'Oh?' said Miss McQueeg.

'Things like the notion that, if a man and a woman spend time alone in them, then they have to get married.'

'And a lot of other tosh on the same lines,' commented the second memsahib. 'To the locals, the caves are a site of great religious significance.'

'When you say "religious",' asked Miss McQueeg cautiously, 'I take it you don't mean . . . Christian?'

'Certainly not!' the first memsahib snorted.

'You mean . . . in the Milkibar Caves . . . there are *heathens*?' breathed Miss McQueeg. Her imagination glowed with the prospect of lots of heathens to throw Bibles at, but she maintained the social proprieties by continuing, 'And, ladies, will Koorbleimee be the extent of your sightseeing?'

'Not if we can help it,' said the second memsahib.

'No,' the first memsahib agreed. 'The longer we can keep away from our dreary husbands, the better.'

Still inwardly glowing at the vindication of her decision to travel to Koorbleimee, Miss McQueeg spent the rest of the journey reading her Bible. And she felt reassured to know that a large crate of more Bibles for distribution to the heathen was safely stowed in the goods and luggage carriage. She read a verse from Isaiah that encouraged her enormously. 'And he shall smite the earth with the rod of his mouth, and with the breath of his lips shall he slay the wicked.'

Yes, thought Miss McQueeg with satisfaction. The heathen of Koorbleimee will be well and truly smitten with Bibles. And the Milkibar Caves sounded like a very good place to commence the smiting.

* * *

171

Blotto was having difficulty getting comfortable. The handcuffs were chafing his wrists and none of the contents of the goods and luggage carriage seemed to have any soft edges. The heat of the train's interior meant he had already sweated through all his (many) layers of clothing. Eventually, he propped himself awkwardly against a crate full of Bibles.

He reflected that he was in something of a treacle tin and no mistake. Nor could he deny that the gumbo was of his own making. His own *making*, he insisted to himself, not his own *fault*. A boddo of his breeding couldn't have acted in any other way.

He reinforced his decision to maintain a dignified silence. Whatever accusations were thrown at him, whatever explanations for his conduct were demanded, his lips would stay shut as tight as a limpet with lockjaw.

Being an English gentleman, he reflected, wasn't all creamy éclair.

To his considerable shock, he actually found himself saying out loud, 'Broken biscuits!'

Thank Disraeli there was no one else in the carriage to hear him.

19

The Maharajah's Palace

Corky Froggett was glad that he had accepted Mr Mukerjee's offer. Though entirely confident of his ability to find his way around anywhere, the Indian roadway system that he encountered was deeply confusing. There were very few signposts and most of the ones they did see were decorated with meaningless squiggles. A knowledge of local languages was required to tell which roads were impassable or simply petered out in the hills. And finding places where petrol could be purchased was a subject requiring a lifetime's study. Though he would never admit it, Corky Froggett and Emmeline Washboard would not have progressed beyond the Bombay suburbs without the expertise of Mr Mukerjee.

He in turn seemed to be delighted to hear from them about life in England. As the depth of reading he'd shared with Twinks demonstrated, he was a man of high intellect and insatiable curiosity. Nothing seemed to interest him more than daily life at Tawcester Towers, and he asked endless questions on the subject. The awe with which he greeted the answers encouraged Corky to tell him more. It was, in his view, only right and proper that someone from a less developed country should show proper appreciation of all things British.

'So, Mr Froggett, your young master . . .' asked Mr Mukerjee, as the Lagonda negotiated a narrow stony track up a sheer mountainside, 'he is not the Duke?'

'By no means,' Corky replied. 'The Duke of Tawcester is his elder brother. That's how it works in England. A title passes to the eldest man.'

'And never to a woman, regardless of age,' Em contributed, with mock resentment.

'Which is only right and proper!' said Corky with a raucous guffaw. She found the idea as amusing as he did.

'And so, if your young master's elder brother were to suffer the misfortune of dying,' Mr Mukerjee continued, 'your young master would become the Duke?'

'Well, yes, I suppose he would. I must confess, it's not something I've ever thought about that much, but yes, that's what would happen.'

'And then, if your young master were also to suffer the misfortune of dying, who would become the Duke then? Not his delightful sister . . . ?'

'No way,' said Em.

'. . . in spite of the fact that she is one of the most intelligent young women I have ever encountered?'

Corky's lips wrinkled wryly beneath the bristling moustache. 'Intelligence has never been thought that important in the British aristocracy,' he replied. 'No, under those circumstances there's no one in the immediate family who would become the Duke. I guess it'd be some cousin or something.'

'Do you have the name for such a cousin?'

'No. There's a bunch of them. All chinless idiots, nothing like the young master.'

'And are there social occasions when the whole Tawcester family, cousins and all, gather together?'

'It's the "Lyminster family", actually.'

'I beg your pardon?'

'Though it's the Duke of *Tawcester*, the family name is Lyminster.'

'Why is this?'

Corky was thrown by a question he'd never considered before. There was a moment of silence before he said, 'It's just how it is.'

'Right then ... so are there social occasions when the whole *Lyminster* family, cousins and all, gather together?'

'Not many. Only time that happens is for the Duke's birthday.'

'And when is this?'

'January. There's a big dinner party for all branches of the family then.'

'And at this ... ducal birthday dinner ... does the Duke's mother ... what did you say she was called, Mr Froggett?'

'The Dowager Duchess.'

'Yes, yes, of course. And would she attend this dinner?'

'No. For one thing, she's never had much time for her children. And for another, the dinner is stag.'

'"Stag"? I'm sorry, what is this? Are you saying at this dinner they eat venison?'

'No, no, matey. "Stag" means, like, only men present. No women.'

'Surprise, surprise,' said Em sardonically.

'Ah, thank you. I understand.' Mr Mukerjee nodded. 'So, this means your young master's delightful sister would not be at the dinner either?'

'Too right, mate.'

'And so, Mr Froggett ... I am not suggesting this as a likely – or desirable – scenario ... I ask only for information. But, if at this dinner in January for the Duke of Tawcester's birthday, some homicidal maniac with a gun broke in and shot everyone dead ... it would be the end of the line for the Dukedom.'

'I doubt if it would,' said Corky. 'The British aristocracy has far-reaching tentacles. They all intermarry so much they've got relations everywhere. If the unlikely events you describe were to happen – and there's no danger of that, let me tell you – but if it did happen, the lawyers'd get on to it. And there'd probably be some sheep-shearer in Australia who's a very distant cousin . . . and he'd become the Duke of Tawcester.'

'How very interesting, Mr Froggett,' said Mr Mukerjee. 'Thank you for answering my questions so fully. It is, of course, fascinating for me, as an Indian box-wallah, to hear about the customs of your fine and well-established country.'

'I'm sure it is,' said Corky. 'It's a great honour for you, too.'

In the goods and luggage carriage, Blotto was aware of night falling. But though the Indian world outside the train grew dark, it seemed to make no difference to the stifling heat inside. Acutely uncomfortable against his crate of Bibles, Blotto didn't think he slept at all.

He must have dozed off, though, because he awoke to the dazzling, headache-inducing brightness of another day. He tried to stand up to ease the cramp out of his constricted limbs, but the train's motion soon had him toppling down again.

As he gazed blearily around his makeshift prison, he suddenly realised that he was looking at something familiar. Amongst the randomly piled luggage, he saw one of his own suitcases. The one that, on the *Queen of the Orient*, had been 'Wanted on Voyage'.

It was a matter of moments to have the case open and to extract the precious object from within. Its contours felt as reassuring as the handshake of one of his Old Etonian muffin-toasters.

With his cricket bat securely in his grip, Blotto felt ready to face any adversity.

It mustn't be seen, though. Any potential weapon would be snatched from him when the Special Train arrived at Koorbleimee.

Blotto stuffed the cricket bat up his right trouser leg.

It was late afternoon when the Maharajah's train finally reached its destination. The railway terminus at Koorbleimee was only a couple of hundred yards from the palace, but there was still a fleet of Rolls-Royces to transport the Maharajah, his family and honoured guests there. On arrival, they encountered a parade of the Maharajah's army, dressed in exotic uniforms. A military band struck up, possibly in honour of Twinks and Ponky, a rousing version of 'The British Grenadier'. Behind the soldiers, ranks of richly dressed servants lined up to greet the honoured guests. A few gratuitous elephants, garlanded in rich silks and jewels, also formed part of the welcoming party.

Covered palanquins were borne up to the Rolls-Royces containing the Maharajah's womenfolk, so that they could be instantly whisked away, unseen by prying eyes, to the zenana.

The palace itself looked to have been created by a pastry chef who made wedding cakes and didn't know when to stop. From the magnificent central block, crowned by four golden domes, to either side lower elevations spread symmetrically. The stonework, a delicate ivory in colour, and its white marble facings, threw back the sunlight and glimmered like a fairytale castle in a dream.

The opulence of the palace's interior was equally stunning to the eyes of the guests. Everything that could be marbled was marbled, everything that could be bejewelled was bejewelled, and everything that could be overlaid with gold leaf was overlaid with gold leaf.

The suite of rooms to which Twinks was led by a detachment of flunkeys maintained the same level of luxury. The bedroom was big enough to play polo in (with space for spectators).

Two Indian maidservants stayed to minister to her every need, the first of which was to run a petal-scented bath in a marble pool. While she washed off the dust of the journey, they unpacked her trunk and laid out dresses for her to choose what she would wear for dinner that evening.

Presumably, somewhere else in the labyrinth of luxury suites, Ponky Larreighffriebollaux was receiving comparable cosseting.

But Twinks gave not a thought to her 'fiancé'. All she wanted to know was the whereabouts of her brother.

Blotto was in fact in the same palace, though under vastly different circumstances from his sister. The journey from the Special Train to his current accommodation had been different too. No Rolls-Royce treatment, far from it. After the procession of luxurious cars had departed from the terminus, he had been bundled – none too gently – into an oxcart by about a dozen of the Maharajah's soldiery. He had not even seen the palace's magnificent frontage, but had been hustled round the back, down dark steps, along a steamily stygian maze of corridors and into a small cell, whose door was slammed and locked behind him. There were no windows. Minimal lighting came from a guttering oil lamp. Its smell joined others which suggested he was not far from the kitchens. And not far from the sewerage system either.

As he looked round the small space, Blotto realised that it could only be described as a dungeon. A gruesome collection of rusty hooks, rings and chains were fixed to the wall. He heard scuttling sounds from the dark corners.

At least he hadn't been chained up. But he was still handcuffed.

And his whole frame felt cramped and aching. There is a finite amount of time that a boddo can feel comfortable with a cricket bat stuffed up his trouser leg.

The Lagonda had arrived at Koorbleimee a couple of hours after the passengers on the Special Train. As they approached the heavily guarded palace gates, Mr Mukerjee hissed to Corky, 'Say you're driving the car of Lady Honoria Lyminster. Don't mention the young master.'

The chauffeur, impressed by the accuracy of all the other instructions Mr Mukerjee had given over the last couple of days, did as he was told. Clearly, their arrival was expected. Ferociously moustached guards pointed towards the garages round the back of the palace.

Once arrived there, richly caparisoned servants directed Corky and Emmeline to their quarters. Mr Mukerjee, who seemed to know his way around, set off in another direction. Nobody barred his passage.

Of course, the chauffeur still had no idea that the young master hadn't travelled to the palace with his sister in the luxury of the Special Train. And if Mr Mukerjee had known any different, he had not shared that information during their journey from Bombay.

It went without saying that Twinks was the most beautiful woman at that evening's dinner. In fact, on that occasion someone of considerably fewer physical attractions could have qualified for the description, because Twinks was the only woman in the room. The Maharajah's wives and daughters were in the appropriate seclusion of the zenana.

The dining room was another example of gratuitous ostentation, with the usual complement of gold, jewels, carving, marble, ivory, etc. Twinks had found, during her brief stay in the palace, that such display quickly became stultifying.

For the occasion, she had abjured her customary short skirts and wore a long evening gown of cream silk. The fact that it covered the perfection of her legs did nothing to decrease her allure. Above the silver-blonde hair rose a single ostrich feather, held in place by a sequinned band that picked up the sparkle of the sequinned reticule which was, as ever, on her arm.

At the entrance to the dining room, a gorgeously dressed functionary with a high turban greeted her and asked whether she wished to go straight to the table or to wait for her fiancé to escort her. Twinks, who had forgotten that she had a fiancé, said that she would wait. She wanted a moment to take in the gorgeous vulgarity of the room.

The guests were about half and half Indian and European, the former dressed in variegated silks and jewellery, the latter in full three-piece dinner suits. The strenuous efforts of an army of punkah-wallahs, controlling the giant ceiling fans, meant that, for the first time in the day, there was a breath of breeze in the heavy air.

At the head of the table was the Maharajah's throne, which left no one in any doubt who was in control of the proceedings. (Mind you, nobody who was in any doubt who was in control would ever have got past the Koorbleimee frontier guards.) The Maharajah himself was standing beside the throne, deep in conversation. He was dressed like a Cartier Christmas tree, but the emerald at the centre of his turban was a poor relation of the Star of Koorbleimee.

Twinks was considerably intrigued to see that the two men with whom the Maharajah was in earnest discussion were Arnold Wembley-Dither and Mr Mukerjee. The first was no surprise, but she wasn't aware of any connection between the Maharajah and the box-wallah.

Just at that moment, Ponky Larreighffriebollaux arrived, with a predictable greeting. She let him take her arm, as if he really *was* her fiancé (which, she realised, unless she did something about the situation pretty damned quickly, he would be), and they followed the functionary to their seats, which turned out to be very near the head of the table. Twinks would have the Maharajah on her right and Ponky on her left.

As they approached, Twinks heard the Maharajah saying, in a voice of considerable urgency, 'I don't care how it is done, but I want to ensure that she is out of the way during tomorrow's court proceedings!'

Reading a warning signal in Wembley-Dither's eye, the Maharajah turned to greet his dinner guests effusively. With a polite bow, the Resident of Koorbleimee backed away to find his place the other side of the table. The box-wallah also bowed and departed.

The evening's menu and the wines were as lavish as the surroundings. Only the finest champagne was served in the finest Austrian crystal glasses. The food was Indian, of a quality that Twinks had never before encountered. What passed for a curry in England offered a tenth carbon copy of the depth and variety of the Maharajah's chefs' creations. Twinks's tastebuds had never been so cosseted. 'Larksissimo!' she kept crying, as each new dish appeared.

Her fiancé, however, was faring less well. The stomach of a young man, most of whose eating had been done at public school or London's gentlemen's clubs, was not accustomed to gastronomic challenges. Even coronation chicken was a spice too far for a digestive system weaned on roast beef and Yorkshire pudding, steak and kidney pie or boiled beef and carrots. There had only ever been three culinary rules in Ponky's upbringing. Meat should be solid. Vegetables should be soggy. And sauces should be nowhere.

So, the reaction of Ponky Larreighffriebollaux's un-trained stomach to the assault of Koorbleimean curries could only be compared to the Indian Mutiny of 1857. He was forced to leave the table in some disarray.

The Maharajah watched his departure in silence. Then he asked, 'Is that gentleman really your fiancé?'

'Well, I'm wearing his spoffing ring,' Twinks replied, flashing the diamond, which had more competition in that room than it had had anywhere else. 'Back in the home country, if a droplet wears a boddo's engagement ring, it usually implies they're going to twiddle the old reef knot.'

'Yes, but there seems about you a . . . lack of enthusiasm, dare I say?'

'English gels of breeding are brought up to believe that overt displays of enthusiasm are beyond the barbed wire.'

The Maharajah smiled sardonically. 'And this from a "gel of breeding" who this evening has shouted "larksissimo!" at the appearance of every dish?'

It was rare for Twinks to feel discomfited or discom-posed, but at that moment she felt both.

The Maharajah laughed in a slightly patronising way. 'So, Twinks, with the vast experience of two days in this country, how do you like India?'

'I don't feel I've clapped my peepers on much of it yet.'

'No, that is true. India is a huge country.' He spread his hands wide to include all the splendour of his palace. 'But you like this, I think?'

Twinks smiled. 'Maharajah, do the brain cells blip with something you said to me the first evening we met on the *Queen of the Orient*?'

He searched his memory. 'No.'

'You were chuntering on about the way you were togged up.'

'My clothes?'

'Bong on the nose. You said some boddoes were

182

intimidated by their splendour ... and other boddoes found them ... ?'

The memory came back. '"Flashy and meretricious"?' With the memory came anger. 'My palace is flashy and meretricious?'

'I haven't said that,' said Twinks with a charming smile. 'You said that.'

The Maharajah sat back on his throne, still annoyed. 'If you knew how much it was all worth, Twinks ...'

She shrugged.

He played with his moustaches before saying, 'I don't think the one who is even now throwing up somewhere ...'

'Ponky?'

'Yes. I don't believe he is your fiancé.'

'You can believe whatever clips your sock suspender,' said Twinks frostily.

'The offer is still on,' said the Maharajah with a lazy smile. 'You can share all this ...' A wave encompassed the luxury around him '... if you agree to be my favourite wife.'

'Sorry,' she said. 'No biddles.' Her next words did make her feel guilty. 'I'm going to marry Ponky.'

The Maharajah nodded wryly, as though taking her point on board. Then he said, 'I think the English aristocracy and the Indian aristocracy see things differently.'

'Give that pony a pink rosette!' said Twinks.

'What you find flashy and meretricious, we find ... splendid.' Another airy gesture. 'All of this ... is an expression of power. Of my power.'

'If this pedals your perambulator,' said Twinks.

'This ...' said the Maharajah. 'This ... is India. And everything else you will see will be India. The tiger hunt I am arranging for the day after tomorrow: that will be India.'

183

Twinks shook her head ruefully. 'No. This is not the real India. I want to see the *real* India.'

The Maharajah said nothing, but with one imperious finger he summoned a flunkey and whispered something in his ear. The man hurried off down the table and returned within seconds, escorting Mr Mukerjee, who was still wiping his mouth with a table napkin.

'Mr Box-Wallah fellow,' said the Maharajah. 'This lady – Twinks – wants to see "the real India".'

'In that case,' announced Mr Mukerjee, almost as if he had rehearsed the line, 'tomorrow I will take her to the Milkibar Caves!'

20

Blotto on Trial

Blotto wasn't feeling in zing-zing condition. The night he had spent in the dungeon would have been uncomfortable even without a cricket bat stuffed up his trouser leg. And he'd never been a happy hedgehog about sharing his accommodation with rats. To add to his trials, the food served by his guards had featured a great deal of curry powder. And Blotto's digestion, having undergone the same public school and gentlemen's club regime as Ponky's, did not that morning manifest its customary breezy confidence.

Nor did the situation in which he found himself after being let out of his cell bring much cheer. The guards escorted him – again none too gently – up a lot of dingy stairs and through many dingy corridors, into the main body of the palace.

Once they were out of the servants' quarters, the quality of the corridors changed considerably. Now they sparkled with marble, ceramics and gold. And the throne room, into which he was ultimately ushered, was the most spectacular in the entire palace.

But for Blotto, hobbling as only a man with a cricket bat stuffed up his trouser leg can hobble, the splendour of the space hardly entered his consciousness. He looked around the throng of seated Indian grandees, attention-standing soldiers and other functionaries in the hope of seeing his sister. Or even Corky Froggett.

But in vain. Neither was there.

Nor was the Maharajah, but the magnificence of the empty throne suggested that, when he did arrive, it would be quite an entrance.

Blotto was frogmarched into position, standing behind a carved wooden structure just like the dock at the Old Bailey. But it was the only object in the room reminiscent of the British system of justice. He looked in vain for anyone who resembled a lawyer, but there was not a white wig in sight.

Anyway, he had a feeling this might be the kind of court in which people spoke only for the prosecution. And, even if that weren't the case, his determination to maintain his vow of silence meant that he wouldn't say anything in his own defence. He wondered gloomily how many years he would be spending in that rat-infested dungeon. Or how generous the Koorbleimean justice system was with its distribution of death sentences.

Arnold Wembley-Dither came fussily towards him. 'This is most irregular,' he said, his manner an accurate metaphor for colonial ineffectuality. 'As a British citizen, you should be judged only by the British legal system. But once the Maharajah gets a bee in his bonnet – or perhaps I should say a termite in his turban . . .' The Resident started to giggle at his witticism, then realised it wasn't the moment and continued, '. . . about something, I'm afraid it doesn't pay to cross him.' He shrugged at the inevitability of failure.

'Don't don your worry-boots about me,' said Blotto, who was happy to talk about anything other than the crime with which he had been charged.

'But I do worry,' said the Resident. 'As a representative

of His Majesty's Government, I should be protecting the rights of British citizens, but I feel completely useless.'

Blotto sympathised with such accurate self-knowledge. 'Yes, there are lots of situations where I'm a bit of an empty revolver too.'

'I mean, in the Raj the British are meant to be in charge, but in some of the Princely States, there's much more loyalty to the traditional ruling families than there is to His Majesty. There are even dissenting voices which feel the British should go back to Britain and leave the Indians to administer what is rightfully theirs.'

'But,' said Blotto, who'd had drummed into him at Eton the unquestionable virtues of the British Empire, 'surely to Wilberforce – it's rightfully ours?'

Arnold Wembley-Dither looked dubious. 'I sometimes wake up in the middle of the night, wondering if it is.'

On hearing this very nearly treasonable opinion from a representative of His Majesty's Government, Blotto's jaw dropped. Before he could say, 'Well, I'll be kippered like a herring!', though, the Resident, suddenly focused, changed the subject. 'But listen, Mr Devereux, we must get you out of this. The Koorbleimean justice system has some fairly unpleasant punishments for people found guilty in its courts, so it's important this misunderstanding is cleared up as soon as possible. I've now heard the circumstances of your arrest, and I think all you need to say is that the object you threw out of your porthole on the *Queen of the Orient* was not the Star of Koorbleimee.'

'But it was, by Denzil!' Blotto insisted stubbornly.

'Are you saying you stole the jewel?'

'You're bong on the nose there.'

'When?'

Blotto had not been prepared for questioning of this depth. 'Erm . . .' he havered, then came up with an answer. 'During the fire alarm. When the *Queen of the Orient*'s staterooms were as empty as a Scots restaurateur's tipping-box.'

'But that's not possible, Mr Devereux.'

'Why not, in the name of snitchrags?'

'It is not possible because a witness observed you during the only time you could have committed the theft from the Maharajah's stateroom. When the siren sounded, you were sitting in a deckchair on the bridge deck. You went straight from there to the muster station, where you remained until the emergency was declared to be a false alarm.'

Blotto knew the answer, but he still asked, 'And who's this witness when they've got their spats on?'

'Lettice Sandwich,' came the reply. 'So, Mr Devereux,' the Resident went on, 'what do you say now about the Star of Koorbleimee?'

'I spoffing well stole it!' Blotto persisted.

'But I have proof you couldn't have—'

Further argument was stopped by a triumphant battery of fanfares, announcing the arrival of the Maharajah of Koorbleimee. Blotto's guards nudged him – none too gently – to stand to attention.

The Maharajah took his time. Other rulers might have got sick of being the centre of attention, but not this one. He relished every moment of it. There was a lot of bowing to him, some of the grandees going so far as to place their foreheads on the marble floor. Blotto was encouraged by his guards – none too gently – to do the same (though the movement was quite difficult for someone with a cricket bat stuffed up their trouser leg).

Only Arnold Wembley-Dither stayed vertical. It would not do for him, as a representative of His Majesty's Government, to bend the knee to the ruler of a vassal state. But he looked extremely uncomfortable about his act of defiance. Again, he took on the shifty demeanour of a schoolboy who'd been caught smoking behind the cycle sheds.

The Maharajah luxuriated in these displays of adoration before eventually subsiding into his throne and gesturing to the throng to resume their former positions. The splendour of his costume matched the splendour of his throne, but again the large emerald at the centre of his turban acted only as a reminder of the Star of Koorbleimee's absence.

Silence reigned, and the Maharajah let it reign for a full two minutes before he spoke. The void was filled by the sound of Blotto's uneasy stomach, rumbling at the volume of the *Queen of the Orient*'s engine room. The breakfast curry had not so much disagreed with him as challenged him to a duel.

When the Maharajah finally did speak, it was not with the lounge-lizard charm he had demonstrated during the passage to India. His voice thundered with the legacy of history. It was the voice of power which had ruled these territories for centuries before the depredations and whole-scale robberies inflicted by the East India Company. The voice would perhaps have been even more daunting had he been speaking in his native tongue but, given the nationality of the accused, he spoke in English.

'I am here today,' he boomed, 'in this court, to find guilty the perpetrator of a crime against the very heritage of our nation. The Star of Koorbleimee has been passed down for generations from Maharajah to Maharajah. It is the soul of our nation. And anyone who steals the Star of Koorbleimee insults not only me, but also all of my forefathers. Stealing the Star of Koorbleimee is more than a crime. It is sacrilege. And the perpetrator of such sacrilege will be punished with the most extreme penalties of the Koorbleimean judicial system!

'The man accused of this horrendous theft stands in the dock before you. Prisoner at the bar . . .' Blotto was not even granted the dignity of a name '. . . you stand accused of the heinous crime of stealing the Star of Koorbleimee. How do you plead – guilty or not guilty?'

It probably would not have made much difference what the answer had been, but Blotto made things simple by replying, 'Guilty.'

A rumble of suppressed anger ran around the room.

'While on his Britannic Majesty's Royal Mail Ship *Queen of the Orient*, you stole the Star of Koorbleimee?'

'Yes, I spoffing well did!'

The anger which greeted this statement was hardly suppressed.

'And,' the Maharajah demanded, 'do you feel any remorse for the crime you have committed?'

Blotto wasn't 100 per cent certain that he knew what 'remorse' meant. He knew what the Morse Code was, but . . . He decided to play for safety, replying, 'No, I spoffing well don't.'

The anger that greeted this threatened to take physical form. Among the Maharajah's soldiery, steps were taken forward and hands were placed purposefully on sword pommels. Had their commander himself not gestured for calm, Blotto might have been shredded to confetti on the spot.

'Since you admit to the crime,' the Maharajah enunciated, 'and since you show no remorse and express no apology for committing that crime, I have no alternative but to pronounce the harshest sentence which the Koorbleimean laws allow. You will be taken from this place and—'

What Blotto's fate was to be after he had been taken from this place was not revealed, because at that moment a soldier in the uniform (as everyone except Blotto recognised) of a Colonel in the Koorbleimean Army, burst into the room and ran towards the throne.

He shouted something in his native language which stopped the Maharajah in mid-sentence (and mid-sentencing too, as it happened). The ruler leaned forward and allowed the Colonel to whisper in his ear.

190

'Excellent!' the Maharajah cried. 'Let him come forward!'

Soldiers at the door parted to form a guard of honour through which the newcomer approached. It was M. le Vicomte Xavier Douce, stepping in his customary unhurried, meticulous way.

A couple of yards from the throne, he stopped and offered the Maharajah a flamboyant bow.

'So, Monsieur le Vicomte, is what I have just been told true?'

The diamond merchant was not familiar with the correct forms of address in India, but he had found that being extravagant never raised any objections. 'Mighty Prince,' he began, 'it is indeed true!' He reached into his waistcoat pocket and produced a small velvet bag. 'I am here to return to its rightful owner, the Maharajah of Koorbleimee ... the Star of Koorbleimee!'

As he spoke the words, he lifted the stone out of the bag. Its facets sparkled with rays from every light source in the room.

'This is wonderful!' cried the Maharajah, reaching forward to the familiar jewel. 'How did you find it, Monsieur le Vicomte?'

'I heard,' he replied, 'that the stone had been hurled out of a porthole when the *Queen of the Orient* had docked in Bombay. I then organised an extensive dredging operation in the harbour.' This was a slight exaggeration. The 'extensive dredging operation' had involved one half-naked boy diving to the bottom. But the Maharajah didn't need to know that.

'And I was lucky enough,' the Vicomte continued, 'by this means to find the object which had been thrown out of the porthole.'

'I cannot thank you enough,' said the Maharajah. 'The Princely State of Koorbleimee cannot thank you enough. You are, I believe, a diamond merchant?' The Vicomte inclined his head. 'Then, since you have returned the Star of Koorbleimee to its rightful home, I decree that you may visit my jewellery vaults – and help yourself to anything you like there.'

'The Mighty Prince is too gracious,' said M. le Vicomte Xavier Douce, with a flamboyant bow and a sly smile. He had just been granted what he had made the journey to Koorbleimee for.

Arnold Wembley-Dither took advantage of the momentary hiatus to step forward and say, 'Maharajah, now you have your property returned, surely there is no need for the proceedings of this trial to continue? For you to start proceedings against a British citizen was never going to be popular with His Majesty's Government, and this seems a wonderful opportunity to put a stop to any potential awkwardness. The last thing any of us wants is a diplomatic incident.'

The Maharajah looked across towards Blotto. Then he boomed, 'Nonsense! The fact that I now have the Star of Koorbleimee back in my possession changes nothing. The miscreant in the dock still stole it from me! And he must pay for that crime! These proceedings will resume another day. Guards, take the prisoner back to his cell!'

The guards did exactly as they had been instructed – none too gently.

And it was borne in upon Blotto once again how uncomfortable it is to be manhandled when you've got a cricket bat stuffed up your trouser leg.

21

The Milkibar Caves

While in Bombay, Miss McQueeg had organised accommodation at a temperance hotel in the capital of Koorbleimee
(which, coincidentally, was also called 'Koorbleimee'). The
remainder of her arrival day was spent drinking tea,
reading the Bible, and preparing her smiting campaign.
The heathen didn't know what was going to hit them.
(Well, they'd be Bibles, actually.)

The Maharajah had graciously granted Mr Mukerjee and
Twinks one of the palace Rolls-Royces, together with
chauffeur, for their excursion to the Milkibar Caves. They
left before seven, to avoid the midday heat. (Twinks was
unaware that the early start was also to ensure that she
was completely unaware of anything going on later that
morning in the throne room. She had still heard nothing of
her brother's whereabouts.)

The Maharajah had also arranged for an Indian maidservant to accompany them, as a chaperone. The local belief
about the consequences of a man and a woman spending
time alone in the Milkibar Caves was a strong one.

It was only a half-hour's drive to their renowned and
mystical destination. On the journey, they chatted idly

about the philosophy of René Descartes and its relationship to Aristotelianism. Mr Mukerjee expressed the
well-worn view that saying, 'Cogito, ergo sum' was putting
Descartes before de horse.

But, once the Rolls-Royce had deposited the three of
them at the foot of the incline leading up to the caves'
entrance, the box-wallah concentrated on providing his
guest with the history of the site. The construction dated,
he explained, from the third century BC, when the caves
had been carved out of the solid granite. No scholar had
satisfactorily identified the technology used to achieve this
monumental feat of engineering (or this feat of monumental engineering, if you prefer). Nor had anyone
explained the method used to bring the surfaces of the
interior walls to an almost glass-like polish. He talked a
little about the religious significance of the caves and
various Koorbleimean superstitions surrounding them
(though not the one about a man and a woman found
alone in the caves having to get married).

Appropriate to her status, the Indian maidservant stayed
a few steps behind the visitors as they climbed towards the
intricately carved doorway. Twinks was not aware when,
clearly by prearrangement, the girl stopped halfway up, so
that the Englishwoman and the box-wallah entered the
caves alone.

She was instantly aware, however, when she felt herself
gripped in a tight embrace and heard Mr Mukerjee hiss
ferociously, 'Now you have to marry me!'

She struggled but he was too strong for her. Who could
say what might have happened, had they not suddenly
been interrupted by a Scottish voice, shouting, 'I have seen
the fires of hell! I have seen the fires of hell! All will be
engulfed in the mighty flames!'

As these words were uttered, Mr Mukerjee felt a heavy
blow to the forehead from some substantial object. The
pain forced him to release his hold, and Twinks instantly

wriggled out of his clutches. She made good her escape, scampering fleetly back to the sanctuary of the Rolls-Royce.

Mr Mukerjee looked down at the floor of the cave to identify the missile that had smitten him. It was a Bible.

He turned to face the wrath of Miss McQueeg.

Such was the force of Twinks's personality that the Maharajah's chauffeur did not question the order to drive her back to the palace, alone.

Once there, after more fruitless questioning as to the whereabouts of her brother, Twinks retired to her suite. She was not upset by the physical assault on her person in the Milkibar Caves. From the time she had started wearing stockings, she had found herself the target for the wandering hands of many amorous swains and had got very adept at dealing with them. Usually, the icy *hauteur* of her voice had been sufficient discouragement but, when required, she too could get physical. Her hands had delivered stinging slaps to many red cheeks and other parts of the male anatomy.

No, what had really put lumps in her custard in this particular incident was the identity of her attacker. She really thought, once she had announced her so-called engagement to Ponky Larreighffriebollaux, that Mr Mukerjee had given up all amatory ambitions. And she had relished his company as – if not an intellectual equal; such creatures were rare – at least he was someone with whom she could share an intelligent conversation. And now, in yet another of myriad examples of men misreading women's signals, such dialogue could not continue.

Twinks threw herself on her bed in a state of Himalayan dudgeon.

* * *

195

Many floors below, her brother languished in his dungeon, like a jockey in a steam bath, trying to get as comfortable as a man with a cricket bat stuffed up his trouser leg ever can get. Which is not very.

M. le Vicomte Xavier Douce's revelation of the Star of Koorbleimee in the throne room that morning might have been dramatic, but it had not changed his predicament one iota. And Blotto was more determined than ever to stick to his story about having stolen the diamond.

Twinks must have dozed off, because she was woken by a tap on the door of her suite. She was informed by an Indian maidservant with an excellent command of English that the Maharajah requested her presence downstairs. When she demurred, it was made clear that a request from the Maharajah was in fact an order.

The study into which she was ushered was considerably smaller than the staterooms where she had been previously entertained, but profligate gold leaf and jewels still adorned any surface that hadn't managed to escape them. The Maharajah sat behind a desk of carved ivory. He was wearing his day clothes, which meant half a dozen fewer rubies and emeralds than his evening wear. His countenance was stern. Standing beside him, looking as tentative and embattled as ever, was Arnold Wembley-Dither.

The Maharajah waited until the maidservant had left the room, backwards, closing the door behind her, before pronouncing, 'I have heard what happened in the Milkibar Caves.'

'So?' said Twinks. 'No icing off my Swiss bun.'

'Everyone in the palace has heard what happened in the Milkibar Caves.'

'Still not going to put me in the mope-marshes.'

'Soon everyone in Koorbleimee will hear what happened

in the Milkibar Caves. Then, in no time at all, everyone in India will hear what happened in the Milkibar Caves.'

'No skin off my rice pudding,' said Twinks. 'Why should I give a tuppenny butterscotch what people in India know about?'

'Because it concerns you deeply,' replied the Maharajah. 'It concerns your reputation.'

'I don't give a figgy pudding for my reputation.'

'It also concerns *my* reputation!' the Maharajah thundered.

'I think, if you'll pardon my interrupting,' said Arnold Wembley-Dither, as assertive as overcooked pasta, 'what the Maharajah wishes to impart is that you, Lady Honoria, do not understand the importance of the Milkibar Caves in the Princely State of Koorbleimee. In this country, they are a shrine with an exceedingly long history.'

'So?' asked Twinks combatively.

'So, there are traditions connected with the Milkibar Caves. Traditions which must be observed or there will be unrest among the people of Koorbleimee.'

'I would obviously, in a general way, regret any incident of unrest among the people of Koorbleimee but, in this instance, it is about as relevant to me as a tail-curler is to a Manx cat.'

'Listen, Miss!' roared the Maharajah, deliberately downgrading her title. 'You are in the Princely State of Koorbleimee! Which means that you must abide by the practices of the Princely State of Koorbleimee! You were alone in the Milkibar Caves with a man. The traditions of my country demand that any woman who is alone in the Milkibar Caves with a man must marry him!'

'Rein in the roans for a moment there,' said Twinks, totally unfazed by the Maharajah's vehemence. 'How do you know I was alone in the Milkibar Caves with a man?'

'Because you were seen alone in the Milkibar Caves with a man!'

'By whom?'

'By a Scottish missionary lady called Miss McQueeg.'

'Ah. Well, Maharajah, I think I see the teensiest logical anomaliette here.'

'What do you mean?'

'I know English isn't your first language ...' The Maharajah's eyes bulged at the potential insult '... but I do think we might have the tidgiest clarification of the meaning of the word "alone". If there are only two people in the Milkibar Caves, they are undoubtedly "alone". If, however, their "aloneness" is witnessed by a third person – be she Scottish missionary lady or the seventh wife of Henry the Eighth – then by no definition can the original couple be said to be "alone". Read my semaphore ... ?'

The Maharajah was not accustomed to having his logic chopped in his own palace. Or anywhere else, come to that. And least of all by a mere chit of an English girl. His face red with fury, he smashed his hand down on to a bell on the desk. Instantly, a Colonel of the Koorbleimean Army appeared in the study.

'Escort this upstart,' the Maharajah bellowed, 'to the zenana! Which is the proper place for all women. Ensure that she is kept there and made ready for her wedding, which will take place tomorrow afternoon, following our return from the tiger hunt!'

'I refuse to go!' said Twinks with steely determination. 'I refuse to go anywhere until you spoffing well tell me what's happened to my brother!'

But the Maharajah of Koorbleimee was immune to impressions of the Dowager Duchess of Tawcester. 'Your brother,' he replied, 'is safely secured in a place where you will never see him again!'

Twinks turned to Arnold Wembley-Dither. 'Come on, put a jumping cracker under it! You're meant to be a repre-sentative of His Majesty's Government. Surely you can—'

But her words were drowned by the voice of the Maharajah ordering his Colonel to 'Take her to the zenana!'

And, unceremoniously, she was taken there.

The Maharajah turned his ferocious eye on the Englishman, daring him to challenge his authority.

'You know best,' said the craven Resident of Koorbleimee.

Inside the Maharajah's palace, one in the dungeon, one in the zenana, Blotto and Twinks were both in the deepest individual gluepots in which they had ever found themselves.

22

Boiled Beef and Carats

Having been educated at home by a series of quickly outpaced governesses, Twinks had never shared the madcap adventures of a girls' boarding school, and was thus unprepared for the seclusion and restrictions of the zenana.

The Colonel had led her straight from the Maharajah's study, through tortuous bedizened corridors, until they came to a row of carved screens, which were the outer defences of the women's quarters. There Twinks was passed into the custody of a gorgeously dressed chubby man with a very high-pitched voice who, from her extensive reading, she instantly recognised to be a eunuch.

Before the handover, the Colonel pointed to the large rock on her wedding finger. 'Give that to me,' he said in excellent English. 'In our culture, a woman is not allowed to be engaged to two men at the same time.'

'She's spoffing well not allowed to be in our culture either,' said Twinks with some spirit.

She looked down at the ring. She had no desire to keep it for aesthetic reasons. It was far too flashy and meretricious for her highly sophisticated taste. But she couldn't be unaware of its value. At the back of her mind there lurked some thought of the diamond's sorting out forever

200

the problem of the Tawcester Towers plumbing. But that would, of course, have involved marrying Ponky Larreigh-ffriebollaux – she was far too honourable a woman to consider keeping the ring under any other circumstances. And the thought of all those pom-tiddling breakfasts ... With only slight reluctance, she handed the ring across to the Colonel.

She was then greeted by the Maharajah's Senior Wife, who clearly ran everything inside the zenana. Twinks was told she must change out of her Western clothes to dress in sari and veil. She did as instructed, having recognised in the manner of the Senior Wife certain qualities of her own mother.

The women of the zenana were perfectly pleasant. With another Englishwoman, there might have been a communication problem but, though rusty, Twinks's command of the Varhadi dialect of the Marathi language was expert. In conversation with the women, though, the impression she got of the life in the zenana was that it must be stultifyingly boring.

Not that those who spent their time there complained. For them, it was all creamy éclair. They didn't seem to think it odd that they were veiled most of the time, and their servants all of the time. They approached every routine banality of life with enormous enthusiasm. And they were terribly excited about the idea of getting Twinks ready for her marriage.

Twinks, meanwhile, focused every smallest cell of her remarkable brain on how she could avoid that marriage. She also cased the joint, but escape from the zenana looked like an impossibility. The windows were barred, and eunuchs guarded every door.

She wished Blotto was with her. Not that he'd be any use in planning an exit route, but she always found her brain-box functioned better when he was there.

Also, she missed her brother, and was desperate to know what had happened to him.

Corky Froggett, too, was wondering what had happened to the young master. Since arriving in Koorbleimee, there had been no sign of him. Mr Mukerjee who, even if he hadn't known on the Lagonda journey there, must by now know of Blotto's fate, had disappeared somewhere into the vast maze of the palace.

And Corky, though he had been given perfectly adequate accommodation in the servants' quarters, had not yet encountered anyone who spoke English. And his attempts to find Blotto or Twinks in the main part of the building had been frustrated by palace guards who would not let him enter.

This caused some frustration but did not surprise him. Spending his entire life in the aristocratic enclave of Tawcester Towers, Corky Froggett knew his place.

When they arrived, he and Emmeline Washboard had been sent to separate accommodation, Corky to the male servants' quarters, she to the female. He did not get the impression that the kind of companionship they had enjoyed so vigorously on the *Queen of the Orient* would go down well in the Palace of Koorbleimee.

The chauffeur found he did not mind too much about this enforced separation. And it gave him an opportunity to consider his relations with the governess.

He could not deny that they'd had a good time on the *Queen of the Orient* – in fact, on almost every vacant surface of the *Queen of the Orient*. Then Em had apparently saved his life after events in Port Said – and that's the kind of thing that puts a bloke in someone's debt. The interludes in Blotto's stateroom had also been extremely gratifying, as the governess had deployed considerable dexterity in bringing him back to life. He could not deny that he had enjoyed her capacious generosity – the generosity which had prompted such a shocked reaction in Miss McQueeg.

But he couldn't see theirs as a relationship with a long-term future. There was no way he could take Emmeline Washboard back with him to Blighty. It would upset the very delicate equilibrium of a mutually rewarding 'arrangement' he had with one of the Tawcester Towers kitchen maids.

No, they would just have memories of 'ships that passed in the night' (or, perhaps more accurately, 'nights which were passed on a ship'). He hoped she would recognise that fact as easily as he did.

Anyway, Corky reminded himself, his first duty was always to the young master.

If only he could find the said young master.

Dinner that evening was different from the previous night's. Among the many things that he wasn't, the Maharajah was a gracious host. He had no wish to make another frontal assault on the digestion of Ponky Larreighffriebollaux. He therefore decreed that the evening's menu should be of English food. His chief chef, who had worked extensively for gentlemen of His Britannic Majesty's Army, had suggested, as a main course, the delicacy known as boiled beef and carrots. To capture the essence of the *cuisine* aspired to, the chef advised that this dish should be preceded by thin soup with no discernible taste and followed by jam roly-poly with custard (made from powder, not eggs).

Not only was he indulged by the menu, but the Captain of the Peripherals was also given the seat on the right hand of his host's throne. On the Maharajah's left sat another guest of honour, Miss McQueeg. What was called locally 'A Milkibar Caves Marriage' carried considerable symbolic importance for the people of Koorbleimee, and anyone involved in facilitating such an event was treated with great reverence.

Next to the missionary sat M. le Vicomte Xavier Douce. He was also being honoured, in his case for organising the return of the Star of Koorbleimee, which sparkled brilliantly on the front of the Maharajah's turban. The diamond merchant wore the complacent smile of someone who, that day, had taken his reward from the pick of the Koorbleimean jewellery vaults.

The Maharajah was prepared for a potential awkwardness during the dinner. The presence of Miss McQueeg at the table must almost inevitably lead to the disclosure of what had happened at the Milkibar Caves. So far as he could tell, Ponky Larreighffriebollaux remained blissfully unaware of this event, continuing under the illusion that he was still engaged to Twinks. At some point the Maharajah might have to inform the guest on his right of the changed state of affairs. In one of his pockets he carried the Port Said engagement ring, ready to be returned to its disappointed purchaser.

In the meanwhile, as he and his guests tried to discern some flavour in the soup which had been served as a first course, the Maharajah talked about the first entertainment of the following day, the tiger hunt.

The second entertainment, of course, though Ponky did not yet know it, was Twinks's wedding to Mr Mukerjee. Her new fiancé, incidentally, was not present at the dinner. Maybe he, like his unwilling bride-to-be, was being prepared for the next day's ceremony.

'Tiger hunting,' said the Maharajah, 'is one of the great sports of India, and nowhere is the game better than in the Princely State of Koorbleimee.'

'Well, tiddle my pom!' said Ponky. And then, proving that he had a wider vocabulary in male company, he asked, 'How do you know where the spoffing tigers are going to be?'

'My gamekeepers,' the Maharajah replied, 'are highly skilled. They study the habits – and habitats – of the beasts. And, of course, we set out bait for the tigers.'

'Bait? What kind of bait when it's got its spats on?'

'Many kinds have been tried but the most effective remains a tethered goat.'

'Well, tiddle my pom!' said Ponky, reverting to type.

'The tiger never fails to come for a tethered goat. So, a goat is tethered in a forest clearing, we have tigers, and everyone is happy.'

'Except possibly the goat . . . ?' Ponky suggested.

'The tiger does not end up very happy either,' said the Maharajah. 'But my guests are very happy. They have a nice hearthrug to take home with them.'

'Good ticket,' said Ponky. 'And do you do the actual hunting on horseback?'

'No, no, Mr Larreighffriebollaux. You are thinking of pig-sticking.'

'From shooting brakes then?'

'No. For tigers, we follow tradition and hunt from the back of elephants. The Koorbleimean elephants are the most highly trained in all of India.'

'Oh, what, so the hunters go in one of those little wodjermabits on the back of the elephant? What do you call one of those?'

'Howdah.'

'Oh, I'm in zing-zing condition. Thank you for asking.'

'But I—'

'Much better than yesterday. I was distinctly wobbulated then. But the boiled beef and carrots are excellent.'

Beautifully brought up, of course, the Maharajah did not draw further attention to Ponky's misunderstanding of 'howdah'. Instead, he decided it was time to include the guest on his left. 'I hope you too are enjoying the boiled beef and carrots, Miss McQueeg.'

'It is excellent, thank you,' she replied, before dropping into her habit of quotation. '"The Lord shall give you in the evening flesh to eat."'

'Which is exactly what I am doing,' said the Maharajah, 'as the Lord of Koorbleimee.'

'No, you weren't the Lord I was referring to.'

'I beg your pardon?'

'I was quoting from Exodus, chapter sixteen verse eight. From the Good Book.'

'Ah. The Bible.'

'Yes. The Good Book. Have you read it?'

'I started it once, but I gave up.'

'Oh?'

'Too much "begatting" in the first half for my taste.'

'Oh.' Miss McQueeg was suddenly intrigued by the Maharajah's turban. 'I can't help noticing that stone you have fixed there.'

'I am not surprised you notice it. It is the Star of Koorbleimee, one of the largest and most famous diamonds in the world.'

'Ah.' Miss McQueeg was silent for a moment, then she said, 'You know it's fake, don't you?'

'FAKE!!!' the Maharajah roared.

'Yes,' Miss McQueeg continued coolly. 'My father was a jeweller. Before I saw the Light, I worked with him. I have an extensive knowledge of jewels, particularly diamonds. I know a fake when I see one. And that stone on your turban, though quite a convincing one, is definitely a fake!'

Seated on the missionary's other side, M. le Vicomte Xavier Douce overheard this conversation and was instantly on his feet, running towards the door.

'Guards, seize him!' the Maharajah bellowed, rising to his feet in fury. As he did so, the sudden movement dislodged something from his pocket. It fell on the table in front of Miss McQueeg – the engagement ring that the

Vicomte had persuaded Ponky Larreighffriebollaux to buy for Twinks in Port Said.

The missionary cast her expert eye over it and announced, 'That's a fake too.'

'Tiddle my pom!' said Ponky. Which was all he could say, really, in the circumstances.

The condition of having a cricket bat stuffed up one's trouser leg is not one that becomes more comfortable with time. And the discomfort is not improved by being hand-cuffed in a steam bath of a dungeon with only rats for company. Nor is the distress alleviated, for a stomach trained to English nursery food, by being fed only curry. Blotto's emotional barometer, whose default setting was 'Sunny' was moving inexorably towards 'Stormy'.

He had become accustomed to the background noises of his incarceration – the clanging, the clattering, the laughter, the crying, the sounds of speech, all completely incomprehensible to him. After less than forty-eight hours, he was also used to the fact that footsteps only came towards his door twice a day, to deliver more food, specifically designed to burn small holes in his intestines.

So, he was quite surprised on the second evening of his imprisonment to hear heavy boots very definitely clumping towards his door, unlocking sounds, and the sight of a tall man in immaculate evening dress being pushed into the dungeon. Thin light from the oil lamp reflected from his monocle. Blotto instantly recognised his new cellmate as M. le Vicomte Xavier Douce.

'Stay in there till we find somewhere permanent for you!' said the guard who'd done the pushing, mercifully in English. The door was clanged shut and locked.

'So . . .' The Frenchman looked at Blotto as he staggered to his feet (not an easy thing to do with a cricket bat stuffed up one's trouser leg). 'Here we are, both in prison . . . and for the same crime.'

'Sorry? Not on the same page?' Solitude had not increased Blotto's intellectual powers.

'We are both being imprisoned for the crime of stealing the Star of Koorbleimee.'

'Ah. Tickey-tockey.' Blotto was curious. 'How did you actually manage to filch the flipmadoodle?'

'Of course, I took it at the same time as you were supposed to have taken it. When there was the fire alarm on the *Queen of the Orient* and when all of the staterooms were empty.'

'Well, I'll be jugged like a hare!'

'You see, my jewellery skills extend to the manufacture of undetectable replicas of certain diamonds. *Almost* undetectable, I should say. It was just my bad luck that, at the Maharajah's dinner table tonight, there was an expert in diamonds who recognised that the Star of Koorbleimee I had returned to him was a fake. *Zut alors!'*

'Tough Gorgonzola,' said Blotto, always ready to sympathise with another boddo's troubles.

'Incidentally,' the Vicomte went on, 'I did organise a boy diver to retrieve from the harbour in Bombay the object which you threw out of your porthole window. Would you like to have it back?'

'Well, I suppose no icing off my Swiss bun if I do.'

The Vicomte handed it across. 'And perhaps, in exchange, you will tell me why on earth you insisted that it was the Star of Koorbleimee and thus got yourself into this terrible predicament?'

'Ah. Yes. Good ticket. Well, you see, the reason was—'

But the diamond merchant never heard the explanation because at that moment the guards reappeared and took him off to the dungeon in which he would be more permanently incarcerated.

* * *

Expecting no further interruptions that night, Blotto tried to settle down to sleep (no easy thing for a man with a cricket bat stuffed up his trouser leg). But just as he let out his first uneasy snore, the door to his dungeon was unlocked and he heard an accented voice announce, 'I have come to rescue you.'

It was Mr Mukerjee.

23

In the Forest

'Don't make a sound,' hissed Mr Mukerjee urgently, as he led Blotto through the bowels of the palace. 'If the guards catch you trying to escape, you'll be back in that place for life.'

'You're a good greengage, Mr Mukerjee,' Blotto whispered. 'And you'd be a Grade A foundation stone if you actually unlocked these handcuffs.'

'No, we don't want to do that yet,' said the box-wallah.

'Why in the name of snitchrags not?'

'In the unlikely event of our being seen by the guards, if you're still handcuffed, I can say I am taking you, on the Maharajah's instructions, to another place of confinement.'

'Ah. Beezer brainbox! Give that pony a rosette!'

'In fact, to make that scenario even more convincing, I think I'd better attach *this* to the handcuffs.'

Blotto felt the extra weight and looked down to see that the 'this' which had been attached was a heavy chain.

'Now we don't look at all suspicious,' said Mr Mukerjee.

'Good ticket,' murmured Blotto.

He looked across at his Indian saviour. Mr Mukerjee must have been more nervous than he appeared, because sweat was pouring down from his hairline, leaving runnels of dark fluid on his cheeks, which he kept mopping with a discoloured handkerchief.

Mr Mukerjee had clearly planned ahead. They were fortunate, in that they didn't encounter any guards, and were soon out at the back of the palace by its garages. A nearly full moon gave the scene a magical quality, silvering the outlines of the many roofs and towers. The Indian night did not feel a lot cooler than the Indian day, but Blotto got a great charge just from breathing fresh air. As well as the smells of civilisation, he detected the fragrance of some exotic but unknown flower.

'You really are the panda's panties, Mr Mukerjee,' he said, 'playing the Galahad like this.'

'It is my pleasure,' said the box-wallah. 'I do not like to see the suffering of a fellow human being.' He moved towards an Armstrong Siddeley shooting brake, which had clearly been brought out of the garage in readiness. 'Hop in the front seat and I will take you to a place of safety.'

Hopping was not easy for a man encumbered with handcuffs, a heavy chain and a cricket bat stuffed up his trouser leg, but Blotto managed to get settled in the car. Mr Mukerjee pressed the self-starter and they drove off into the night. Soon they were in deep forest, where only trickles of moonlight penetrated.

Blotto looked across at the box-wallah, who was still sweating heavily and constantly taking one hand off the wheel to wipe his face with the handkerchief which seemed to be getting grubbier by the minute. He had his sleeves rolled up and Blotto noticed a dark mole on his right forearm.

'Tell me, Mukerjee me old gravy boat,' he said, 'have you seen my sister recently?'

'Indeed, I saw her today.' He didn't mention that they had been in the Milkibar Caves together. 'And I will be seeing her tomorrow, for sure.' He did not mention that that would be on the occasion of their wedding.

211

'Oh? 'Cause I wouldn't mind clapping my peepers on the old troutling.'

'I am sure you will be reunited soon,' said Mr Mukerjee reassuringly. 'Ah, we are here.' He slowed the car down.

'The spoffing "place of safety"?'

'Exactly. The place of safety.'

They got out of the shooting brake and were suddenly aware of the night-time sounds of the forest. Rustles of unexplained movements high in the trees and low in the undergrowth. Squawkings and chatterings from animals Blotto had never heard before. And one he very definitely had heard before.

The bleating of a goat.

The poor creature was tethered to a tree by a chain that went all the way round the trunk.

What happened next happened so quickly that Blotto didn't have time to react – particularly given that he was hampered by a heavy chain and had a cricket bat stuffed up his trouser leg. Mr Mukerjee produced a key from his pocket and undid the padlock attaching the goat's collar to its chain. Within seconds it was locked on to the free end of Blotto's chain.

'You lump of toadspawn!' roared Blotto. 'What do you think you're doing?'

The box-wallah came close and hissed in his ear, 'I am ensuring that you will never inherit the Dukedom of Tawcester!'

'I don't want to inherit the fumacious Dukedom of Tawcester!'

But there was no response to Blotto's words. He heard the sound of the Armstrong Siddeley driving back to the palace. He heard the sound of the bleating goat going away from him in the opposite direction.

Then there was a terrible roar, a shriek of anguish from the goat . . . and a crunching noise.

24

Happy Endings?

On the evening before his young master's tethering as bait in place of a goat, Corky Froggett was polishing the Lagonda in the palace garages, surrounded by Rolls-Royces, and thinking gloomy thoughts. The unexplained absence of Blotto was his main anxiety, but also, he was not looking forward to the inevitable – and probably awkward – ending of his liaison with Emmeline Washboard.

Almost the moment he thought of her, by some magic of synchronicity, the governess appeared, in a state of some distress. 'Corky,' she said, 'I have just heard what has happened to Blotto and Twinks!'

She had proved more fortunate than he in gleaning information. Among the female servants, there was one who spoke excellent English. What had happened in the Milkibar Caves was big news in the women's quarters, and the maidservant had told Em all about Twinks's predicament . . . though that was not the word she used. All the female servants thought the English girl was extremely fortunate to be having 'A Milkibar Caves Marriage'. It was the fate they had all dreamed of. Their predominant emotion was envy.

The other great bonus, Em explained, was that the English-speaking maidservant had access to the zenana

213

and, for a financial consideration, was prepared to take a message to Twinks.

It was Corky's view that getting a message *from* Twinks might be more useful. He had had many years to build up confidence in the uncanny powers of the young mistress's brain. If Twinks knew she had a contact outside the zenana, he felt sure she could devise a plan of escape.

Em wrote the note. She was better at that kind of stuff than Corky. And she entrusted it to the English-speaking maidservant, promising an increase in the agreed fee if the woman returned from the zenana with a reply.

It was only then that Corky had a chance to ask if Em knew anything of Blotto's whereabouts. The news she brought on that front was dispiriting. The chauffeur's first thought was that he must rush down to the young master's dungeon and rescue him. But, as Em pointed out, every part of the palace was guarded by the Maharajah's soldiers. Corky would be arrested before he got through the first door. She recommended that they should get Twinks out first and, if her brain power was as good as Corky said, she'd come up with the perfect scheme to rescue her brother.

He assured her that he hadn't overestimated the young mistress's genius, but he still didn't feel as confident as he sounded. 'Anyway,' he said, 'all we can do now is wait till we get the message from Twinks.'

'Yes,' said Em. There was a silence. It was almost dark, but there was a moon and light from the back windows of the palace. She went on, 'There's something I think I ought to tell you, Corky.'

'Oh yes?' he said, his moustache quivering. That was never a very promising opening line from a woman.

'The fact is, I have very much enjoyed the time we've spent together, you know, on the *Queen of the Orient* . . .'

'Certainly. Cracking time.'

214

'But there is something I should probably have told you earlier . . .'

'What's that then?' he asked uncomfortably.

'I told you I was going out to take up a position as a governess in Pondicherry . . .'

'You did indeed.'

'And I said that the appointment had been arranged in London, when the father of the family – a military man – was over there.'

'You did say that, yes.'

'And I implied that the arrangement was purely a business one . . .'

'That was the impression I got, yes.'

'That was perhaps slightly misleading . . .'

'Oh?'

Em decided she was fed up with prevarication. 'The fact is that when I and my future employer met in London, we struck up . . . a very close relationship . . .'

'I see.'

'With plans that it should continue on that basis once I reached Pondicherry.'

'Right.'

'In other words, I will be seeing to the needs, not only of his children, but of him as well. Do I make myself clear?'

'Clear as daylight, Em.'

'So, I'm afraid, Corky – pleasant though the interlude we shared was – it is now at an end.'

The chauffeur could not believe what he was hearing. He'd never thought he'd be let off the hook quite so easily.

'So,' asked Em, 'how do you feel, Corky?'

'I will learn to live with my grief,' he said with nobility, silently rejoicing.

It was shortly after that the maidservant returned, with a note from Twinks. Corky Froggett's confidence had been justified. She told them exactly how her escape should be engineered, and Emmeline Washboard immediately set about following the detailed instructions.

Fluently, in the Varhadi dialect of the Marathi language, Twinks had explained to the other women in the zenana the English tradition as to how a young woman should spend the last night before she gave up her single status. On the eve of her wedding, she should be allowed to be alone, to contemplate the great change her life was about to undergo. She should be allowed to dress as she chose and be fed with her favourite food. Above all, no one should talk to her, unless she initiated the conversation. This was how, throughout the British Isles, the wedding eve had been spent since time immemorial – or at least since the Norman Conquest.

Twinks asked if, on this night of all nights, she might be allowed to follow the traditions of her own country. The request was taken to the Senior Wife, who graciously agreed. With considerable relief, Twinks changed back out of her sari and veils into the clothes she had been wearing for the ill-fated expedition to the Milkibar Caves.

Having discovered, mostly from the appalled laughter of the women, what was being served to the Maharajah's dinner guests in the dining room below, she asserted that her favourite food, in which she wished to indulge that special evening, was boiled beef and carrots.

And she waited for the next stage of her plan to unfold.

Emmeline Washboard had never before worn Indian dress. The head-covering and veil hid her hair and skin colour, her hands were invisible in the gloves with which she pushed the tablecloth-covered food trolley towards the zenana.

216

The eunuchs at the various doors had been warned of her approach and forbidden to engage her in conversation. They led her to the suite in which, completely alone and dressed in her Western clothes, Twinks was apparently contemplating the excitement and serious import of her forthcoming marriage.

Once inside the suite, the boiled beef and carrots were moved from the top to a side table and Twinks hid herself on the lower level of the trolley, shrouded by tablecloth from prying eyes. Em pushed the trolley back the way she had come, and the silent eunuchs obligingly opened all the doors for her.

(If anyone had challenged Twinks about the unoriginality of her escape plan, complaining that the person-smuggled-out-on-the-lower-level-of-a-trolley routine had been a feature of every screwball comedy since Hollywood began, they would have received a very crisp response. Twinks's mighty brain could of course have come up with something infinitely cleverer, but she was always economical in the use of its powers. If the simplest solution worked, there was no need to construct anything more elaborate. So, the person-smuggled-out-on-the-lower-level-of-a-trolley routine it was.)

As instructed, Emmeline Washboard continued her journey all the way to the garages at the back of the palace. Though there was no sign of Corky, the gleaming Lagonda stood waiting for them.

'All right, you can get out now,' said Em.

Twinks sprang from under the tablecloth, looking lovelier than ever.

'Larksissimo!' she whispered. 'Now let's go and find Blotters!'

As she spoke, a tall figure, who'd been smoking a

cigarette by the back door, stepped out of the shadows. 'Is that you, Twinks?'

The women froze. Had someone witnessed the escape? Was Twinks about to be taken back into custody?

But when the man stepped forward, she saw it was a very distraught Ponky Larreighffriebollaux.

'Twinks,' he said dismally, 'how can you ever forgive me?'

'Ponky, what have I got to forgive you for?'

'I've behaved like the worst sort of oikish sponge-worm,' he said bitterly. 'I've asked a girl to marry me and I've given her a leadpenny engagement ring!'

'What – that diamond?'

'It was a fake. A replica. Made by that absolute stencher, M. le Vicomte Xavier Douce. I cannot live with the shame!'

'Ponky, don't don your worry-boots about that.'

'I have to. What I have done is way beyond the barbed wire. Only the worst kind of slugbucket would give a girl a counterfeit engagement ring and expect her to stay engaged to him!'

'Oh,' said Twinks, beginning to see that there might be a good side to the situation. 'Well, if you really feel that we should end the engagement . . .'

'I've behaved like such a four-faced filcher, I can't see any alternative.'

'If that's the way you feel . . .' Twinks appeared to struggle ferociously with herself before announcing. 'Our engagement is at an end.'

'Thank you for being such a Grade A foundation stone about it,' mumbled Ponky Larreighffriebollaux, staggering back towards the palace. 'We won't meet again, Twinks.'

She felt a relief very similar to that experienced by Corky Froggett earlier in the evening. And it struck her that Ponky had only found the articulacy he'd always lacked in her presence when the relationship was over. A whole conversation without a single 'Tiddle my pom!' Give that pony a rosette!

218

But she hadn't time to dwell on anything, because Corky Froggett came rushing out of the palace towards them. 'Somebody saw the young master – in chains – being driven off in a shooting brake!'

'Where to?' cried Twinks, as she leapt into the passenger seat.

'To where they hunt the tigers!' replied Corky, gunning the great engine into life.

Emmeline Washboard watched the car's taillights wink away into the darkness. It had been a nice little interlude, she thought, as she made her way back into the palace.

25

Tiger, Tiger

There was enough moonlight in the clearing for Blotto to see the blood of the former goat glistening round the tiger's jaws. The mighty creature moved slowly towards him, eyes glowing, evidently interested. The goat had been an appetiser. It was eying the main course.

But the tiger didn't have to rush. It had taken in the chain and handcuffs. Its entrée wasn't going anywhere.

The only good thing that had happened, during the goat's consumption, was that Blotto no longer had a cricket bat stuffed up his trouser leg. He had managed to shake it out and the familiar handle was now in his hands. He wasn't using a conventional grip, the handcuffs precluded that. But it did feel wonderful to hold the thing and breathe in the nostalgic tang of linseed oil.

'This,' he said to the tiger, 'is my cricket bat. And it's played some spoffing good innings in its time, let me tell you. There was one that always tinkles the cowbells for me. It was the first time I was given a berth in the Eton and Harrow match. I was just a spriglet then, new bug at the school, a tadpole in a field of frogs, and I was way down the batting order . . .'

* * *

While the Lagonda wolfed down the road into the forest, Corky brought Twinks up to speed with what had happened to Blotto since she last saw him on the *Queen of the Orient*.

'And did you get the SP on why he insisted that he was the pot-brained pineapple who filched the Star of Koorbleimee?'

'I did not find that out, milady.'

'It'll be something to do with Blotto's misplaced sense of honour. He's always Galahadding up the wrong drainpipe.'

'I couldn't possibly comment, milady.' The light changed as they passed a clearing. 'I think we're getting close. Third clearing on the left, that's what my informant said.'

'Then put a jumping cracker under it, Corky! Blotto's life is hanging by a cobweb!'

'. . . and then this blunderhead on the Harrow side flung down a full toss, aimed straight for my spoffing tooth-trap. But I edged the ball to leg, where their fielder threw himself at it like a flying fish, but no dibbles. Another four, and the oppo's starting to think I must have had a limpet for a grandpa, so they put their speed merchant back on from the pavilion end . . .'

The eye of the tiger began to glaze over.

'. . . but by now, you see, the pitch has got some boing in it, and I'm starting to settle in the crease like a cat on a comfy cushion. And the Harrow greengages are getting as frustrated as mice in a milk bottle, so I think I can loosen up the legs and try some new strokes. I've been playing cagey too long and, reckoning the cup's already in the cabinet, I open up with some leg-drives and, well, I'll be battered like a pudding if I didn't invent a version of the leg-drive that's still talked about in . . .'

The tiger slunk back into the forest.

* * *

Moments later, the Lagonda arrived with Corky and Twinks aboard. They released Blotto. Brother and sister did not embrace – they weren't into that kind of moozy stuff – but they both felt seeing each other again was heaven on a pickle-fork.

Though the siblings had luggage back at the palace, they reckoned reclaiming it represented too much of a risk. They had had enough of the Maharajah's machinations.

'I think the bounciest thing we can do,' announced Twinks, back in her role as decision-maker, 'is return to Bombay as quick as two ferrets in a rabbit warren, and catch the first boat back to Blighty.'

'Toad-in-the-hole!' Blotto agreed. And he took the wheel of the Lagonda.

After they'd been driving in silence for some minutes, Twinks sighed and said, 'I still don't feel I've seen any of the *real* India.'

'I still don't feel I've seen *any* of India,' Blotto agreed plaintively. 'Except for the inside of a fumacious dungeon.'

There were more signposts pointing to Bombay than there had been pointing to Koorbleimee on the way over. Corky, having driven the route in the other direction, knew where they were going, so they made good time. They didn't stop anywhere overnight, master and chauffeur taking turns with driving and sleeping.

It was well into the following day before Twinks asked her brother, 'Why did you actually insist that you had stolen the Star of Koorbleimee?'

'It was to protect someone's spoffing honour.'

'I thought it must be. Give my pony a rosette!' A silence. 'It was a lady's honour, I assume?'

'Bong on the nose, sis. You see, on the *Queen of the Orient* there was all kinds of chittle-chattle going round about Corky and his nurse . . .'

The chauffeur pricked up his ears.

'. . . and suggesting that what they'd got up to in my stateroom went beyond standard Florence Nightingale practice.'

'Did they say that?' asked Corky, convincingly shocked.

'And then that Scottish woman came in with her own muckspreader and, anyway, I thought the Stilton was getting distinctly iffy. So, when that Captain Barnacle slugbucket comes in, asking who filched the Star of Koorbleimee, and I saw something under his chair that belonged to Corky's charming nurse, I thought, "Oh-ho, Blotters, scandal alert if anyone sees that!" So, I decanted it out of the porthole zappity-ping. And when the Captain asked if what I'd jettisoned was the Star of Koorbleimee, I nodded the noddle. Quick thinking, eh, sis?'

'Oh yes, Blotto,' said his sister wearily. 'Very quick. Give that pony a rosette.'

'And, of course, once I'd uncaged those particular ferrets . . . well, a boddo can't go back on his word, can he?'

'No,' said Twinks, again weary.

'I couldn't have done anything else. Could I, Twinks?'

'No, Blotto. *You* couldn't.'

Corky thought about the situation. The fact that the young master had leapt to the defence of the honour of a woman who . . . well, who'd been passed around more times than a salt cellar . . . well . . .

'Thank you, milord,' he said. 'I find myself more in your debt than ever.'

'Oh, Corky, don't talk such meringue.'

'Incidentally, Blotters,' asked Twinks, 'what was the object that you threw out of the porthole?'

'Ah,' said her brother, remembering. 'As the custard drips off the spoon, I actually have the little wodjermabit with me.' He reached into his pocket and pulled out something in a small velvet bag. 'I think you'd better have it, Corky.'

223

'Thank you very much, milord,' said the bewildered chauffeur, taking the proffered gift. He opened the bag to reveal the perfume bottle he'd bought for Em in Port Said. The perfume bottle whose two ends had been squashed and misshapen by assassins' bullets. The perfume bottle that the Vicomte had had salvaged from the harbour in Bombay. Knowing that the real Star of Koorbleimee was safely stowed in Twinks's sequinned reticule until he chose to retrieve it.

Blotto waited for a reaction to the perfume bottle. 'I must get it back to her,' said Corky fervently.

'I think you've got a cad's chance in a convent of achieving that,' said Blotto. 'And it did save your life. Something for your mantelpiece. I think you should keep the flipmadoodle.'

'Thank you very much,' said Corky. 'I think I should, too.'

There was a liner leaving for England the evening of the day they got to the Bombay docks. But it was absolutely booked solid. No space for two aristocratic siblings, a chauffeur and a Lagonda.

Or no space until Twinks went into the shipping office and once again exercised her charm. When their ship left the quay, one of the last sights of Bombay they saw was a very angry Spanish family standing on the dockside beside their Hispano-Suiza, which had been moved out of the hold to make room for a Lagonda.

After recording one of the shortest ever visits to the sub-continent, Blotto and Twinks's passage back from India was uneventful.

The two of them – and Corky – remained very cheerful. The only sad sight they saw on board were some of the Fishing Fleet who had failed to find husbands in India. They were universally – and rather cruelly – described as 'returned empty'.

* * *

The Nawab of Patatah arrived at the Palace of Koorbleimee the day after the Lyminsters' departure. He was delighted to meet up with his old muffin-toaster, Ponky Larreigh-ffriebollaux, and with a will they set about organising the first match of their cricket tour. Fortunately the Nawab managed to line up a few ex-pats to fill the gaps in the visitors' team.

In the event, the Peripherals beat the Koorbleimean eleven by seven wickets. The Maharajah, who was used to getting his own way in everything, was not best pleased. The loss just added to the bad mood he felt about losing the Star of Koorbleimee. And the punishments his system of justice imposed on M. le Vicomte Xavier Douce were only a small compensation.

The diamond merchant – or should one say 'diamond thief' – knew where the missing stone was but, as the years of his incarceration stretched ahead of him, thought there was little chance he'd ever be able to reclaim it.

Meanwhile, Ponky and the Peripherals moved on, from Indian city to city, playing some of the best cricket that had ever been seen on the subcontinent.

Ponky's figures improved, both for batting and bowling, and he put that down to the confidence boost he'd got from being engaged to the most beautiful woman in the world.

The fact that the engagement had ended, before reaching the ultimate destination of marriage, worried him not a jot. Ponky Larreighffriebollaux had had his moment in the sun.

As he put it, gleefully, 'Tiddle my pom!'

Miss McQueeg stayed in India until she'd got rid of all her Bibles. Then she too sailed back to the home country. And, having found God, on the voyage home, she managed to lose Him. She found Sin instead. In the form of one of the lower deck stewards. And she found she enjoyed Sin more. (God was quite glad to be shot of her, too.)

26

Birthday Fireworks!

That January evening, at Tawcester Towers, the Dowager Duchess went to bed early, leaving no one in any doubt as to her disapproval of her elder son's birthday celebrations.

The Duke of Tawcester himself was in a much better mood. The dinner being a stag event meant that Loofah would not have to spend time with either his mother or – more pertinently – his wife, universally known as Sloggo. This was a relief, as time spent with Sloggo too often involved trying to impregnate her with a male heir to the title. The failure of this endeavour could be measured in the number of daughters they had.

So, he looked forward to a predictable evening of alcoholic consumption leading to incapability. His younger brother shared this ambition. It was the only way Blotto could cope with all the male Lyminster relations, young men whose chins seemed to recede in proportion to how distant their connection with the family was.

Tomorrow's headaches did not need to be considered. Blotto's priority was surviving the evening, and he only knew one way to do that.

* * *

Twinks, meanwhile, had not been idle since their return from India. There were details about their journey which, to her acute mind, still needed explanation.

She had picked her brother's brains (which never took long) and also consulted Corky Froggett. She asked them to remember incidents which they thought unimportant, but which had great significance for her.

And most of her questions concerned Mr Mukerjee. He had undoubtedly engineered their encounter in the Milki-bar Caves, knowing full well the potential consequences. Why was he so keen to marry her? Twinks wrinkled her exquisite brow a great deal over that question.

Other droplets of information began to join together until they formed a strong stream of logic. She asked Blotto in great detail about his ride with Mr Mukerjee in the Armstrong Siddeley shooting brake. He relived the journey for her, mentioning the dark fluid the driver had kept wiping off his face, and the round mark on his forearm.

Twinks questioned Corky about the conversations he'd had with Mr Mukerjee on the drive from Bombay to Koorbleimee. How interested the box-wallah had been in the details of the Duke of Tawcester's birthday party. More links of logic started to form.

Then she approached the local police. Chief Inspector Trumble and Sergeant Knatchbull of the Tawcestershire Constabulary were not the sharpest knives in the cutlery canteen. In any investigation, their default position was bafflement. But Twinks had found in the past that, if she provided them with all the proof of why someone had committed a crime, they were perfectly competent to do the arresting. Which is how she planned to use them in this case.

Of course, her plan did carry a certain level of risk – the risk of multiple deaths, in fact – but she couldn't see another way of securing a conviction.

So, Twinks watched and waited.

* * *

The Duke of Tawcester's birthday dinner took place, appropriately, in the Ducal Dining Room, a space that was rarely used at other times of year. It was on the ground floor, commanding a fine view over the estate. And beneath it was a cellar, one entrance to which was in Tawcester Towers's external walls. In the weeks running up to the birthday dinner, Twinks watched that entrance intently, and was rewarded by observing exactly the kind of covert activity she had anticipated.

She just had to get her timing right on the night of the dinner itself.

For some formal feasts at Tawcester Towers, pre-prandial drinks would be taken on one of the terraces, but not in January. The Duke's guests started their drinking where they would finish it, in the Ducal Dining Room. They would all have arrived and be seated by eight o'clock and that was when Twinks planned to unleash her *coup de théâtre*.

To cut off any escape route, she would use the exterior cellar entrance rather than the one inside the building (though she saw to it that trusty footmen were guarding that too). Flanked by a bewildered Chief Inspector Trumble and Sergeant Knatchbull, on the dot of eight o'clock she pushed open the door and the Sergeant directed his broad torch beam into the cellar.

Caught in the act, a tall man stood with a box of matches in his hand. A long fuse led to a pile of barrels. The method of blowing up a large number of people hadn't changed a lot since the Gunpowder Plot.

'We meet again,' said Twinks.

The tall man said nothing.

'Barrington Flexby-Cruise, as I live and puff. Or would you rather be called . . . Mr Mukerjee?'

Still no reply. But an expression of resignation took up residence in the man's face.

'I should have realised that all that chittle-chattle – about Sanskrit texts, and Confucius and Nietzsche – was remarkably similar to discussions we had here about iambic pentameters, alexandrines and *ottava rima*, shouldn't I?'

'Perhaps you should,' he conceded.

'But seeing you out of context, with the darkened skin and the flattened-down hair . . . and the accent . . . You had me for the complete gooseberry fool.'

'Thank you.' He inclined his head in acknowledgement of the compliment.

'Bit beyond the barbed wire, though, donning a disguise . . . for someone of your supposed breeding, Barrington.'

He said nothing.

'So, for your fumacious planette to bring home the silverware, you had to marry me and eliminate Blotto. You knew the Koorbleimean tradition about the Milkibar Caves, so you reckoned that would sort out the wedding. And you paid those slugbuckets in Port Said to try to coffinate my brother – they nearly did coffinate Corky Froggett. When that murder plan failed, you bided your time until we reached Indian shores and then dabbed your digit at a tiger to do your dirty deed. Little did you realise the low boredom threshold of tigers when it comes to cricket.'

'Congratulations, Twinks,' said Barrington Flexby-Cruise. 'You've got it all worked out, haven't you?'

'Yes, I think I have pinged the partridge here. So, having failed to blow Blotto on the quick route to the Pearlies in India, you came up with this Guy Fawkes rombooley. In the room above are all the Lyminster males with even the most distant of claims to the Dukedom of Tawcester. With all of them coffinated, you'd be the only one left to inherit.'

'You read me like a book, Twinks. You always did.'

'Except when you were disguised as Mr Mukerjee,' she said with some annoyance. She was still kicking herself for not having seen through his subterfuge. 'Oh, and incidentally,' she went on, 'was twiddling the old reef knot with me still in your sights?'

'Yes. I was of the view that, with all your male relatives dead, you wouldn't be able to resist your mother's pressure for us to get married.'

'Then you underestimate me, Barrington.'

'I'm not so sure.'

'Are you jiggling my kneecap? Do you think the mater, with all her male relatives dead, would want me to share an umbrella with the stencher who coffinated them?'

Barrington Flexby-Cruise shrugged. 'That kind of thing has happened many times before in the Lyminster family history. And I regret to inform you that your mother knew all about my plans and positively encouraged me.'

'Don't talk such toffee!' Twinks snapped. Though, when she thought about the Dowager Duchess's customary level of sentiment towards her children, she wouldn't have put it past the old battleaxe.

Anyway, the confrontation had gone on long enough. Turning to Tawcestershire Constabulary's finest, she said, 'Enough circumstantial evidence to make an arrest, don't you think, Chief Inspector Trumble?'

'On what grounds?' asked the Inspector, reverting to his customary bafflement. As is obligatory with representatives of any local constabulary, he and Sergeant Knatchbull had been at the end of the queue when the brains had been handed out.

'Attempted multiple murder . . . ?' Twinks suggested.

'Oh yes. That should do it,' the Chief Inspector agreed.

And so it was that the criminal career of Barrington Flexby-Cruise, a.k.a. Mr Mukerjee, ended. His attempt to kill all of the Lyminster heirs who stood between him and the Dukedom of Tawcester had been thwarted. He was clever, but nowhere near as clever as Twinks. Nobody was anywhere near as clever as Twinks.

The attempted murderer was detained at His Majesty's pleasure for a satisfyingly long time. And no one regretted his absence.

Except possibly the Dowager Duchess. She thought Barrington Flexby-Cruise would have made rather a good Duke, and still couldn't understand why Twinks hadn't married him. To the old woman's mind, he would have made a better Duke than Loofah. And an immeasurably better one than Blotto.

Whether, as he had claimed, the Dowager Duchess actually knew of Barrington Flexby-Cruise's plans and encouraged them, Twinks was never sure. And it wasn't something she wanted to ask her mother about.

The morning after the birthday dinner, which had ended with the traditional fireworks and alcoholic stupor, the Dowager Duchess summoned all of her children into the Blue Morning Room to complain about the night before. This was a bit unfair on Twinks, who hadn't been involved in the dinner and had in fact ensured that it didn't end in a massacre.

But it was just as well she was present. Because, as the Dowager Duchess started tearing strips off her two sons, Twinks reached into her sequinned reticule for a handkerchief and found her hand closing round an unfamiliar object. Something hard, contained in a velvet bag.

She thought back to the dinner on the *Queen of the Orient* the night after the theft of the Star of Koorbleimee. She had been sitting next to M. le Vicomte Xavier Douce, the man she now knew to have stolen the jewel. He must have had it about his person at the time. She remembered he'd drawn attention to her sequinned reticule, and she had asserted forcibly that she'd never let anyone search

231

inside it. Then she'd left it on the table to go off and talk to Blotto.

It would have been a matter of seconds for the Vicomte to pop the jewel into her sequinned reticule, with a view to collecting it from her later. Which, of course, he'd never had a chance to do.

In the Blue Morning Room, she lifted the Star of Koorbleimee out of its bag and held it up. The way it refracted the light cut off the Dowager Duchess in mid-dressing-down. It even cut through the hungover haze of the two brothers.

'Well,' said Twinks, 'I think perhaps we have a way of sorting out that fumacious plumbing.'

Some weeks later, Blotto received a letter with an Indian postmark. It was from Lettice Sandwich.

'I wanted to write to say it was such fun to spend time with you on the *Queen of the Orient*. I am writing this from the home of my brother, Reuben Sandwich, but I will soon be moving into my own house, when I marry his great friend, Major Ginger Biskett. He and I are just right for each other. I will always have fond memories of you, Blotto, but I knew nothing could ever work out between us. I would have been constantly aware of my intellectual inferiority to you. Yours affectionately, Lettice.'

Blotto glowed from a feeling he had very rarely experienced, but he supposed his sister must have all the time. And he felt no guilt for the fact that he'd completely forgotten Lettice Sandwich's existence. After all, he had his Lagonda. And Mephistopheles. And, though he hadn't managed to play a single game in India, he had his cricket bat. Few men were so blessed.